The Mysterious Secret Guardians:

The Owl Mountain Doomsday Solution

Books by Dorothy McCoy

Mysterious Secret Guardians series
The Mysterious Secret Guardians in the London Underground
The Owl Mountain Doomsday Solution

Coming Soon!
Final Chapter of the Mysterious Secret Guardians

The Mysterious Secret Guardians:

The Owl Mountain Doomsday Solution

Dorothy McCoy

SPEAKING VOLUMES, LLC
NAPLES, FLORIDA
2023

The Owl Mountain Doomsday Solution

Cover design by Hannah Linder

ISBN 978-1-64540-863-5

To my beautiful Sophie, who was my constant beloved companion
in the best of times and the worst of times.

Even the thief Dark Death could not take my faithful Big Soph away.
She is free in spirit to watch over me, as she did so devotedly in life.

God's blessings on you, my dearest friend.
My Harlequin Great Dane Sophie.

Acknowledgments

Since my distinguished characters did most of the work, they deserve credit:

Sir Winston Churchill, Former Prime minister, WWII Hero
Dr. Albert Einstein, Genius
David Smythe, Former WWII Air Marshall and MI5 Agent
Admiral Stallings, WWII Royal Navy
Thelma Dove, Former SOE and Freedom Fighter
Angus Snowden, Retired MI5 Agent
Abigor, Former Demon
Dr. Raven "Bones" Wyndot, Psychotherapist Extraordinaire
Father Antonio, Exorcist
Sophie, Great Dane and so much more

A huge thank you to the talented author, Jeffery Deaver.

Thank you to my fabulous editor and fellow Mysterious Secret Guardian, Rita Kitenplon. She rocks!

My beautiful publishers, Kurt and Erica Mueller, Speaking Volumes.

My dedicated Agent, Nancy Rosenfeld.

And, finally, the Big Guy.

Chapter One

The Blackness

Absolute darkness, a blackness I did not know was possible. It is disorienting and terrifying. I cannot see a trace of light or shapes. Am I standing? Where am I? What has happened to me? I try not to freeze in terror, sensing the darkness trying to absorb me. Wait! What is that? I strain to hear an almost imperceptible dragging, slithering sound; Dear God, I am not alone in this Hellish black hole! I am excruciatingly aware of everything, and Instinctively, I feel a malevolent presence moving toward me. Horrifying!

I turn to the power of my survival instinct, ingrained boldness, and blind faith to counter the darkness and whatever slithers toward me. My body shivers as the entity tries to overwhelm me with an essence of pure evil. Its iciness is biting into my skin. I must defeat this encroaching evil by shielding myself from the greedy darkness. Enduring the formidable double onslaught is slowly ebbing away my strength. Can I resist? I am fearful I will die or worse here in this ravenous black hole. Just breathe. My iron will is threatening to explode into scattered, impotent shards. Words by Poe flash across my feverous brain, "Deep into that darkness peering, long I stood there, wondering, fearing . . ." Why did I remember Poe's words? A fog is overwhelming my brain. Clarity fades, and time has become ominously slothful. Did time stop? Is that possible? Fresh waves of terror sweep over my brain!

If only I could understand where I am and the ghastly battle within and around me. What manner of nightmare is this that feels so real? David, where are you? Please help me!

I don't know what to do, and my senses deceive me. I hear a faint sound. No, you imagine it. Come on, Bones, breathe deeply, concentrate, or you will die. Listen. A voice from deep within the darkness? Listen. David, David, are you here? Please be here!

Dear God, what touched me?

Chapter Two

The Team

I run to the door of the Royal Suite at the Savoy in London, our lavish headquarters, and throw it open, expecting to see my Guardian Team members: Sir Winston, tall, hunky Air Marshall David Smythe (WWII), and Dr. Einstein. Abruptly, I come face to face with a terrifying monster, stumble backward, and almost fall over an oversized ottoman. Great Dane Sophie is with me, emitting a menacing snarl, lips pulled back from razor-sharp canines.

Instead of the Team we expect, the handsome green-eyed Demon Abigor looms in the doorway. We had deadly encounters with him on our last mission. Abigor is cold, calculating, and soulless. He can appear charming and likable, but he wears a mask to deceive. Abigor is a demon; all demons are pathological liars and merciless killers. Abigor gleefully threw an 80-year-old retired MI5 agent down a flight of stone stairs. He lured me to a deserted pub—I was fortunate to escape. Be aware there are worse things than dying. Demons harvest souls from unsuspecting humans and condemn them to "unquenching" fires in Hell.

Consequently, I am not in the mood to be hospitable. I won't be inviting Abigor in for a chatty visit and high tea. Sophie moves between the Demon and me. I am safe from him because the powerful immortal, Big Soph, guards me.

We stand facing each other as I wait for Abigor to threaten me or tear me to pieces. Sophie would vigorously object to the former and destroy him if he attempted the latter. Sophie is much more than a Great Dane. She is an ancient entity from Beyond with formidable powers. Abigor is perfectly aware of this, and I doubt our visit will become a good versus evil wrestling match. He would lose, and I believe he senses this.

Abigor walks right past us and makes himself at home on the plush leather sofa. Honestly, I am losing patience with the psychopathic uninvited Demon. In Demonology legends, he is depicted as a goodly knight on a prancing, snorting steed. He is supposed to command seventy legions in Hell. We are aware that demons embellish their legends. Since Abigor's last visit to London was during Shakespeare's time, he speaks in broken, sometimes inaccurate Old English, which is maddening, but not the worst of his traits. The worst is strutting around with thousands of damned souls harvested from unsuspecting humans tied to his belt. One such soul belongs to the vile Dr. Josef Mengele, the Angel of Death. A wicked, murderous physician at the infamous Auschwitz concentration camp.

The last time I saw Abigor was when my heavily armed Team stormed Mengele's laboratory in London. Thelma Dove was there on another mission. She offered Josef Mengele and Abigor a chance to follow her into the light and save their filthy souls. This offer was their one opportunity to avoid spending eternity sweating in Hell. A grand bargain, right? Mengele refused Thelma's hand when she reached out to him. He died unremorseful and unrepentant. Hence the loss of his soul. Abigor struggled to choose his path and disappeared without replying. I think Thelma might be an angel; if not, she is a saintly ghost. She is a lovely woman with a halo of golden hair framing a Helen of Troy face. Reflecting on these highlights from our last meeting, I sense something in Abigor has shifted.

Finally, Abigor speaks, "I know thou art not pleased to see me, Bones. We have an unpleasant history. Aye, I did throw thy friend Angus down the stairs at the Old Royal Navy College. Verily, I did threaten to destroy thee at the Hoof and Barrel Pub when I tried to take the cursed Sunstone Compass from thee. Hear me; I followed the path Thelma offered me and returned to my heavenly home. I spent many days tortured by hideous demons fighting to keep me chained to Hell. Thelma stayed by my side throughout the excruciatingly painful struggle. My eternal soul was at stake, and we won. I wast greeted with wondrous joy and celebration when I ultimately walked back into the light. I have repented, and I shalt never return to my former path. Ask Sophie. She knows." He points to the growling, highly ticked-off Harlequin Great Dane.

Sophie slowly nods but with great reluctance and a distinct lack of enthusiasm. Her memory is quite good and incredibly long. She had hoped to castigate him for his many transgressions against Angus and me. However, Big Soph knows he is telling the truth, which is good enough for me.

I have never known a demon who returns to his righteous roots. Truthfully, Abigor is my first demon experience. I am unsure about the protocol for congratulating a recovered monster. Sophie shows me the way. She licks Abigor's hand and sits at his feet. I am going to have to adapt her behavior somewhat. I shake his hand, still angry about his treatment of Angus. He was once in paradise as a rogue angel, and God's loyal legions threw him and his rebellious cohorts out along with their creepy leader, Satan.

Abigor says quietly as if to himself, "Michael and his angels fought with the dragon: and the dragon and his angels fought, but they did not prevail, nor was a place found for them in heaven . . ." A brief silence passes between us, and I don't know if our Demon, aka reconstituted angel expects a response from me, but I don't have one. I am just a country psychotherapist, not a theologian.

All right, I will accept him into the fold. "We are grateful you are on our side, Abigor, I guess. We can use all the heavyweight fighters we can get. You and Druid are heavyweights." Druid joined our Team in our last mission. Druid was sent to us from Beyond with no resume. He is hard to miss at a colossal six feet and 7 inches. Also, contributing to his startling appearance, Druid habitually wears a black suit, more fashionable in the 1890s, with a bowler hat perched jauntily on his massive blond head. Well, let's see, he is not young, but clearly not middle-aged. At first glance, his exceptional physical strength is unmistakable and striking. Yet, there is something more, much more, that holds the eye of even the most casual observer. Thugs move to a distance—little old ladies in purple cross themselves before hurrying away. Druid is a riddle, an enigma who, when not busy with other things, had saved my life when he frightened away a gunman about to puncture my head with a .357 caliber bullet. As a semi-Team member, he mostly pops in and out, giving us dire warnings of coming calamities or scolding us.

Abigor warns me, "Thou wilt not see Druid as often for a while. He covers the Old and New World and oversees two potentially troublesome situations. One is Kim Jong-Un in Gojoseon, excuse me, now North Korea, and the other is in Persia, now Iran. Many more men than you realize art of an autocratic and volatile nature, art destabilizing the world. They plan to make someone, perhaps, the Antichrist, dictator over all humanity. We must stop them to prevent the extinction of freedom and democracy. Druid and I art also charged with protecting God's chosen people in Israel. We pursue a peaceful settlement for all though we cannot ensure yond outcome. Also, they art attempting to use a power they doth not understand and cannot control. The dunces might kill millions in their folly. Druid and I art on high alert now. Verily, we art always on a high-alert adrenaline rush."

With a switch in demeanor, Abigor smiles fondly at me, "It is good to see thee, lovely, willowy, raven-haired Bones." Now, this is suspicious and creepy. Abigor is flattering me. In our previous encounters, he wanted me dead. I don't answer. Sophie yawns.

"I owe thee, dear Bones, Angus, and Sophie, an apology, and I hath heard that Dr. Mengele's crazed assistant Franz killed Angus. I am sorry for thy loss. I shalt beg for his forgiveness in the next world."

A male voice says, "What do you owe me an apology for, Abigor, you stinking scum? I gave as good as I got, mate. You still look like a disgusting, loathsome demon to me."

I pivot around and see a young Clint Eastwood look-alike standing behind us. Oh, my God! It is Angus, a much younger Angus! He was eighty the last time I saw him on the night he died, saving my life. He took a bullet with my name etched on it. Yes, that often happens to me, so I warn mortals not to hang out with me. I jump up and throw myself at him. He grabs me up and swings me around with the strength of a young man. I start weeping with joy and cannot stop. He offers me his handkerchief. He is a man from the 1960s with a handkerchief for a sobbing lady.

The four of us sit down to chat. I order lunch for one since, apparently, Angus is no longer mortal.

Abigor appears confused. His startling green eyes squint as he looks to me for answers, "First, I am grateful to have Angus back. Bones, I know naught about you and the others. Since I am now a member, I would like an explanation. What is the Team, and what do we do? I am in the dark." I smile at that reference. Abigor is right; he should know about us and our mission. Angus chimes in that he is interested as well.

Something is troubling me, and I need an answer, so I ask, "Abigor, there is something I must know. When we were at the pub, would you have killed me if I had given you the Compass?" This incident happened in our last mission; instinct saved me. I refused to give him the Sunstone Compass, and that decision was crucial. Fortunately, he did not have the power to take the Compass. I was unaware of it at the time, but it protected me from evil forces as long as I held it in my possession. I still have it safely tucked away in my purse. I hold my breath as I wait for Abigor's answer. Angus and Big Soph snarl at Abigor.

Abigor holds his head in his hands and looks at his feet as he whispers, "Dear Bones, please do not ask me about these things. It wounds me to think about the Demon who wast me. I would die, if I could, to save thee now. I make this promise to thee. Never be fearful if I am near." He grabs Angus' handkerchief from me and wipes his eyes. Angus grabs it back. Sophie leans toward Abigor, showing teeth and gums. She does not like the first part of his answer, which comes down to a hellish—yes. I shall try to forget, but I take it personally when someone plans to kill me. Call me sensitive.

I leave that memory. I will do my best to loop Angus and Abigor into our mission, "I can tell you what I know; some of this will not be new to Angus since he was involved." They are both leaning forward toward me; I have their complete attention.

I begin with nail-biting ancient history, "David Smythe joined MI5 after WWII. Angus had just become an agent when David was Deputy Director-General at MI5 in 1965. Both David and Sir Winston died that year. Sir Winston died in his bed surrounded by loved ones, and David was shot to death by a treacherous IT guy." I must pause; my heart is pounding. Even now, remembering David was murdered in cold blood deeply wounds me. I take a deep breath and continue. "Wentworth, the techy MI5 cretin, had gone to the dark side with the Nazis. We are confident Dr. Mengele's Neo-Nazis and WWII Nazis were behind David's, uh, assassination." Breathe, Bones.

I ask Angus to interrupt me if he wants to add anything. Then move on. "Angus, an excellent investigator, worked on David's case briefly but could not investigate a case without leads." Angus bows to me.

"The only person who knew about the Mengele Code, a hot lead on the case, was MI5 Director-General Ogden. Lo and behold, he died in an automobile "accident" attributed to a "heart attack" soon after David was murdered. We don't know why Ogden was driving David's 1939 Rolls-Royce Phantom. Angus also investigated the "accident" until shadowy thugs threatened his wife. The new Director abruptly shelved the case without an explanation. Investigation reports were stuffed into a dark file cabinet in the basement, never to see the light again. Intriguingly, rumors circulated in the Intel Community that the CIA had created a heart-attack drug."

Angus' tight jaw spoke volumes; he spat through clenched teeth, "That never sat well with me, Bones! Damn it, I don't think it was an accident!" He calms down as he explains the technical aspects, "I asked a medical doctor outside the agency to look at Ogden's body at great risk to my career. The cardiologist doubted the official diagnosis. Some traitorous dog at my agency was involved! I feel it in my bones!" His face grew redder as he relived the shameful experience. Fighting back the tears mixed with fury, he uttered, "They crossed a huge line when they threatened my beloved wife!" Amen. Someone left a message on their phone saying Angus' wife might have an accident if he pursued the case. The case became history.

I am moist-eyed, too, as I thank Angus for filling in that part of the story and reply, "Indeed, infuriating, dear Angus. Decades later, I became involved with the Team when Sir Winston suddenly appeared in my office without an appointment and demanded brandy. Churchill told me that in 1964, he and David Smythe acquired a tattered notebook inside a canvas bag circa WWII. Written on its yellowed pages was a complex code they could not decipher. A name was printed in bold black letters on the bag. Mengele! That hated name stopped them in their tracks. They worked on the code briefly and could decipher a few lines. Then, death gatecrashed. Churchill died in January. By then, they had learned that an odious Nazi organization planned to clone Hitler and a couple of his loathsome pals. Mengele planned to bide his time until biotechnology research advanced to a critical phase, allowing Mengele's research goals to become a reality. Seventy-five years later, the advancements in biotechnology became a reality, and the Powers from Beyond formed our Mysterious Secret Guardians Team to stop the fiends. Our team is not alone; I don't know how many Guardian teams are out there protecting the world, but I know there are several."

Angus raised his hand, "Uh, Bones, I didn't know there were other Teams. That is fascinating information. Do we know who leads the other teams?" I told him I was privy to only two leaders, Agatha Christie and John F. Kennedy. He stared at me, mouth wide open. I suppose he is a mystery fan.

I get back to my story now that I have shocked Angus, "The Team recruited me because I owned a unique copy of Churchill's book *Gathering Storm*. Days before David was killed, he had written the entire Mengele code in that book for safekeeping. It is a tediously long story, but the book ended up with me in North Carolina. Short version, I paid big bucks for the book, purchasing it from a rare books dealer in London. Neither of the guys knew why Einstein was included in the Guardian Team. Beyond is unfathomable, enigmatic, and vexing. Churchill, Einstein, and David are immortal, powerful, and quite brilliant. Me? Well, I am a cool psychotherapist. Our Team, which now includes both of you, is working on let's-save-the-world, part two."

I ask for questions. They wave at me to carry on, but my story is almost finished.

I have urgent questions for Angus, "How are you here? How are you young? Are you mortal? Can we keep you this time? Do I have to eat alone now? I am so excited to see you!" It had been so much fun having another mortal with whom I could share coffee and meals. The ghosts don't do food or drink. Sir Winston pretends he is drinking Scotch, brandy, or Pol Roger champagne. He was notorious for his alcohol consumption in life. Truthfully, it was more modest than the legend he probably encouraged. We typically see him with a snifter in one hand and a fine Cuban cigar in the other. Dr. Einstein "smokes" a pipe and wears glasses he doesn't need. My true love David Smythe is rock solid and has no odd habits other than devotion to me. I love that!

Angus laughed, "Those are a lot of questions, dear Bones. The last thing I remember is you begging me not to die when Franz, the murderous sewer scum, shot me." We both shudder as we relive the horror of that night.

His reflection takes on a somber tone as he continues. "We shall meet again, Franz, and the rules have changed." He paused and appeared to be shaken by something. "I just remembered tears falling on my face." His tone again changes as he brings himself once more into the present. "Today, just a few minutes ago, I found myself standing outside the door in the hall here at the Savoy. I felt full of energy and thirty-five again. I don't know what happened, but I don't think I am mortal. Maybe Sir Winston will have some answers for us when he returns. By the way, where is the Team?"

Sophie is sitting next to Angus on the sofa; she is as thrilled to see the dear man as I am. It was Sophie's tears he felt on his face as he died that nightmarish evening. That was not his first time. Angus died once before in a car crash. Axel the creep ran him off the street, and he hit a light pole. Sophie brought Angus back to life. She could not save him from the Grim Reaper twice. That is one of the rules imposed by Beyond. If someone dies, Sophie can bring that person back, but only one resurrection per person. Oddly, the rule may not apply to me. The car crash happened during our previous mission when we tracked the Neo-Nazis to their nest in a rough neighborhood in London.

Since Angus has recently been dead, and Abigor has been a demon, I fill them in, "The Team is conferring with Spears Westbrook at the Met Police. He thinks he may have a lead on Franz's whereabouts. Spears will share the tip with Miles at MI5. We want Franz badly for shooting you and incidentally trying to kill me. Damn cutthroat! And, of course, we must get the journal back before some other mad scientist wannabe decides to finish Dr. Mengele's mission and clone the three monsters. Also, Franz may have the viable cells essential for cloning them. We can hope he does not. Without the cells, Dr. Mengele's work died with him. Spears says Hitler, Goebbels, and Himmler's cells, which Mengele had safeguarded all these years, were not in the lab when they raided it. Yet, he is positive their cells were there earlier that day; one of the scientists swore to that. I think it was the guy who had a panic attack when we invaded their facility."

The guys are hanging on my every word, I remark, "Sir Winston, David, and I interviewed the scientists working in the lab that night. As you know, the police academy trained me in Neurolinguistics, so I watched the researchers for signs of deception and saw only a few instances. Unfortunately, their knowledge was compartmentalized and very specific to their particular task. We continue to put those bits and pieces together. We have heard that another team of scientists was working with Mengele at an undisclosed location. Angus, you remember the older scientist who scolded us when we entered the lab, a feisty guy?" Angus nodded his head cheerfully; he remembered the feisty guy. "He said he heard Mengele talking with someone on the phone; he thought Mengele said the name Dr. Wagner. We believe vile Doc was sharing their recent breakthrough in boosting the healing process with the Youth Drug." Big Soph has gone to sleep. This is rerun time for her.

Abigor, the new angel, is at a loss since much of this is unfamiliar to him, "Bones, I wouldst love to understand more about the Youth Drug. Can it be used to help humankind? Verily, it wouldst be a wonderful blessing for which we could be thankful!" I assure him Dr. Einstein will work on that as soon as we complete our mission. Abigor crosses himself in gratitude. My former Demon really has changed. Perhaps.

Warming to my subject as we get to the good part, I press on, "If Franz took the cells, there is a possibility, however remote, that they may still clone the Nazi monsters. So far, we have nothing of substance to locate him. On a positive note, Spears has a couple of potential leads he is pursuing. We have not given up, and neither have Spears and Miles. Spears has been a demon working without sleep, trying to track Franz. He was furious about your murder, Angus. Wait until I tell him you are alive!" What am I saying? Spears would not understand about Beyond and returning spirits. Uh, no . . .

Where was I, guys? Oh, yes, "We have been working with Spears in all of our recent missions. It is much easier for him to process evidence with his high-tech labs, arrange for crime scene professionals, and use his extensive list of law enforcement contacts around the globe. David and Spears are friends. Spears thinks David is an intel spook, a highly classified intel spook, still alive and working with MI5. Oops. Spears has no idea who Churchill and Einstein are; a talented makeup artist, Madame Dubois from the Royal National Theater, reimaged them. As two of the most famous men produced in the 19th Century, they were entirely too recognizable. Neither man took the reimaging with good grace."

Sophie wakes and nods her great head vigorously in agreement.

I take time to grab a cuppa from the silver teapot on the coffee table. I add, "Angus, you know most of this, but the saintly Abigor does not." The saintly Abigor gave me a dirty look that was not at all angelic. I laugh and continue, "We had tracked down Dr. Mengele and his creepy assistants Franz and Hans in our first mission and detained them in a cell in the London Sewers. We were under the optimistic illusion that they were alone in their mad scientist plans to clone the most sinister criminals from the Third Reich. We were incredibly mistaken. This unwarranted optimism seems to happen frequently. Vile Doc and henchmen had an army of Neo-Nazis around the globe and a group of brilliant but highly unethical research scientists at their beck and call. Mengele needed time to pursue his mission, so he created a youth drug concoction that slowed the aging process to a virtual halt. Naturally, Mengele's unscrupulous scientists were immensely interested in this stunning breakthrough. Financially, the drug would be worth billions."

Angus is pacing and taking in the intel; he stops mid-pace and asks, "Do we have an estimate of the number of degenerates in the Neo-Nazi organization? I knew they were involved with Dr. Mengele. Indeed, they were there at the lab when Franz absconded with the Journal. They also caused me to wreck the really cool Aston Martin. By the way, I owe those thugs, especially their bosses, Axel and Weber, a hefty thump or two. I would think Miles and MI5 would have information on the guttersnipes. I shall talk to David about this. Our investigation is global and convoluted. I am eternally grateful we have this huge team of six to handle the mission." Angus smirks, and Sophie and I smirk back. Abigor is squinting at me again. Angels are too serious.

I am starving. Where is lunch? I responded to Angus. "The subjects who received the youth jab did not age, and their healing was enhanced. Reflecting on the lesson of Frankenstein, yes, there was an oops. Their hearts continued to age one tick at a time. Tick, tick, tick. Those ticks started to add up by the time they reached the century mark. The Nazis who died of myocardial infarction, Dr. Mengele and Hans, were over 100 when they dropped dead. Ok, can either of you tell me, just for fun, how many heartbeats would tick off in one hundred years?"

Abigor jumps up, waving his hands. "I knoweth, dear lovely Bones, that wouldst be about 3,004,560,000 beats!" Wow! I am stunned by our former Demon! Angus stares at him.

Wide-eyed in amazement, I move on, "Good job, Abigor! Guys, let's jump back to the bad guys. Mengele had hoped to fix this annoying heart deficiency in the drug's promise and had come quite close with a group of researchers in Austria. Sadly, for him, that was when we caught up with him and secured him in the London Sewer." That turned out to be much less secure than we thought. Sigh.

"As we know, this intractable cardiac detail killed Dr. Mengele and his henchman Hans. Hans died on a prior mission when he aimed his cannon size gun at me. He fired before heart failure dropped him. Thankfully, Sophie lept across the room and shoved me out of the projectile's path. I took Han's murderous intent very personally. Before that, he had tried to dislodge my head with an antique long gun at a bookstore in London. I found myself in trouble with Beyond when I fought back—vigorously. Another Beyond rule, members of the Team cannot kill a human unless they are saving an innocent—The Prime Directive. The Team members, except for me, are immortals. Our enemies are normally human." I glare at Abigor; he had been our only Demon enemy. I return to my story. "Hans and Franz had a misguided and inexplicable prejudice against me. As far as we know, Mengele, Hans, Franz, Wentworth, and their small Hit Squad were the only ones treated with the youth concoction. All are dead now, except Franz and the Hit Squad. The brutal Hit Squad was deemed necessary due to their highly specialized skill set—punishment. The Neo-Nazis are terrified of those monsters, so traitors are few. That is all I have, for now, guys." Both, uh, men, clap in appreciation, and I take a bow. Sophie slides the silver teapot toward me.

I open the floor for questions and comments.

Abigor ignores me; he is anxious to mend fences with Angus, "I am delighted to see you again and in the prime of thine youth, Angus. Thou were a worthy adversary, and I hope to call thee a friend one day. I have been assigned to your team for now. I cannot explain by whom or under what circumstances; I was sworn to silence. Know this; I shalt make up for our previous unpleasantness. I shalt not fail you." Angus frowns as he observes Abigor. He does not appear convinced that Abigor is a rehabilitated former Demon. Who can blame him? It doesn't happen every day. To be honest, since I joined the Team, these Twilight Zone experiences are likely and generally accepted with a yawn.

Abigor continues, "It is not universally known that I hast, well, changed sides. Secrecy is essential because it allows me to access the dark side when advantageous. That advantage will not last long." He paused in thought, and eyebrows lifted above those startling eyes. He shook himself and continued,

"My history with the Nazis is long and dark. I heard rumors about Hitler's deep depravity and forays into the occult and technology, and I used that to gain an audience with him. I planned to harvest his smutty soul; he wanted to win battles and defeat his enemies. We made a wicked contract. I shalt always sorely regret helping that despicable man. Recently, I sought and gained Mengele's soul on my final mission as a demon. Then thanks to Thelma, I was immersed in mine own spiritual struggle. I can never adequately express mine deep gratitude to that saintly spirit."

He stares at us, looks around the room, then whispers, "I have two words to share with thee, Owl Mountain. Those two words art vitally important, and an extreme urgency is attached."

No sooner were the words out of his mouth than the room began to shake and rumble loudly. In the center of the room, flames shot up through a hole in the floor. Shocked, I jumped away from the flames and retreated to a safe distance. From the middle of the flames, a hideous creature arose. I have never seen anything as horrible, even in nightmares. It is mottled browns, greens, and tans as if it were in an advanced state of decomposition. The monster's eyes are large and rimmed in black. Its mouth is a red slice that could have been cut by a surgeon's scalpel, framing decaying teeth. Slimy, squirming vipers rise from its head. Its nose is large and bulbous, with blood oozing from it. The closed eyes slowly open, black and gangrenous red. I am too terrified to breathe.

When it spoke, words slithered out, and it looked directly at Abigor. It hissed, "Demon, you are watched, and we shall utterly destroy you and everyone around you. You will leave now and never return! There will be no mercy after today!" I wasn't feeling the mercy part.

Abigor laughed and said, "Surgat, you do not intimidate me with thine magic tricks and dramatic entrance. Consider, I worked with the great Shakespeare, you amateur! I was a demon for centuries, and I am not frightened. Thou cannot harm me. I am stronger than I have ever been. I order thee to depart now!"

The apparition parried, "You risk destruction. I warn you, Abigor! Join us or be annihilated." A thought appears to enter his mind. "Ahhh, yes, and what about the puny woman?" He looks at me and smiles the most horrid smile possible on this side of Hell's gates. Apparition snarls, " I can turn her into a tower of flames with one breath." Abigor, Angus, and Sophie move as one defensive unit to stand in front of me.

Sophie is doing her creature from Hell thing. Her red eyes throw off sparks. Angus rushes toward the flames, but Abigor jerks him back and throws himself over the apparition. It disappears through the hole from whence it came. The hole in the floor closes as if the entire incident were a shared nightmare or mass hysteria, though I am the only one who is a tad hysterical. I fall on the leather sofa hyperventilating. I put my head between my knees and started breathing slowly. I usually don't react this way to danger. I am pretty used to being attacked as the only mortal on the team. Yet, in my defense, the thing was massively disgusting and smelled of rot and decay.

I am wild-eyed, and stuttering overwhelmed with shock. Yet, Sophie, Angus, and Abigor are perfectly calm and at peace. Their calm annoys me.

Abigor explains calmly, "That was all theatrics to try to intimidate us. Naturally, Sophie and I hast superior powers. We art on the side of good. He is a horror in appearance, though he is no more dangerous than yond coffee table unless one is mortal. His appearance was contrived. Yes, he is awful to look upon, I grant thee that, but not that hideous. The snakes art for effect—overdone, I should think.

"Honestly, he could have turned thee into a pillar of fire." I am not happy. He is taking that possibility entirely too lightly. Maybe there is still a little demon hiding in there.

As he spoke, the door to the suite flew open, and Dr. Einstein and Sir Winston, distressed and disheveled, rushed into the room, expecting danger. Dr. Einstein dropped his pipe as he swung around, searching every corner. Sir Winston almost swallowed the cigar in his mouth. They were followed by David, distraught but in alfa male control. The three spirits checked the room and then inquired about what had just happened. They had sensed the danger to me. The guys have powers that I do not understand. They can teleport, or something, from one place to another in the wink of an eye. They can sometimes influence humans to do their bidding. They "talk on a phone" without a device—tremendous savings in phone plans and data rates. When necessary, my Team members can become invisible. No, I cannot do any of these things. Sigh.

Their powers came from Beyond (I am not privy to that information.) and were given to them when they accepted our mission—save the world. They had all died and were relaxing in Beyond when the world and humanity were threatened by villainous deviants one more time. From what David told me, several teams like ours fight daily to save humans from the stupid and malevolent among us. I met Veracity Hall-White from another Team on our last mission. She is an expert on all things mariner, and I hoped to learn more about the ancient gold Sunstone Compass. The Teams have an encouraging track record, but success is never guaranteed. Hitler was never supposed to reach the pinnacle of global power. As Abigor confessed to us, he was partially responsible for that abject failure on our part. He aided Hitler in becoming a world power. Churchill likes to refer to Hitler as the Corporal.

As soon as the guys were sure the danger was over, we sat down to discuss the monster. David sat beside me, put his arm around my shoulders, and held me close. If he still had a heartbeat, I would feel it now. No matter, he is and always will be the love of my life until I no longer have a heartbeat, maybe forever. We fell in love when our eyes met so many months ago. That was the first day our team came together. We knew we would never have a life together. As Tevye said in *Fiddler on the Roof*, "...a bird may love a fish, but where would they build a home together?"

I am still traumatized by the Demon from the Abyss pyromaniac and his threats against me. Undoubtedly, David has eased my blood pressure, and my breathing is returning to some semblance of normal. Yet, I need to tell my story to calm down.

Sir Winston looks worried. "Dear Bones, you seem to be in a high state of excitation. Are you well? What do you want to tell us? Please calm yourself, my dear, and tell us what is wrong. Have you eaten?" All the guys seem to think I constantly need a burger.

The whole story about the monster started tumbling from me. "Guys, there was a monster. A real smelly monster threatened to turn me into a tower of flames. He seemed serious about that! He rose from the floor, maybe from Hell; flames were all around him! The hideous creep threatened to ignite me. Abigor said the monster could burn me to a crisp, but he didn't seem to care." David, Einstein, and Sir Winston all turn a withering glare toward Abigor. Assaulted by their disapproval, Abigor visibly shrinks.

I take a breath and continue, "The smelly monstrosity threatened Abigor with destruction. But, I suppose his ability is not as strong as his words and horrid appearance. Sophie, Abigor, and Angus jumped in front of me when he threatened to turn me into a tiki torch. Abigor smothered him. Anyway, he disappeared." I stop, exhausted by my terrifying tale, and reach for a cuppa. David jumps up and pours the hot restorative liquid into my cup. My cup shakes as I try to find my mouth.

Everyone is still glaring at Abigor. He sighs and says, "Surgat is a powerful demon of ancient origin. He is first seen as a flame, then in human form. He rules 36 legions in Hell. He wast sent to intimidate me. Verily, I do know his tricks. Thus, they do not work on me, although he knew tricks would be effective on Bones. He must have bethought we wast alone. He would not come when the entire group art hither because that would lessen his impact. Aye, I admit he can harm mortals. Somehow, he knew I wast sharing information on Owl

Mountain. On the dark side, demons guard the secret. Be aware that while I am part of the team, demons shalt be watching." I shiver.

Worried and angry, David asked, "Abigor, what is Surgat capable of? What are his powers? How do we stop him?" We are eager to hear Abigor's answer.

Abigor seemed reluctant to talk about powers. Finally, he said, "He can change to any shape he wishes, shapeshifter. What we saw was not the true Surgat. He sought to terrorize. He can perform some magic and take possession of humans. Possession by demons is real, and it always has been. Exorcism often worked. He art an expert at destruction. Surgat art fully capable of turning our dear Bones into, what did she say, a tiki torch without a moment's hesitation. Each demon art different, and he art iron-handed. We cannot kill him. We must protect Bones from him." We sigh in unison. Nothing is ever easy on our missions.

Dr. Einstein is concentrating; his forehead is deeply creased in thought. Finally, he says, "If you don't mind, I shall change the conversation to powerful weapons. I know nothing of demons. "He adjusts the glasses he doesn't need and peers at us. I had a professor of Biology in undergraduate school who did that before he yelled at us. Einstein does not yell. He says, "I have heard of a secret facility or lab at Owl Mountain. It has been many years, and the stories contradict each other. However, I strongly suspect something is there, furtively draped in the shadows. It would be beneficial to investigate. If I am not mistaken, Riese is the code name for the project. Underground structures are nearby. Let me think. Yes, it was at Ksiaz Castle in Lower Silesia, Poland. What have you heard, Abigor?" All eyes turn toward our former Demon.

Abigor says, "I hast heard a fearsome machine there is capable of destroying much of the world. Aye, I admit that sounds fanciful. Even more fanciful, another machine or door is capable of unimaginable wonders. I know not what. Maybe it can stop the disaster." He asks hopefully, as much to himself as to those in the room.

David joins the speculation, "Yes, I remember wild stories back during the war suggesting Hitler had a doomsday machine tucked away in Owl Mountain. No one really took it seriously, and the War ended, and we all went home to start new lives without bloody wars and their shocking destruction. What did you hear, Sir Winston?" Sophie is a statue as she listens.

Sir Winston leans forward and chomps down on his cigar, "There were rumors and reckless conjecture at that time. Hitler was insane and invested resources in all manner of wild inventions and even the occult. One man seemed to know more about a secret weapon than anyone else. He was a young man who was familiar with the Owl Mountains. His name was Andrew "Red" Biggers. He had begun an investigation into the rumors before the War ended. In 1943, Red and many other stalwart Brits were recruited as volunteers in my newly formed Special Operation Executive or SOE. As a country, we stared annihilation in the eye while watching Hitler's thugs ravage Europe. My SOE operatives trained at country houses, such as Wansborough Manor, and Guildford, in espionage, sabotage, and reconnaissance. They were a handpicked group of extraordinarily courageous and resourceful men and women. Their existence was a well-guarded secret for obvious reasons. We chose Red because he was familiar with the Owl Mountain area in Poland and spoke the language. I believe his maternal grandparents lived in the area. The SOE members had to fit in and hide in the open for their success and survival. In plain sight, so to speak. If the Germans or their local supporters had discovered SOE operatives, they would have immediately executed them. Red would be nearly a hundred years old. He may still be alive. We must determine where he might be if alive. It is more likely he died long ago, so we will contact his close companions and search his papers. He may have left written documents that could further our knowledge. We will return to the investigation of Owl Mountain momentarily."

We circle back to what Sir Winston was going to say before he called on me about my state of "excitation." But first, we engage in a verbal free for all. I am anxious to discuss the miraculous circumstances surrounding our returning and new Demon members. Angus has questions about his new state of being. Abigor wants to warn them. Naturally, the guys already knew everything we were clamoring to tell them.

Sir Winston, the Greatest Statesman of the 20th Century, spoke directly to our former MI5 agent, "Angus, my dear boy, we are delighted to have you back with us looking in fine fettle. Youth suits you! I know you are wondering what happened after you died. There was a worthy meeting in Beyond where David, Albert, and I participated. The Powers wanted to know what to do with you after your death. We were quite passionate about defending your importance to our team. They wanted to reward you for your sacrifice when you stopped a bullet meant for our dear Bones. She would not be here today if not for you stepping in front of her at the opportune moment for her, not so for you, my boy. I am rarely without words, yet I do not have the eloquent phrases to express our gratitude adequately. The Powers decided to bring you back to us and reward you with youth. Naturally, as an immortal, you will not suffer the ravages of advanced age. This was your age when you worked with David and later investigated his murder and the Director-General's death. Therefore, this was your reward which you so richly deserve. Welcome back, dear boy!" Sir Winston wipes away tears with his linen handkerchief and reaches for his brandy snifter.

We all shake Angus' hand, pat his back, hug him, and show our love and appreciation for his courage and commitment. Then Sir Winston turns his attention to our new member, the former Demon.

Smiling at Abigor, Sir Winston continues, "Abigor, we knew you would be joining us, and we know how that came to be. We are aware that you possess information to which we are not privy. The Powers have assured us that you are a friend and will use your exceptional abilities to further our mission. We owe a debt of gratitude to Thelma Dove for making this possible. She and Admiral Stallings have been quite beneficial to us in the past. You are acquainted with the resourceful Admiral." Sir Winston smirks. He referred to their little battle of wills on the stairs when the Admiral and Abigor first met. The Admiral won a neat victory in that emotive wrestling match. And hence another entity on that seemingly endless list of those to whom Abigor must apologize. Of course, hundreds of years as a demon is a long time. Abigor sighs in resignation.

David tersely interjects, "I understand you will be taking your orders directly from your superior. We are pleased to add you to our Team, and we will work together for the good of humanity. We appreciate your willingness to assist us in our daunting but worthy mission."

Harshly, David adds, "That said, you did try to kill Bones. I am struggling not to destroy you, which is my first instinct. Your behavior will determine how I relate to you. You have been warned." His words are spat out rather than spoken. David is now looking very much the indomitable Air Marshall from WWII. His face is solid granite, his broad shoulders are squared, his dark eyes flash, and his gaze is laser-focused on Abigor's fathomless green eyes.

Dr. Einstein, ever the peacemaker, says, "Welcome to the Team, Abigor. Our mission is tremendous in scope. We have many impressive resources at our disposal, but our mission is still an enormously formidable undertaking. I assume you know about the worldwide system of determined, evil enemies we must overcome." Abigor nods. David snarls. I smile. Sophie snorts, albeit gracefully.

Sir Winston returns to the subject of Red Biggers. "Abigor tells us the Owl Mountain investigation is imperative. I shall call on a few of the men of my acquaintance who were involved in SOE leadership. Sadly, most of them are dead. As you are aware, that does not always close the door for us. I invite you to look around this room. Some of us never give up, never, never, never." Sir Winston smiles and trades the cigar for the snifter, which he puts to his lips. He salutes the never-give-up guys. I don't think Abigor counts.

The doorbell rings, and Angus answers; my food has arrived delivered by the affable Fatima from room service. I never answer the door; it can be dangerous. I munch on my well-done roast beef and cheese sandwich with sweet potato fries as they converse.

In mid-munch, I have an idea. "Sir Winston, I have been thinking while you were talking, and I will pay our splendid Admiral Stallings a visit at the Old Royal Navy College. He seems to be looped into everything about the Nazis and WWII. He is more reticent than I would like, but I don't have another source at the moment. I haven't traveled on bus #188 in a while." Everyone nods in approval except Abigor. Bus #188 takes me to the Old Royal Navy College. I have repeatedly encountered the lovely Thelma on the bus, patiently waiting to hand a book about demons to me. She seems to have an inexhaustible supply. The Admiral was very helpful in our last mission with information about the Sunstone Compass and its link to the Dark World. The Dark World remains a mystery. It appears that one cannot enter the Dark World without the Compass, assuming someone was mad enough to want to open that door. He undoubtedly knows about Owl Mountain and what they may have hidden there.

David says, "I have a colleague or two who were assigned to that project in the 1960s. There were still concerns about a possible weapon our enemies could use against us. World War II was over, but the Cold

War was still going strong. Sir Winston played a significant role in the Cold War until he left office. It began in 1947 and ended in 1991. It was a tensely uncertain time."

Angus looks interested. "They assigned me to that project. We were concerned the Soviets would hear the rumors and try to take advantage of the situation if such a weapon existed. We could never find reliable data confirming the likelihood of a super weapon at Owl Mountain. I discussed this with Sir Winston's contact Red Biggers, who was working with MI5 after the War, and we had planned to go on an expedition into the mountains, but we could not get permission from our government officials." Angus paused as his countenance took on a slightly perplexed look. "Biggers was an odd duck. He was very secretive, even for an MI5 agent. Red seemed convinced there was something to fear, yet Red never gave me supporting data. He was a bulldog of a man, low to the ground but powerfully built; he lost an eye on the Front and wore an eye patch. He was intimidating at first glance—and at second glance. No doubt that worked well for him when he was in SOE. It was a busy time for MI5, and the agency didn't have sufficient reason to pursue the Owl Mountain rumor. Biggers died in the mid-1960s from a heart attack. Odd that. He was in excellent health and not yet 50 years old. You must have seen him about, David." We were all thinking the same thing. We have known too many people who died because they had information dangerous to someone willing to kill for silence. Perhaps, we are simply paranoid. David, the Director-General of MI5, the policeman in Brighton Beach, Heather, and Wentworth, the IT geniuses from our first mission, were all killed because they knew too much. No, we are not paranoid.

Sir Winston looks troubled but plows through. "Angus, old man, please ascertain when Biggers died and acquire a copy of the autopsy report and the death certificate. I am suspicious. We are reasonably certain that MI5 Director-General Ogden was given a drug developed by the CIA that mimicked a heart attack. He died—convenient. The official report on the accident implied the driver suffered cardiac arrest and rolled David's car. We never learned why the Director-General was driving the Rolls. What are your thoughts, Albert?"

Dr. Einstein considered what we had discussed before answering, "I have little data on which to base an assumption. However, as I have said repeatedly, logic will get you from A to B. Imagination will take you everywhere. I agree with you, Winston; we should learn more. I believe life is like riding a bicycle. To keep your balance, you must keep moving. We must continue our forward momentum by asking questions, collecting data, and applying our imaginations to understand what we learn." Dr. Einstein is a genius. He drops his glasses, and Soph retrieves them for him.

David is already moving toward the door before he tells us, "I knew Biggers slightly. He was on assignment out of the country quite often. I want to know why he died. I think it is time for Angus and me to nose around at MI5. At least we don't have to worry about anyone recognizing the younger Angus since he is supposed to be dead. That would be a tough one to explain." David winks at me and smiles his crooked smile as he and Angus leave on their assignment. Yes, my heart flutters.

Sir Winston and Dr. Einstein will pop over and chat with Veracity Hall-White at the National Maritime Museum. They hope she can add to our meager knowledge about the Compass and Owl Mountain. Sir Winston suspects the two are connected in some elusive way we cannot imagine.

Abigor smiles as he says, "Well, it art time I start earning mine bread. I shalt talk with a couple of unsavory demons who might know something about the Doomsday Machine if it truly exists. I shalt hope they art not yet aware of my transition." Sophie watches him closely as he walks through the door. At least he doesn't just pop out of rooms anymore like the giant Druid. That reminds me, we have not seen Druid for quite a while. You would think he would pop in to scold us loudly more often. I miss his booming voice. Since he saved my life on the last mission, I have become quite fond of him. Everyone except Sophie has retreated to complete their tasks.

I grab my well-loved long black cardigan from the chair by the door and head downstairs to walk the few blocks to the bus stop to catch bus #188. It is time to have a little visit with Admiral Stallings at the Old Royal Navy College. Perhaps the angelic Thelma Dove will be there if I am lucky.

I notice the temperature has changed today. My cardigan and jeans are a bit warm for my walk. I shed the sweater and march on more comfortably with my black cotton turtleneck and jeans. I really must learn to check the temps for the day.

My bus ride is uneventful. I am a little disappointed Thelma is not aboard waiting for me with a new Demon book. Sometimes I wonder if I had dreamt all of this since from the very beginning when Sir Winston showed up in my office without an appointment demanding brandy. I suppose I could have fallen and hit my head. Brain damage happens.

It is a lovely short walk from the bus stop to the Old Royal Navy College. When I first visited the good Admiral here, I also encountered Abigor for the first time at the reception desk. He did not bother to mention that he was a demon. He winked at me, pointed toward the stairs, and said, go to room 666. Obviously, I thought that was his little joke. It was not.

I head for the same stairs, quite confident that I am the only one here today who can see these stone steps and certainly the only one who can climb up to the Admiral's office. It is quite a tiring hike even though Admiral Stallings' office is supposed to be on the third floor. I am astounded by the number of steps I must climb. Realistically, I climb much farther than three flights of stairs. I expect a high-altitude nosebleed. Finally, exhausted, I arrive at the Admiral's office. I stand outside the door, which currently has the number 316. It changes. I wait, knowing he is aware of my presence in the hall. After a few minutes, I hear, "Come in, Doctor." The door opens itself, and I enter the captain's cabin. It looks as one would expect it if this building were an old sailing ship. There is minimal furniture besides a couple of battered wood chairs, an equally battered enormous desk, and the Admiral sitting behind the desk. He is an alarmingly handsome man in the tradition of a Clark Gable. Tall, dark hair, tanned from much time at sea eighty years ago when he was alive. He motions for me to sit in one of the wood chairs.

Admiral Stalling's attention is razor-sharp and riveting. He says, "So, you have come back to visit me, have you, Doctor? Did you destroy the Sunstone Compass as I advised you to do on more than one occasion? More than your life is in danger when you possess that indescribably evil, corrupt device. Ah, I see from your expression, Doctor; you have not been wise. You are childishly easy to read." He seemed to lose interest in me and looked toward an antique leather book on his desk. Shades of the lovely, cryptic Thelma and her book collection?

I sit down, take out my notepad and pen, and answer, "I am delighted to see you too, sir. I heard your words when you warned me, and I took your wise counsel seriously. The compass is not mine to destroy. We need your help again. We have heard whispers, disturbing stories, a doomsday machine, or something dreadfully frightening at Owl Mountains. Abigor tells us something has shifted there, and it is now urgent that we investigate. Rumors have been circulating for decades. Everyone in our team had heard of the Owl Mountain Doomsday Weapon, though the stories vary in content and detail. Most of the rumors are vague and unsubstantiated. Can you tell me anything, anything at all, that will help our Team? Time is of the essence. We would be forever grateful." I try to look properly chastised.

The Admiral leans back in his chair and studies the mysteries of the white clapboard ceiling again, singularly focused on teasing out the threads of the inexplicable hidden there. Finally, he answers, "Why do you want to know about Owl Mountain? What has happened?" I always get more questions than answers from Admiral Stallings. Patience, Bones.

I consider staring at the ceiling in my best Zen pose. I don't. "Admiral, Abigor told us there is a weapon capable of incredible destruction hidden away in the dark recesses of Owl Mountain if only one knows where to look. It can be found. If possible, we must find it and render it harmless before our enemies decide to turn it against humanity. Dr. Einstein thinks there may be another machine or door there as well. He has no idea what it is capable of, but he suspects it may have mighty powers. He heard about it during WWII. Is there anything you can tell us to help on our journey?" I notice the ship's lantern hanging above the Admiral's desk sway.

The good Admiral studies the mysteries of the white clapboard ceiling again. There is only one small window in the ship's cabin, which is too high and small for me to look outside. I presume he found the desired mystery in the ceiling since he returned his attention to me with those penetrating blue eyes. "Doctor, I have also heard whispers from long ago. Hitler was mad, of course, and he reached out for the bizarre, occult, and fantastic. This Doomsday Machine and the other, uh, device are manifestations of that madness. The Nazis twisted Technology and science into an unnatural Frankenstein monster. I believe you referred to that name recently." I sway, shocked by his prescience! How did he know? He could not have known that! Impossible! He smiles as he observes my reaction. Truthfully, I didn't think his lips could do that maneuver.

As soon as I can collect myself, I soldier on, "Please continue, Admiral. I would like to hear what you know. Your words concern me. Correct me if I am mistaken. You appear to verify what Abigor has told us. The possibilities are alarming. I must admit I suspect extreme urgency is appropriate."

The Admiral cannot be rushed, no matter the urgency. I suppose he is past that. After an appropriate pause, he picks his words carefully and with precision. He says, "Doctor, I am not a man subject to flights of fancy. I am a man of facts and due consideration of all plausible options. Recently, the noise around these issues has grown louder than in many years. I have heard three things, and none are pleasant to my ears. Firstly, the group behind the recent interest in the Nazi and Neo-Nazi groups are leaders in the New Global Agenda movement. They furnish the financial backing and seem to think this is acceptable. The NGA members think a resurrected Hitler is the man to bring about their dream, authoritarian despotism. In plain words, the world elites enslave the peasants. Secondly, they have made an unholy alliance with a powerful partner. Thirdly, what is the most disturbing whisper? He delivers the answer in a sharp whisper of his own. "A mighty Demon is at the heart of the scheme and pulling the strings without anyone understanding the danger. Destruction may be the Demon's goal. His home is in Owl Mountain, and he has no scruples about destroying much of the planet if necessary." In a more matter-of-fact tone, he elaborates. "If mass destruction is his goal, the Doomsday Machine is the appropriate weapon to annihilate much of humanity. I hear that he has something that NGA desperately desires, but I have no idea what that might be.

Foolishly, they think they can control him. Have you not noticed the direction governments have been moving in recent years? There is a worldwide push for more central control to create a universal dictatorship. They extinguish voices of disagreement. Silencing everyone who would fight against them is part of their plan.

"Are these whispers accurate? I cannot answer that question. But I am convinced the world is in great peril."

I am distraught by what the Admiral told me. No, he is not a man of fancy or hyperbole. He is deliberate in his thoughts and words. I wish, at this moment, it was not so. Yes, I have noticed a more authoritarian movement in governments worldwide. I must get back to the Savoy and share this information with the Team.

I thank the Admiral for his time and information. He watches me closely as I turn to leave. As the door opens, his parting words chill my soul. "Doctor, your extraordinarily formidable Team has vast resources to battle evil in all its many forms. But I must be honest, so you will have an opportunity to make preparations. I sincerely believe you will lose this battle. I am sorry, my dear." There was an additional reason for his warning I did not understand at the time.

His parting words, equal parts regret and maybe even pity, hit me like a sledgehammer. I stumble through the door. It closes and disappears as I walk to the stairs. I don't bother to look back at the ever-changing number on the door.

Chapter Three

Meeting at MI5

When I returned to the suite, Sophie was the only one there. She immediately knows I am distraught and gives me a sweet knee hug to mend my black mood and restore me to warrior mode. It works. I am back in a never, never, never surrender attitude, and I desperately need food. I order a pot of coffee and a ham and cheese sandwich with sweet potato fries made by the lovely folks at room service, especially for this Southern girl.

After a few minutes, Fatima, a friendly Pakistani lady, delivered my order. She typically brings my food since she has learned my taste and preferences. So, she provides a massive pot of the blackest, most robust coffee possible. We chat about her son and his incredible soccer team for a few minutes. Her dark eyes sparkle with pride when she talks about his prowess on the field. Our chat is perfect; I desperately need a normal human conversation.

I bite into my luscious sandwich, and, with a little stab of pain, I am reminded of how much I miss eating with Angus. Breaking bread with another human was such a delight since the guys don't indulge. That sharing door has closed, and I am on my own. Maybe we will add another mortal to our team. We certainly need all the help we can get if Admiral Stallings is even marginally close to being accurate. This mission is enormous and annoyingly complex in both depth and breadth. Every time I try to get my head around the big picture, the room starts to spin.

As I am chewing the last morsel of my delicious sandwich and sipping my third cup of coffee, Sir Winston and Dr. Einstein return. I don't know whether to immediately blurt out The Admiral's most recent gloomy prognostication or wait until the entire Team is together. I decide, instead, to ask them about their chat with Veracity Hall-White before I throw a shadow over the day.

I give them each a warm hug and ask about their visit with the maritime expert. Sir Winston looks gloomy and begins, "It was most interesting, dear Bones. Veracity is always a delight and very well connected to the peculiar and historical, including the ancient and extraordinary. She had heard of the Owl Mountain 'Curiosity,' as she called it. Alas, she was adamant. She had no intention of delving into the occult or demonology. She does not open dark doors. We attempted to impress Veracity with the gravity of this mission to us, not only to us but, more critically, to humankind. She did admit she had heard that a demon is in residence at Owl Mountain. She obstinately refused to be a fellow traveler on our journey into the mountain's demonic bowels. Undeniably, she was quite unnerved conversing about the 'Curiosity' with Albert and me. We soon found ourselves dismissed and shown unceremoniously to the door. I haven't felt that unwelcome since I lost the national election on July 05, 1946. Would you say that covers our peculiar conversation, Albert?" Sir Winston found his matches and dropped them to the floor. Big Soph, again, retrieved the matchbox for the Great Man.

Albert took his glasses off, ran his hand through his unruly hair, causing it to stand up straight, and replied, "I wish I understood why Veracity, who is not a squeamish woman by any means, reacted so uncharacteristically." The good doctor seemed genuinely perplexed before continuing. "Our conversation frightened her. Of what would she be frightened?" He looked at each of us questioningly as if one of us might suddenly have the answer. He tried to reason his way out of his bewilderment. "Nothing of which I am aware can harm her. She is protected, just as we are, from demons and everything else mortals would fear. As I have always said, if you cannot explain it simply, you don't understand it well enough. Obviously, I don't understand it." He ends emphatically!

Their conversation awakened a memory; I chimed in, "When I talked to Veracity during our last mission, she said she did not like to dwell on the demonic. That was when I consulted her about the Sunstone Compass. She told me a demon had once owned the ancient compass, and he put a curse on it. She could not tell me more or likely chose not to discuss it." Soph sagely nodded her head in agreement.

We continued debating Veracity's inexplicable reluctance to talk Hell and demons. I can't believe we said that. I am so accustomed to the genuinely terrifying and Twilight-ish that I forget not everyone is as comfortable with the stuff of nightmares. She may be more in her comfort zone with the purely academic aspects of our missions. We are lucky to have access to her extensive knowledge of the ancient, particularly maritime antiquities, and her impressive research skills. Note to self, no demonic discussions with Veracity.

David and Angus walk in the door, and I rush over to hug them and kiss David on his sensual full lips. After talking to Miles at MI5, they are excited and fill us in on the particulars. David informed Miles that Angus, now introduced as George Clarke, was new to our team, a former Inspector at Brighton Beach, and he would be helping them with the investigation. By the way, there will be a glowing personnel file with the name George Clarke in Brighton Beach's Sussex Police computer, and no, I don't know how they accomplish that. BTW, he has many awards and commendations. They don't do anything unsatisfactorily. Miles has helped us in the past and is a powerful, dependable resource. Angus, now George, asked about getting a copy of Red Biggers death certificate and autopsy report. Miles assured George that since Biggers' was working with MI5 at the time of his death, they would have that information in his file. Since the file is decades old, it would take a while, but Miles ordered it before leaving his office. He warned them that many of the old files were not computerized. We are enthused to hear positive news for a change—score one for the White Hats. David has total recall and can give us a shot-by-shot report on his visit with Miles.

David shared the gist of the meeting with us. "While we were with Miles, there was a knock at the door. A man and a woman joined us. Miles introduced us to them."

David describes the older, a robust man with chestnut hair and a matching mustache. He was probably in his mid-fifties, with a broad toothy smile and clouded gray eyes. Miles told us, 'This is our new Deputy Director-General, Emory Taylor. You may have seen him here before when we had meetings. He has been with us for a couple of months. He replaced Thomas Staggs, who died suddenly. I am sure you have met Thomas." David nodded his head in agreement. "Thomas was a talented, dedicated member of our team for over ten years. Oddly, his autopsy did not explain the cause of death—such an unexpected tragedy. We are in a high-stress business. I suppose I shouldn't be surprised. We appreciate Emory stepping in and taking control of Thomas' duties. Emory, this is David Smythe, formerly with our agency, and George Clarke, formerly with our friends at Sussex Police. They are investigating a private case, and we are assisting them." They had all shaken hands and exchanged polite comments. David had noticed that Emory's handshake, surprisingly, was relatively weak. He said the other person was a woman in her forties, with luxuriant black hair and lovely large dark eyes, perhaps of African descent. She smiled at them, but the smile did not reach her troubled eyes. A burden rests too heavily on her shoulders?

Miles introduced her to us. 'This lady, Emara Davis, is the Head of our Joint Terrorism Analysis Centre. She has been with us for twelve years and runs a tight ship for our organization. The JTAC is a grouping of representatives from sixteen government departments and agencies. As you know, they analyze data for terrorist threats. She has quite the responsibility for numerous representatives and missions. I don't know how she does it. Especially now, with all the upheaval in the Middle East. Her department is vital to our interests. The Taliban and ISIS are unusually active again."

David says, "We did the handshaking and polite conversation again."

David frowns slightly as he recalls the details of the meeting he just described to us, "It was strange meeting the new Deputy Director-General. I had not realized that Thomas Staggs had died. That was a shock. I have not had time to stay abreast of the changes at my old agency recently. Thomas had only been with MI5 for about ten years. He was a good man, meticulous about details, and a bulldog in pursuing cases." David pauses and frowns again.

While looking for his silver matchbox, Sir Winston looks up at David and questions, "Your description of the conversation with Miles about Staggs is terribly interesting, David. Miles's lack of alarm and inquisitiveness about Staggs' death is peculiar. He lost a top-ranking key member of his team, and he yawned and carried on? After saving the world, I want to look into his questionable response." Churchill finds his matchbox and smiles with satisfaction. Angus agrees the Deputy's sudden death doesn't pass his smell test.

After the interruptions, David continues, "I hear what Sir Winston and Angus are saying, and I heartily concur. We shall shelve the investigation into Staggs' death for another time. Miles is still working on finding Franz, and I am grateful to report he has a promising lead. He sent notifications to all the European research laboratories, warning them that Franz was armed and extremely dangerous. He had hoped he would hit pay dirt. One of the labs responded to Miles' warning and reported Franz may have made contact with them. They had seen someone skulking around the facility property late one night recently. Clearly, their security is no better than it was when we invaded. Of course, you will not be surprised to hear the lab is in Innsbruck, Austria." Anticipating our question, David continued. "Our old friend, Dr. Suggs, is still the director. To enlighten our new members, Dr. Mengele, Big Franz, and Blond Hans worked with the Austrian Lab to perfect their youth drug. The scientists had no idea with whom they were working. Since Dr. Mengele was infusing lots of money into their research, they probably did not thoroughly investigate his credentials." We nodded our agreement—money talks.

"Research labs seldom have money thrown at them in large amounts. Usually, they have to compete with other researchers for funding. Mengele was a Godsent to them—so to speak. We found the Mengele gang there after weeks of running down leads. Once we arrived, we had the Gunfight at OK Corral. Not our idea, but that was the way it went down. Fortunately, we were armed, except for Dr. Einstein. Bones barely made it out alive. I am not sure the scientists will be thrilled to see us again—people can be so sensitive. The fact is, this is the only solid lead we have on Franz. I suggest we pop over to Austria and add a little excitement to their lives." David smiles his wicked sexy smile.

The others quickly agreed this was an opportunity we could not afford to miss. Since they were popping, I was not included in the landing party. I cannot pop. I would have to be on a much more time-consuming flight to travel to Austria with them. I am sadly disappointed.

Sir Winston is excited to go. "Gentlemen, we must go back to the laboratory where we first met the Mengele monsters. We were well prepared and fortunate last time, and I am hopeful our luck will hold. Since we must move immediately, Bones will stay here, and Sophie will stay to protect her. With the Demon pyromaniac on the loose, we cannot even contemplate leaving Bones alone. Do we all agree that David, Angus, Albert, and I shall leave at once and meet at the lab in Austria?"

Everyone nodded in agreement except me. I was not nodding or happy. I do not want to be left behind and miss out on the excitement, but I understand the need for haste in investigating our only lead. Miles will probably contact local law enforcement to ask them to check on this information too. Our Team must get there before the cops arrive.

They depart en masse, leaving Sophie and me some time to relax and think about the problem at hand, Owl Mountain. I didn't have an opportunity to tell the guys about my visit to Admiral Stallings. I decided to look at my notes, but when I opened my red leather Sak tote, I found a book not there when I left this morning. I notice the volume is quite fragile as I pull it from my tote, so I am cautious. The title on the front is *The Discouerie of Witchcraft* by Reginald Scott. A note is attached; it says:

> This book was written in 1584, and you will be pleased to know Scott consulted many experts of his day, including Agrippa von Nettesheim's *De Occulta Philosophia,* written in 1531. Knowledge is power. Enjoy your book.
>
> Your friend,
> Jeffrey Stallings

Great, now I am getting occult books from Stallings and Thelma. I am a bit confused. Why has witchcraft been added to my reading selections? Weren't demons enough? They are like Goodreads with a dark spooky edge.

I surprised myself by wishing Abigor was here to help with the old English translation.

Chapter Four

Back to Austria

The Team arrived at the lab in Austria before I could snap my fingers and click the heels of my ruby slippers. David and Angus take the lead as the most experienced law enforcement professionals. They huddled outside in the darkness of night in the lush greenery. The lab security plan did not include viewing the grounds from the lab. Densely packed trees and large shrubs surround the facility. If the scientists have security people, there is no way the guards can see anything, even if Julius Caesar's Roman Legions decide to attack. In all fairness, I must admit the likelihood of an attack by Julius and his helmeted legions is unlikely. I suppose the landscape designer scored over the security consultant. Luckily, this lack of visibility is helpful to our Team. The landing party is armed; they are always armed, except dear kind Dr. Einstein. He is uncomfortable with modern weaponry. A hundred yards from the lab entrance sits a moderate-sized brick shed probably used to store tools and chemicals, fortunately, large enough for the four men and Abigor if he happens to show up. It has windows that allow them to remain hidden but offer a view of the lab. Since the guys can invoke invisibility when necessary, they can use that advantage to take turns patrolling the property.

They decide to wait until all the cars leave the parking lot. Franz is old but human. Thus, he has limitations the Team does not share. He must be seeking shelter. Though it is not winter, the nights are nasty because of thunderstorms in the area this week. Franz will need dry clothing, shelter, and food to survive. They know from prior experience Franz prefers German food. They will look around the surrounding area for a German Restaurant. If they can grab him while he is away from the lab, they can avoid the scientists who may still harbor unreasonable resentment about our previous shoot-out. The guy's time frame to find Franz is squeezed tightly. Local law enforcement will soon learn that the scientists spotted Franz in the area. The Boys in Blue may decide to come snooping. Local law enforcement notification will not include the details or circumstances surrounding Franz's criminal escapades. He probably will not be a high priority. However, the guys cannot depend on that.

They decided to try a local German restaurant called the Shiftskeller. It advertises all the traditional German dishes. They are open until midnight, giving Franz shelter until he decides to return to the facility. Early morning is an ideal time for him to scout out the Laboratory with little chance of being seen. The Shiftskeller is within walking distance of the lab. Perfect. Franz and his gang regularly visited a traditional German restaurant when their lab was in London.

If the Austrian facility has not changed since their last blockbuster visit, it seems likely that the lab's security is minimal, relying on technology that David can destroy in seconds. They assume Franz can do the same. A late-night visit will attract Franz since the probability of entering without being detected is quite good.

The guys pop over to the Shiftskeller to hang out and watch for the deviate, Franz. They enter a tastefully decorated large room with gleaming wood floors and contemporary wood tables accented by bright red chairs for a pop of color. The guys became accustomed to the traditional German restaurant while tracking Franz and creepy friends in London. Pleasantly surprising this restaurant is unique. The rustic timber beam ceiling and engaging murals lend an aura of drama and artistry to the interior. Sir Winston is accustomed to the best and is at peace here. Outside, a long narrow alley separates towering ancient buildings. This is an excellent place to sit where they can watch the entrance door and the passage.

The smiling head waiter, tall, blonde, with a manly beard and suspenders attached to the eponymous lederhosen, shows them to their table by a large window overlooking the plaza and alley. Soon the waitperson approaches their table. She is a cute redhead with a curvy figure shown off to her advantage by a short yellow skirt and a white peasant blouse. Her long, blood-red fingernails give a daring edge to her bold look. She stares at David and speaks directly to him. Dr. Einstein, Sir Winston, and Angus might as well be invisible. She does give a second half-hearted appraising look to the now young Clint Eastwood double. The poor man does not hold a candle to the hunky David in his leather bomber jacket, white button-down shirt, and tight, faded jeans. He exudes an edge of potential danger as in-your-face and solid as his worn jacket.

Staring at David, she says in German, "I am Hannah, and I will be taking care of you, uh, gentlemen. Our special for tonight is, is, uh, uh, let me see, oh, yes, I see it here, Knackwurst with Sauerkraut." Hannah giggles. She stutters while eyeing the delicious David. All four spirits speak German, so they are perfectly at home here. Or they would be if Hannah was not looking at David with that voracious, needy look on her freckled young face. Sadly for Hannah, she is unaware of three things. Firstly, David is dead. Secondly, he is passionately in love with and forever committed to the love of his life, or afterlife, whatever. David thinks of a tall, willowy woman with wavy, habitually mussed black hair and arresting chestnut brown, keenly intelligent eyes. Thirdly, Hannah is not that woman.

Angus seems puzzled by the plan to come here and voices his concern. He asks David, "Why didn't we leave a guard at the lab? I could have stayed, and if Franz had shown up, I could have contacted you. I realize this is a likely place to find him, but just as likely, he could be back at the lab."

David nods his agreement. "I thought about that, Angus. If he is at the lab, we will find him when we return. Franz has to enter the building at some point if he wants to get help for his crazy schemes. If Franz gets inside, we will meet again. Where would he go?

"I must admit I am apprehensive. There is always the possibility it was not Franz the scientists saw, and I fear he has somehow made contact with the Neo-Nazis. No doubt they had an emergency plan to meet if the entire diabolical scheme blew up in their faces, which it did. Remember, there are thousands of Neo-Nazis around the world. Money is not an issue; their funding is quite generous. My long-term goal is to trace their source of seemingly unlimited capital. We must bring a hurting to the sleaze bags financing these creeps."

The four spirits desperately want to escape the salivating Hannah and turn their attention to their mission. They all ordered the knackwurst and a Bevog Hagger Blend 0318.

Sir Winston anticipates his Bevog Hagger. He is enjoying their sojourn at the restaurant. "We must learn not to go to public places with David. He attracts entirely too much attention from the ladies." The former Prime Minister chuckles good-naturedly as he says this. Sir Winston was known for his sense of humor and brilliant wit unless you attempted to conquer his island nation. Then the fight was on, and Sir Winston would always win. In Churchill's life, either this one or the last one, losing is not an option.

Dr. Einstein is shocked and remarks, "I can see things have changed since I was a young man back at the turn of the Century, uh, the 20th Century, of course. Ladies were not quite so bold and audacious as this." His forehead wrinkled in a frown of disapproval. Dear man is a few decades behind the curve. Yet, the Great Scientist was not a prude and appreciated the ladies.

David is red-faced and embarrassed by all the unwelcome attention. The hunky David has no idea why the waitress behaves this way. And he is ecstatically grateful that Bones is not here to witness this shameless display. Angus is simply annoyed. He wants to return to their reason for being there, namely Franz. At heart, he is still eighty.

After the besotted Hannah delivers their meal to the table, they say a polite thank you and pretend to be engrossed in their sausages. Sir Winston enjoys pretending he is sipping the hearty beer. All the food and beer will be left on the table when they leave. This abject neglect of their repast will inspire wild speculation by Hannah and the staff, though not nearly wild enough to approach the truth.

Hannah watches from afar, wishing to get those red nails on David. A horde of other wait staff joins her, riveted on the virile newcomer. The Management hopes David will find another German restaurant to eat at while visiting their lovely village. The staff is completely ignoring the other diners. Their food languishes in the kitchen, growing less appetizing by the minute.

The guys keep watch on the restaurant dining area and the alley outside. They are hidden from view behind a large column. Franz would not notice them upon entering. They would have him before he could escape once he entered the large room. Unless they are surprised, they can move at speed impossible for the human eye to follow. The patrons around them would never know four men apprehended the ill-fated Franz, and poof, they vanished.

The guys manage to linger, pushing their food around their plates and pretending to sip beer until midnight when the restaurant finally closed. They are disappointed Franz did not show. David hates missteps that waste time. He suggests, “We knew there was a possibility we would choose the wrong option, and Franz is at the facility or blissfully eating dinner at another restaurant. Shall we move on to plan B and stake out the research facility? We have a long night ahead of us unless we are lucky. I feel lucky." The dispirited spirits pay their bill and step into the chilled night.

Naturally, there are other German restaurants in the area, but this one reminded them of the restaurant in London frequented by Franz and the other guttersnipes. Robert Burns told us the best-laid plans of mice and men often go awry. Or, in 21st Century vernacular, it is what it is.

They pop back to the laboratory and see nothing of consequence. No police. No Franz. Not even a mildly disgruntled German Shepard. They decide to wait between the tool shed and the lab. They will see Franz if he tries to enter either building. They wonder what his plan might be. Why sneak around the grounds? To get the help he needs, he would have to approach the scientists with Dr. Mengele's journal and the cells if he has them. Franz has spent the past 80 years working for Dr. Mengele, and following his orders, he has not developed planning skills of his own. He has always just followed orders. Mengele sent Franz twice to kill me—he failed miserably. His execution of plans is questionable too.

David turns to Dr. Einstein and Sir Winston. "Why don't you stay here where these well-placed benches and a table make it comfortable for waiting? Angus, you and I will explore the perimeter of the building, checking doors and windows. We do not know if Franz was here while we waited for him in the restaurant. If he is here, we will find him. He is probably getting desperate. Perhaps Franz is wet and hungry and will make obvious mistakes. He has never been the sharpest pencil in the pack."

Angus agrees, "That's a good plan, David. I will start by going around the south side of the building. If you go the other direction, we can cover each side of the building twice per round. We will find him."

David signs a thumbs up.

Angus moves toward the south side of the building and begins to inch his way around it. He inspects every window, door, and dark corner. So far, all the windows and doors are shut fast with locks in place. He peeks around the far corner of the building, now dark with Austrian Pines and massed heather in huge clumps. Angus is kneeling in the heather, looking carefully around. He stops abruptly. A few feet ahead, almost hidden in the darkness of the night, Angus sees a large figure. As he silently moves closer, he sees a massive man with dark hair and a bodybuilder's bulk, barely perceivable as he blends in with all-black cryptic coloring. The stealthy figure reaches for a window. He has a backpack from which he withdraws tools. The whole you-don't-see-me cat thing doesn't work well. Angus immediately knows who this trespasser is and what he must do. He rushes around the corner and grabs Franz from behind with his arm around Franz's neck, and he is under control in seconds. David hears Franz's scream and runs full tilt to help Angus.

David gets there in seconds. He hisses, "What have we got here, Angus? Does this man seem familiar to you, my friend? Hey, Franz, did you think you would meet Angus again on this side of the curtain? Surprised, huh!? My mate looks younger, doesn't he? Oh, you can't see him yet because he is behind you? Gosh, this will be a nice shock for you, be careful. You have a faulty ticker." His light tone disappears, and he nearly spits out the words. "You despicable scum!" David disapproves of despicable scum killing his friends, and his anger is palpable.

Angus is smiling from ear to ear. Karma is hell. Also, he is amazed at his most recent enhancement in impressive physical prowess! Arnold Schwarzenegger, bring it on! He has not felt this strong in decades! Hell, he has never felt this strong! He thinks he may like this new life or whatever it is.

Angus joins David in needling Franz. "Yes, mate, let's turn you around so you can take a good look at me. The tables have turned, you bloody criminal, 'rascal, an eater of broken meats; a base, proud, shallow, beggarly, three-suited, filthy worsted-stocking knave criminal.' As a fan of Shakespeare, I have always wanted to say that, David. Thank you for giving me the opportunity." He releases his chokehold on Franz and turns him around none too gently. Franz stumbles with the force of the spin. He is bewildered by the strange words and crazy men.

Franz looks at the two spirits and frowns, "Let go of me! What are you doing? I have a right to be here. Just ask Dr. Suggs. He knows me—we have worked together. What are you saying, you madman?" Franz squints as he looks at Angus. "What language are you speaking?" He stares at one man and then the other, just inches from their faces. "I don't know either one of you. You mistake me for someone else. Let me go at once!" Franz stares at them and shakes his head. He struggles to place them. They realize he is not faking. Something is wrong with him.

David says harshly, "Come on, old-timer, you remember Angus. You shot and killed him a few days ago when you tried to kill Bones. If you had succeeded in killing her, I would have dragged your ugly carcass to the mouth of Hell myself and watched you burn." Franz saw David often just a few weeks ago in the sewer. Franz is beginning to realize what is happening to him. He is terrified, alone, and abandoned by his benefactors. His eyes open wide, and he starts gasping to get air into his tortured lungs.

Angus is not as angry as he thought he would be about Franz shooting him dead. His new life has definite advantages. Yes, it indeed does! He says, "You are not in danger, old man; we are not monsters like you and your bloody Nazi playmates. We are going to take you to Sir Winston. He will be thrilled to see you, mate. It has been a couple of weeks since you two have chatted." Franz is trying to put all of this together. His faulty heart is not pumping sufficient oxygen to his starved brain. Processing is terribly slow and tortuous. He gawks at Angus and tries to understand what David told him. No, he doesn't know either one of them. Wait, the one in the bomber jacket does look vaguely familiar. Franz is frantically trying to explain to himself what he is witnessing rationally. Wait, they are trying to trick him. Dr. Mengele said they might try that if they ever captured him. What did Herr Doctor tell him to do? As hard as he tries to remember, nothing comes to him. His brain is not online, and Franz's wifi is disconnected. The harder Franz tries to remember, the further away the conversation scurries. His head is aching, and he is fatigued. David picks up Franz's backpack and walks toward Dr. Einstein and Sir Winston. Franz has trouble keeping his balance and stumbles along in front of Angus and David.

Sir Winston is ecstatic as he watches the threesome move closer to him. He says, "David, dear boy, I see you and Angus have successfully rode to the hounds. Tallyho! Well, Franz, I am quite pleased you have decided to join us again. I have not seen you since, well, since the Sewers of London and the London Laboratory. We must catch up on what pandemonium and troublesomeness you have created since shooting our dear friend, Angus." When he speaks the last words, Sir Winston's voice loses its friendly, playful tone. Angus' death was sadly tragic for all of them. His gaze is frigid and filled with condemnation.

Franz seems to be oblivious to everything and everyone around him. He stares off into the darkness, swaying as if being buffeted by a mighty gale. Franz is aging before their eyes. His hair is swiftly turning from dark brown to gray, then white. The spirits themselves are astonished by his rapid transformation.

They immediately teleport, or whatever they do, with him back to the London Sewer cell. Yeah, they can travel with a human in their grip. No, I don't know how they do that either. I do know it is dangerous for humans. That is why I have never dared to try teleporting with them. Naturally, the guys would never do anything that put me in danger, like transposing my molecules in flight. However, they don't appear to be particularly concerned about Franz and his molecules. In their defense, Franz murdered Angus, and he tried to kill me numerous times. I owe my life to Franz's stunning incompetence.

Chapter Five

The Transformation

I am waiting with Sophie for the guys to return from historic Austria when suddenly, Abigor is in the room with me without a polite warning.

I jump and scold him, "Don't do that! You aren't Druid. He is the only one who can just pop in and out. We have a door, Demon; use it!"

Abigor seems surprised. "I am sorry, dear Bones. This art new to me, and I am still practicing. Be at peace, maiden. It seems contrary to open doors."

I am at a loss for patience, "Demon, do not call me maiden. This is not the 16th Century. Get over it! Try catching up with the rest of us!"

His eyes are wide and puzzled. "Please do not call me by that hateful name. I am not a Demon. They art vile and to be despised. Verily, I chose another path." Great, now I have hurt the Demon's feelings, well, former Demon. Who knew they were so sensitive? I decided to soften my approach.

"Ok, Abigor, I understand that you are a former Demon. I shall try to keep that in mind, but please resist just popping up like so much burned toast. It is disconcerting when you do that." Sophie is looking at us bewildered as we have this ridiculous conversation. I am anxiously waiting to hear from the Team. Not to mention, my discussion with Admiral Stallings was terrifying. He said we would lose. What will it mean if we lose? I need to share my concerns with the gang. I didn't have to tell Sophie—she knew everything without being told. Big Soph gives me a knee hug. That helps me to feel in control.

As I counted the possible disasters, the Team came in the door. I point toward the door to remind Abigor how one enters a room. Yes, I know, petty.

I am thrilled to see them. I need conversation, plans, answers, and hugs. David comes over to me, where I am sitting on the red sofa, pulls me up, and hugs me tightly to him. This hug feels different from our usual hug, more desperate as if he thought I might have disappeared while he was gone.

The guys sit down after greeting Abigor and me. David is sitting close to me. Abigor has absolutely no idea about appropriate behavior. He moves close to me on my other side. Truthfully, I liked Abigor much better as a loathsome demon. Maybe I am getting overwhelmed and irritable. It happens.

Sir Winston is beaming. He begins, "Bones, we have excellent news for you. After staking out the lab, that is the right word, David?" David nods approval. He continues excitedly about nabbing the creep. "We were exceptionally fortunate to apprehend Franz. "We had staked out a German restaurant most of the night with no success and returned to the lab hoping we might nab him there." He looks to David again. Sir Winston is getting the hang of police jargon and enjoying the learning experience. "Angus was patrolling the perimeter of the building when he saw Franz. The thug was trying to open a window. Angus grabbed him around the neck, and we immediately returned to London with Franz in tow. He is back in the sewer where he belongs. The Austrian researchers will never know we were there.

"Regrettably, our hope to learn more about the Neo-Nazis and anyone else involved with the Mengele organization from Franz was for naught. A bedeviling Fate shot down our bright optimism. Franz seems to be having a rather bizarre transformation and total breakdown. When we caught him, he looked as he had always looked, approximately 40 years old and quite robust. You would not recognize him now. David, my boy, would you like to continue? I want a cigar and some brandy." I hand his silver matchbox to him and get a dazzling smile for my effort.

David picks up where the Great Man left it. "I don't know what is happening to Franz. It is as if the youth drug suddenly stopped working and reversed itself. That doesn't happen when one ages normally. He has matured to his approximate age of around 100. In the time we have known him, he has been a vigorous, powerful man. You, dear Bones, know that better than anyone since he tried to choke you a few weeks ago and recently tried to shoot you. He nearly succeeded both times. I could have lost you forever." David turns away for a moment to regain his composure. "Thankfully, you were rescued by Sophie and then by Angus later. You have loving, faithful friends when you need them, my love." He does a slight bow and salutes each of them before continuing. "We don't know what triggered Franz's transformation from strong to frail, sick, and elderly. Naturally, we know the youth drug suspended the aging process from about 40 years old until now. This transformation was remarkably fast. By the time we got Franz back to the sewer prison cell, just a matter of a few minutes, he had turned into a man of 100 years. His brain is scarcely functioning, and his heart is under an enormous strain. We do not expect him to last long. Dr. Ansen McCoy, who worked with Miles at MI5 and treated Angus in the hospital, is with Franz now. He is not optimistic that Franz's heart can continue pumping throughout the night."

Angus breaks in, expressing his concerns. "And what is so frustrating to us is Franz did not have the Journal or the viable cells with him when we found him. He had a backpack with burglary tools, his .357, and Oreo cookies with extra filling but nothing else. I remembered the evidence sewn into the lining of Dr. Mengele's black leather doctor's bag, so I brought Franz's backpack with me. It sits by the door until later when I can take it apart. We had hoped to learn more from him about the others miscreants involved. Our frustration is impossible to describe. I know you and Abigor share in this painful moment. Since Franz could not communicate, we had no reason to stay with him. He is certainly not one of my favorite people."

I feel their deep despair and add to it. "Guys, there is something I need to share with you from my conversation with Admiral Stallings. Regrettably, this will not improve your mood. I have been distraught since I talked with him. He agrees there is probably something monstrously dangerous that hides in Owl Mountain. He also said that our enemies are numerous and powerful. The admiral does not think we will prevail this time. I have been replaying his words repeatedly, and I am not sure what it would mean to the world if we lost this battle. It troubles me to think of lives that could be lost."

Dr. Einstein speaks for the first time. He has been taking in everything, and he frowns, as is his habit when he concentrates. He looks over his glasses at us. "Gentlemen and Bones, and of course, Sophie, there is nothing we can do to reverse Franz's decline. We will perform an autopsy to understand what happened when the time comes. It may give us data to determine what is killing him. Yet, we know the basic cause, old age is killing him. I sincerely doubt we shall learn more than that. We may never know what triggered the rapid downward spiral. So, we will leave that for now. The drug may have an expiration date. It simply stops working. In the past, we knew about the heart defect. This inconvenient expiration date is a new wrinkle. Dr. Mengele may not have known about this limitation in his beloved Youth Drug."

Evidently, our genius is as puzzled as the rest of us. "Moving on to what Bones reported. The Admiral is well-informed and quite amazing in his own right. Yet, since the mission has not unfolded, we have not even begun that mission. I see no reason to disquiet myself based on his prediction. You were going to talk with the demons of your acquaintance, Abigor. Did you learn anything of importance?"

Abigor seemed surprised that Dr. Einstein was looking to him for information. He responded, "I made contact with a couple of powerful demons. One, Aamon, is an ugly demon who looks like a combination of a wolf and an alligator. He is a Grand Marquis of Hell with 40 infernal legions and is the 7th Spirit of the Goetia. Do not ask. Curiously, I never noticed how ugly like a toad he wast before. Oh, he can breathe out fire. A word of caution, thou will want to be careful if you meeteth him in person. Providentially, he didst not know about mine new path in life, or he didst not care. He confirmed that one of the mountains in the Owl group hast been used for many years to store a fire-breathing machine. That is how he described it. A connection to his ability, I suppose. He also hast said there is more potent magic hidden there. More unpleasant news, a formidable demon in residence is prominent in the Neo-Nazi movement. They may not know he is a demon." He lifts both hands to show this is the best he can do.

Why can't we ever have just ordinary flesh and blood, non-fire-spewing bad guys? We always have youth-dosed centenarians and demons. Why? Of course, while I am throwing stones, I must admit our team is four spirits, a former Demon, a ghost dog, and me. Well, I guess that does it for my mental whining.

Chapter Six

Owl Mountain Plan

We now had more information about Owl Mountain. Not nearly enough to start our mission, but we were certainly getting closer. We turned the floor over to David since he had the most intelligence experience.

David considers what Abigor shared with us about rumors of danger at Owl Mountain and suggests, "We know there appears to be sufficient information to take a closer look at Owl Mountain. Thanks to Bones' research skills, we know what we are facing. The Owl Mountains are part of the Central Sudetes in southwestern Poland. The Owl Mountains cover about 200 square kilometers. For Bones and Sophie's information, that is approximately 77 square miles. The Great Owl, not that it matters, is 1,014 meters tall. In feet, it translates to 3,329. Definitely not enormous for a mountain range but not something we can cover quickly with only six team members. "He stops momentarily to see if everyone is still following. "We know 90,000 cubic meters of excavated tunnels were carved into the Mountain. Access points to the tunnel systems are located at Walim-Rzeczka, Jugowice, Sobon, Sololec, and Ksiaz Castle. The area is littered with all manner of debris typically found in a war zone, machines, crumbling buildings, and bunkers. I suggest we contact Miles for assistance on this massive project. Naturally, we will be very circumspect in sharing information with him. There are more modern ways of looking for certain weapons than were available after the War. Since we don't know exactly, or even generally, what we are looking for regarding its physical makeup and fuel source, that leaves us with a giant question mark. To further complicate matters, a mountain with ore surrounds our target. Perhaps, geophysical ground penetrating radar, which uses electromagnetic radiation to detect subsurface objects and changes in material properties, would be appropriate for our needs. Not my area of expertise." Arriving at the crux of the matter, David dives right in.

"We must decide how to approach this request with Miles. Questioning him about cutting-edge technology without filling him in on exactly what we are seeking will require, uh, finesse." David looks beseechingly at Churchill. Finesse is not in David's toolbox. "Sending out a plane is more of an undertaking than we have requested from Miles. I would be interested in hearing your thoughts on that." David throws open the Miles dilemma for discussion and winks at me.

Churchill once said, "Tact is the ability to tell someone to go to Hell in such a way that they look forward to the trip. Works for finesse too." He is the master of finesse when he chooses to be.

Sir Winston searches his vest pockets for his troublesome matchbox and carries on. "David, dear boy, you have a relationship with Miles based on trustworthiness and similar goals, that is, of course, protecting the British Empire. Naturally, Miles would have to discuss our request with his superiors. That would be necessary so they could assess the feasibility of using expensive equipment in this pursuit." The former Prime Minister remains pensive as he lights his cigar that had gone cold again. He resumes, "I still have close friends in positions of high authority. I am not unknown to our Queen." None of us bother to mention there has not been a British Empire for many years. The mention of Queen Elizabeth II got our attention. Yes, they have known each other since she was a small child. Tragically, King George VI died in 1952, and the young Elizabeth became Queen when Sir Winston was on his second stint as Prime Minister. They met weekly for the remainder of his time in office, which ended when he retired in 1955. They particularly enjoyed each other's company because of their mutual love of horses and polo. Sir Winston had told me the Queen wrote a touching letter telling him how much she would miss him and how dearly she held his wise counsel. He said he shed tears as he read it.

Queen Elizabeth gave her treasured former Prime Minister a magnificent funeral customarily reserved for royalty. His was the first state funeral for a non-royal since 1935. Mourners lined up along the route weeping as his coffin passed carrying their beloved Winnie. Over 350 million people watched this heartbreaking event on television. Sir Winston said, at the time, he was emotionally moved by the majestic pageantry of his funeral. Stunned, I asked him how he could have seen it. Crickets. By royal decree, Churchill's body lay in state at Westminster for three days before traveling to his final (As it turned out, not so final.) resting place. After much pomp and circumstance, he was laid to rest at St. Martin's Churchyard at Bladon in the company of his parents and ancestors. The Kingdom began planning the massive undertaking, code-named Operation Hope Not, in 1953. Of course, the always-independent Churchill refused to surrender to the Grim Reaper in a timely manner. According to Lord Mountbatten (assassinated in 1979), the plans had to be revised numerous times because the pallbearers, much to everyone's annoyance, kept dying. As Churchill so modestly said, he was not unknown to the Queen.

We decided to shelve the Queen for now unless we get incredibly desperate. Hey, crises happen.

Sir Winston adds a shocker. "Ksiaz Castle was built in the 13th Century and has evolved into the majestic Baroque-Neoclassical structure it is today. I am connected by marriage to the owners, the Hochberg family. Hans Heinrich XV Hochberg married Maria Teresa Olivia Cornwallis-West (Daisy) in 1891. Her brother, George Cornwallis-West, later became my stepfather when he married my mother in 1900. George was a decent chap, and I enjoyed his company. I may take a trip to visit that side of the extended marriage-related family under an assumed name." His eyes twinkled as he said this. It is hard to know when he is serious. I can certainly imagine him haunting the castle, searching for clues.

Dr. Einstein, missing the humor altogether, says, "David, I have no idea how we could accomplish this essential task in our mission. Also, I can see no other way to find the facility in the mountains unless there is a record of its location. Indeed, I would think there would be records. If so, Miles may be aware of their existence and location. We would be wise to try that avenue first. We must press forward. The world is in greater peril from those who tolerate or encourage evil than those who commit it. We cannot be a part of the passively uninvolved." Our mission is very personal to the eminent scientist. Einstein renounced his German Citizenship in 1933 as he quickly saw the terrifying writing on the wall. He realized the direction Hitler, a rabid antisemitic, was taking Germany. Tragically, he lost friends and colleagues who could not quickly grasp the danger or flee.

Angus scratches his head, thinking aloud, "First, I agree with you, Dr. Einstein. I seem to remember a plan of the facility and looking at it with Red Biggers. It was there in the Director's Office at the time. No doubt, it has been moved since then. It would be advantageous to check with Miles and determine if he has found the personnel file on Biggers, including his autopsy and death certificate. We can ask about the Owl Mountain Facility too." Angus is ready to get past the planning stage into the mission itself. He is excited to try out his newfound super youth in action.

David is energized by what he sees as a path ahead. "We have a couple of plans of action to advance our mission, and I am confident we can find the target location without much delay. Angus, why don't you and I pop over to see Miles now? Hopefully, he has Biggers' file.

Whether Red died of natural causes or not, our mission remains unchanged, but it would be interesting to know. I am distrustful by nature, and I wonder if the reason Biggers was killed was to destroy all roads to the Doomsday Weapon. If that is true, I am convinced it is unlikely the map still exists." As much to himself as to the group, he poses a question. "Why would someone at MI5 want to stop Biggers from investigating the possibility of such a dangerous weapon?" The implications of the answer that popped into his mind left him dumbfounded. "There is only one reason, to take control over it. That means an inside job. Inside MI5!" David grimaces in pain at the thought that someone in his old agency is corrupt. "Of course, that was a long time ago. What that means, for now, I don't know." We all look at David with our mouths open. Corruption in MI5 is a disheartening theory, yet Angus implied the same thing. It also means we cannot trust everything they tell us.

"We shall return soon. Sir Winston and Dr. Einstein, would either of you gentlemen care to join us in this little hunting expedition? If you want to remain unseen, you can concentrate on listening and observing without the distraction of engaging in conversation."

Both of our esteemed senior Team members grabbed their hats and ran toward the door. Sir Winston has never missed a daring adventure in his long, illustrious life. Just ask Detective Walter Thompson, Churchill's bodyguard during both Wars. According to Thompson, they barely slipped out of the jaws of death on at least 20 occasions. Again, daring death to catch him, Churchill had insisted he would be in the thick of things on D-Day, watching and shaking his fist at Hitler from the bow of the HMS Belfast. King George persuaded the fiery Churchill to remain home by threatening to stand beside him on the deck of that mighty ship. Sir Winston refused to endanger the King. Foiled!

Abigor and I are alone with Sophie in the suite. I am too excited about finally starting this mission to sit there and have an idle conversation with the retired Demon. Abigor wants to explore my chat with Admiral Stallings. "Bones, I am confused. If the Admiral doth not know our plan, why is he certain we will not prevail? What doth he knoweth that we do not?"

I am taken aback by his skepticism. "That is a good question, Abigor. I wonder if Stallings knows something that would help us to bring down our Demon and the Doomsday beast. Shall we take the #188 bus, go to the Royal Navy College, and ask the good Admiral himself? That reminds me, I have not had time to look at the last book he gave me. Witches? Why Witches? Any idea about the relevance of witches, those pointy-nosed, broom-riding, fictional creatures?"

Abigor was walking away, preparing to leave for the Old Navy College, and turned swiftly and faced me. "Bones, I do not know where thee got that idea. Witches use witchcraft to cause harm or death. They have the most wondrous powers, and they art not fictional. Most of the women tried for witchcraft during the early witch hunts in England, from about 1600 until the mid-18th Century, were not witches. To a much smaller degree, witches doth exist. They art quite real. Witches and demons have always been linked in committing evil deeds." I am not buying this without solid evidence. I shrug my shoulders and continue to move toward the door.

The #188 is crowded today with people shopping, visiting London, going to and from work, and, of course, unbeknown to them, Abigor and I are on a mission to save the world. I wish for once I was going shopping, maybe a new shade of red heels and a matching leather purse. Yes, that would be lots of fun and so darn normal. Alas, that is not the reason for my excursion. We sit behind women excited about visiting the Murder Museum at the Met. They share gruesome details about a bloody fingerprint on a cashbox that convicted the Stratton brothers, Alfred and Albert, of killing an elderly couple in a 1905 robbery. Justice was swift for the siblings. They were executed in the same year. The unlucky brothers were the first murderers convicted in England using the newfangled fingerprint technology.

We learn from bits and pieces of the overheard conversation that the women are from a police department in New York. They are in London to work with the Met Police to create a new database of pedophiles. Silently, I wish them the best of luck on that honorable task.

We exit at our stop and walk a short distance to the College. I feel like Bill Murray in *Groundhog Day*. I can't seem to get away from Admiral Stallings and his ship's cabin. I am terrified I will still be coming here to learn whatever about one monster or another when I am a little old lady wearing pearls, comfortable shoes, a shapeless dress, and a shawl. Purple would be the perfect color for my old age. Yet, even when I try, I cannot imagine myself as old. I am reluctant to consider what that might mean.

It is late, so the building is closed and locked. Security is diligently patrolling the grounds at regular intervals. Fortunately, since I am with Abigor, we can get in, or rather, Abigor still has his powers, like walking through doors and letting me in. He can disable a security system with the wave of a hand. As long as he uses his powers for good, he is still fully functional. Abigor disconnects the security system and opens the side door for me. We begin our trek up the virtually never-ending steps, which is easy for him. One would think I would have built up my leg muscles due to my many trips up these steep stairs. Nope.

We arrive outside the Admiral's door. The number is now 413, which seems to mean something to Abigor. He crosses himself and bows. I hear the Admiral's booming voice from the other side of the door telling us to enter. The door opens, and we walk in.

The Admiral turns toward us in his chair. He, of course, knows about Abigor's conversion since Thelma was involved. Thelma and the Admiral were planning to marry in 1939. WWII began in Europe on September 01, 1939, when Hitler invaded Poland. Stallings knew he would be fully engaged in the war effort, and his work would be life-threatening. They discussed their future and decided to wait until after the war to get married. Stallings was right. War is perilous. German soldiers shot him as he and his crew were helping targeted Jews escape from Germany by boat. She joined the SOE and the Free French, aiding and supporting the Resistance fighters. Later Thelma died in an automobile accident.

Admiral Stallings purses his lips, annoyed at my persistence. "I did not think I would see you again so soon, Doctor. I see you brought a visitor, a new team member. Congratulations on your salvation, Abigor."

"Now, what can I do for you at this late hour?"

I gather my confidence around me and reply, "Your last words to me were frightening, Sir. I cannot get them out of my mind. Abigor asked a question that made me think. We have not begun our mission yet, we don't even have a comprehensive plan, and you clearly believe we will fail. What specifically makes you think that Admiral? As you said, our resources are formidable, and our benefactors are all-powerful. What must we do to win?" I would love to hear something that alleviates my fears.

He looks at Abigor as he answers, "You have the answer, Abigor. You know about the immense power of the Sunstone Compass and its connection to the Dark World. Why don't you enlighten Dr. Wyndot?"

Abigor replies, "Aye, yes, I do know about the Sunstone and the Dark World, but what hast that to do with Bones' question?" I was not aware Abigor had this valuable information; he has never volunteered it. I knew he had wanted to take the Compass from me when he was a demon. I am left wondering what his reticence means to our mission. We will chat later!

Admiral Stallings continues to probe, "Abigor, where is the opening to the Dark World? You have the secret words that must be spoken to open the door to that horrible place, and Bones still has the ancient Compass. I think Sophie advised Bones to keep it in her possession to protect her. It protected her from you when you tried to acquire it. Surely you have been told about the location of the door to the Dark World. Also, no one has been able to find the entrance to what you call the Doomsday Weapon."

Abigor and I look blank, but he presses on. "I am confused, Admiral. What are thee trying to tell us, and why does it make thou think we shalt lose this war? That is my concern. We cannot lose. There is too much hanging in the balance."

The Admiral takes the bait. "The opening to the Dark World is in Owl Mountain, and it may hold an antidote to the weapon you seek. You are the only two people who can open that door together. Once you are in, I cannot predict what will happen. I have been told that you must find the door to the Fantastic Machine. The map of the tunnel's location is at MI5. Some individuals at MI5 whom you trust may belong to the dark side—be cautious. Franz has the key. That is the information I have, and I cannot verify it. Do with it what you will. Be warned. I hear many things. Does the Fantastic Machine exist? I begin to wonder. I can say no more." Well, that settles it. We are totally perplexed.

"The Demon will try to stop you, and he has magic in his armory. As one would expect, he is unadulterated evil. Of this, I am quite certain a Demon is there, and he is powerful. You must pass his chambers to reach the doors you seek. He poses as a man, and his followers may not know with what they are dealing. They want a New Global Agenda with Hitler in control. He is the most charismatic psychopathic villain the world has seen in the last two centuries. He could bring disgruntled diverse people together. First, they must get Hitler back, and with Mengele gone, that will not be without its virtually insurmountable challenges. They will also need Himmler and Goebbels to accomplish their goals. Goebbels will control the disinformation. There is no freedom without a free exchange of information, thoughts, and ideas. Your task is twofold. Stop the Hitler plot and his autocratic supporters and stop the Demon who would destroy much of humanity. Even if they cannot recreate Hitler, they will find another charismatic psychopath. There seems to be no shortage of brutal maniacs.

"The NGA and the Demon are not pursuing the same goals. The NGA is in for quite a surprise if he destroys the world." They would not be the only ones.

Abigor and I look at each other, arriving at the same thought. The Admiral says the same thing about MI5 that David and Angus suggested. They are implying a plant may be in-house that will attempt to stop us if possible. We must be careful with whom we speak and what we say.

I answer quickly. My alarm is climbing from bad to worse. "You know, Admiral, I liked our previous conversation better. I was hopeless, but I understood your words. Let me see if I can summarize this. We must get the key from Franz, who is dying. Whatever the key might be, you have not specified that. Then we must grab the map from a very well-armed, quite secure MI5 who may not be in the mood to be generous or even on our side. If we accomplish those two rather daunting tasks, we must get past a powerful and terrifying Demon. He probably won't be in a good mood, either. That has been my experience with demons. If we can find and enter the Dark World, there is no guarantee a fantastic machine is inside. Did I summarize your words correctly?"

The Admiral solemnly nods his head.

Abigor, who has been listening and looking more gloomy by the minute, interjects forlornly, "This cannot be the only way to the monster, the Doomsday Machine. The tasks which art overwhelming and ill-defined art virtually impossible to achieve even with our fearsome powers. Verily, you have assured us a ghastly Demon and probably his minions from Hell shield the Machine. Alas, I know not what key we must acquire from Franz or how we accomplish that before he dies—at any minute." I don't like Abigor's synopsis any better than the Admiral's more lengthy soliloquy.

Admiral Stallings replies, "Isn't that what I told Bones in our last conversation? You asked me why I said you would lose. I just told you, but understand there are possibly two machines. The fantastic machine, if it exists, will nullify the Doomsday machine if you are lucky. I am not supposed to tell you all of this. I just broke several restrictions. There is more. If you are without hope or resources, come back. I am not supposed to help you. That is against the restrictions Beyond placed on me. Yet, I will do what I can at that time. I cannot just allow your vessel to hit an iceberg and sink, especially if humanity is onboard. We have already done that, and it didn't work out well. You may go now and make your futile plans." We thank the Admiral for his time, not so much for his prognostication.

Abigor and I walk out feeling more defeated than when we arrived. Being told we will lose is one thing. Pointing out the inescapable reasons we will fall in defeat has battered our meager hopes. Maybe we are taking the Ancient Mariner's cautionary tale too literally, and there are loopholes in his logic. My head is spinning. I can't analyze each task without a cup of coffee and help. I am hungry, and that always affects my ability to think clearly. Yeah, right, that is the critical issue. A steak with fries and everything will clear up. I have to chuckle at my absurdity because I don't know what else to do.

I am still thinking about the former Demon's less-than-full disclosure about the Compass and the door to the Dark World. I dive in, "Abigor, I want to chat about Owl Mountain and what you know."

As we walk down the stairs, Abigor turns back toward me to answer my pointed question. Something grabs my arm from behind. Surprised, I swing around and see Surgat. How could I forget the snakes? I am uncontrollably furious with this abomination. Righteous anger storms through my brain, crushing all logical thought and fear in its path. Insanely, I lunge for Surgat and trip him with a leg sweep. He falls forward. I kick his legs with my red high heels executing a few well-placed savage kicks. Crumpled from my furious assault, he rolls down a couple of steps shrieking like a jilted banshee.

As I assess the damage I have done, Abigor screeches, "Get away from him. What art thou doing? He will turn thee into a tiki torch! Stop it! I shalt handle him!" Abigor reaches for me, but I quickly move away from him. I will handle this one!

I don't care what happens. I throw myself at Surgat, using all of my 125 pounds to my advantage. As he lies crumpled on the steps, I tackle the ungodly creature savaging him with a powerful kick to his hideous head as vipers reach out to nip me. I sweep my leg again and trip him as he tries to rise. He falls, then I kick him full in the stomach knocking the air out of him. The triumphant whooshing sound is music to my ears.

I screamed at the top of my voice range, "You terrified me before, not this time, freak! I have had it with you monsters!" I am sure I am wild-eyed and look like a deranged lunatic, but I smile as I think how much worse the demon looks.

As I am about to kick him in his awful face again, Abigor grabs Surgat from behind, lifts him over his head, and throws him toward the bottom of the stairs. The throw was powerful enough that Surgat would have crashed through the wall if he had hit it. Damn demon! He disappears halfway down the stairs in a cloud of sulfur smoke.

I yell after him, "Damn stinking coward!" I can't breathe without great effort. The smell of sulfur is overwhelming. As my rush of adrenaline subsides, I can take little gasping breaths. What happened to me? From where did that raging fury come?

Abigor is so furious he can barely speak. "What wast thou doing? Thou were lucky thou took him by surprise, or he would have slaughtered thee in seconds. How would I explain to the Team, especially David, that I let a demon slaughter thee? How? Thou shalt never do that again! I would have jousted with yond demon with no harm to thee."

Frustrated by his interference in my fight, I yell at him, "You do not tell me what I can do, Demon! I am tired. My soul is withering as I try to grasp the false illusions of safety. I shall fight alone if necessary. Though, I don't believe it will be necessary. I have fought before tonight. I battled with both Hans and Franz, I did not always win, but I gave them something to think about in the dead of night. Just ask Blond Hans about our fight in the bookstore. Oh, never mind, he is dead. Never again will I back down from a righteous fight, no matter the consequences. Fear will not cripple me! Never!" I am too irate to make sense.

We are surprised by a sound, and Admiral Stallings is standing at the top of the stairs, hands on his hips, watching and listening as we scream at each other. He yells down to Abigor, "Tell your ugly Demon fiend never to show himself in my building again. I will destroy him no matter how safe he thinks he is from righteous retribution."

"Oh, excellent fighting form, Bones! Never let fear rule you. Bravo!" He shakes his head, smiles, and walks away.

We begin our journey back home after this incredible visit, incredible even for us.

We suddenly realize that Druid, the giant, is standing before us. He is in his usual state of righteous indignation. He glares at Abigor and snarls at him, "Well, Abigor, I see you are keeping Bones safe. She is the only living human on your Team. Amazingly, without your help, Bones is still alive. I have warned your Team before, do not endanger the mortals. Remember, not long ago, Angus was alive too. Amateur!" His snarl is fearsome to hear. An enraged giant is a rare sight. Blue eyes are literally flashing in his state of fervent outrage. Gently, he looks at me and says that a traveler in the tunnel may stop Armageddon. Then he is gone. Again, this is his usual disappearing act. Abigor has never seen a wrathful giant. He blinks twice and continues to walk in a sort of trance. What a day this has been!

We walk back to the bus stop without further adventure. We have said all we have to say. We ride back to the Savoy on the #188 in silence. I will address my question to Abigor on another day.

Chapter Seven

The Gathering Storm

When Abigor and I walk in the Savoy's suite door, the guys and beautiful Sophie huddle together, passionately discussing something of dire importance. They completed their tasks faster than I thought they would. I am anxious to hear their stories, especially after being privy to Admiral Stallings' alarming theory concerning MI5. Though I don't suppose it was that alarming since David had implied the same lack of confidence in his old organization. I know this is a painful realization for David. Of course, the treacherous Wentworth worked for MI5 as IT support staff, not an agent.

Both Abigor and I are almost breathless from our recent traumatic experiences. I don't think former demons can be traumatized. But let me tell you, psychotherapists can be! We pounce on the guys armed with incredible information and warnings.

They are taken aback by our state of excitation yet again. Ok, let's be truthful about my state of agitation, not Abigor's. I run to the sofa to sit beside David for comfort, not safety. He obliges with a tight breath-catching hug and a kiss on my forehead. It appears that his GPS is off a bit.

His next words make me forgive all. "I am so glad to see you, sweetheart. I missed your lovely face and sunny smile." David stops abruptly; his features take on a look of concern and alarm. "By the way, dearest, you are not smiling. What happened while you were gone? Did Abigor do something to upset you?" Raising his voice, he said, "What did the ruffian do to you?" Abigor, standing cautiously at a distance, moves back a few steps—anticipating an imminent explosion.

Sir Winston intervenes, calming the situation quickly, "David, let's not surmise. Bones, what has distressed you? Please take your time and tell us. Would you like a nice pot of coffee? What about a delicious dinner from room service? Angus, would you please call them?" Angus goes to the phone and lifts the receiver to call room service. I hear him ordering a huge meal and coffee. Before he can ring off, I yell, "A piece of carrot cake too . . . no, make that two pieces. Oh, Hell, I want the entire cake! I earned it!"

I finally get an opportunity to explain. "Just give me a minute. There is much to tell. We chatted with the Admiral again. Abigor had a good question that begged for an answer. Why was the Admiral so confident we would fail when we had not even begun to fight? We asked him and got more of an answer than we had anticipated. He said there are four reasons we will lose. First, we must get the map from MI5, and as David suspected, a treacherous plant might make it challenging to find the map. I hope he has not destroyed it.

"It appears the Dark World and the Sunstone Compass are tied to the Doomsday machine in some crazy way. The Compass opens the door to reach the Fantastic Device in the Dark World. However, that has shifted, and the Fantastic Machine may not exist. If it does not, we would have to use other methods to neutralize the Doomsday Machine. Whatever those methods might be. We must pass the powerful evil demon who is behind this chaos. His chambers are between the opening of the access tunnel and the Machine. If we get into the Dark World, we don't know what will happen to us or if we can ever leave. Sophie said I must keep possession of the Sunstone for whatever reason." Sophie nods vigorously in agreement.

"The totalitarian New Global Agenda villains want world domination, and they think Hitler and his buds can make that happen for them. Hitler will be repackaged, of course. The villains think the Demon running the show is human, maybe. Oh, and Franz has the key, dying Franz. We do not know what "the key" means. The key to what?

My voice is rising as I arrive at the finale, "And, to add to a thoroughly obnoxious day, a demon attacked us. And you can be sure I fought back like a savage beast. I will not be a victim again. I was winning, too, when Abigor threw the demon's ugly arse down the stairs, and he disappeared in the usual sulfur smoke. Oh, Druid showed up and raked Abigor over the coals for not protecting me. He said something strange, too. A traveler may help us. End of story." Whew!

The guys appear to be in disbelief as they try to process my *Friday, the 13th* story. David appears unwell. Can a ghost turn pale? Angus is blinking rapidly as his brain tries to reboot. Sir Winston almost choked on his faux brandy. Only Dr. Einstein takes the fateful day in his stride.

Sophie approaches and stares at me with focused intensity. Her eyes drill into my brain, and I hear, "If you had not carried the compass in your purse, you would have died." Is this real, or am I beginning to have hallucinations? Either option is certainly possible. As a psychotherapist, I know how likely we are to start having hallucinations at any moment. No, this is real.

The guys are staring at us. I don't know if they can hear what Sophie is telling me. Sophie's sending thoughts never happened before except when she was in celestial form, and I am almost astonished. Truthfully, nothing will reach the level of astonishment ever again.

Sir Winston breaks the spell and reveals, "I heard what Sophie, uh, said, and I assume the others also did." Everyone except Abigor nods. "I shan't repeat her statement. Abigor, you were present at the meeting. Would you like to add anything to Bones' report?"

Abigor is obviously confused by Sophie's message to us since he did not hear it. "Thank you, Sir Winston. I confirm everything Bones hath said. The meeting with Admiral Stallings wast enlightening, confusing, and dispiriting. He also said he was forbidden to share his knowledge with us. He knows something else but shalt not make that known unless we are at a dead-end without hope. I doth not know if his warning that we shalt lose our righteous battle with evil is true. I wilt not believe we have been defeated before we begin." Abigor hesitates for a moment of contemplation before he continues. "He also told Bones I know the location of the door to the Dark World. That is true. I do not know if the Fantastic Machine art there. Again, even with the good Admirals' words of gloom, I still pray we can prevail in our mission. Miracles happen, and I am one of those miracles." He crosses himself. David discreetly rolls his eyes at this dramatic display, and Sir Winston chuckles at David's behavior. Dr. Einstein misses it completely. His brain is processing E=mc2 or some such thing.

Strangely, no one shares Sophie's message with Abigor, who did not receive it. We do not discuss it by silent mutual agreement. A wildly peculiar moment in an unquestionably weird existence. What does it mean?

Fatima arrives at this moment with my scrumptious dinner, so my attention is focused on my food. Angus ordered a gold medal dinner, mackerel appetizer, BBQ monkfish, hard bread with tomatoes, and a double-layer carrot cake for dessert. The bold, brash coffee is the perfect compliment—absolutely amazing culinary delights to calm my soul.

While I am savoring my heavenly feast alone, the guys discuss our predicament. I hear the word "dark" several times.

Dr. Einstein has considered our reports and processed them with his incredible IQ and says, "Bones and Abigor, I have heard everything you reported to us. Thank you for obtaining this information. I have tremendous confidence in our friend, Admiral Stallings. He has very succinctly described our current mission and tasks. Shall we tackle one task at a time? We must find the access tunnel to the machines, wherever it might be in the Owl Mountains. David reported the daunting size of our target area. Though several tunnels are well known, we can enter those tunnels. David reported on the challenges we may encounter earlier today. Something Stallings said intrigues me greatly. He said about a traveler. What is that supposed to mean?" Abigor and I nod in agreement. The statement is incomprehensible.

The genius is shaking his head in puzzlement while loading his pipe. He continues, "Our visit today with Miles was noteworthy in one regard. David asked if he knew anything about Hitler's weapon, rumored to be at Owl Mountain during WWII. I thought he was guarded in his reply. I would be interested in hearing your thoughts about our meeting before I say more, gentlemen."

Angus speaks up for the first time. He is getting used to the whole being dead thing, "Since I worked at MI5 for many years until I retired in 1990, I am familiar with their lack of candor at times. I don't know Miles well, but he seems to be solid. I got the impression Miles was concerned about someone hearing our conversation. He kept looking around the room. That was very odd, I thought. When I think about Director-General Ogden, I wonder if someone has approached him also from the Dark Side. Admiral Stallings suggested a plant—we don't know what position they occupy. Or Miles may simply be concerned about confidentiality. I wish Bones had been there. Her skill in Neurolinguistics might have helped us detect deception."

Angus explains what is concerning to him. "I was disappointed that he had not yet found Red Biggers' personnel file. I don't know if Miles or someone is stalling or if the file is hard to find. He said he had heard about the secret facility but knew nothing about a map. Again, I don't know what to believe."

David affirms agreement with both Angus's and Dr. Einstein's assessments. "I have known Miles for a long time now, and he has been a reliable resource when we needed help. Something was wrong today, and I smelled fear in the air. We don't need another dead Director-General on our watch. As we push closer to an answer and find that answer, it gets more dangerous for the mortals involved. We have already seen that with Bones. Druid is right; we have been lax in providing safety. I thought Abigor could protect Bones. Clearly, I was mistaken. I won't make that mistake again." Abigor looks down at his shoes in mortification.

"And what about this? Are they the only two who can go into the Dark World? Why can't Abigor give magic words to one of us? Considering what the Admiral said today, I don't know if that is an issue anymore. Things keep changing. I shall wait for the next version of the "Fantastic Machine" from the good Admiral." David is not the only one confused.

Vindicating David's claim of smelling fear, I threw out some animal psychology. "Smells are processed and interpreted in the limbic system, which offers another clue. One of the limbic system's primary organs, the amygdala, is directly responsible for perceiving and responding to fear. Of course, scientists believe we can only smell fear in another member of our species." Everyone seemed baffled by my timing and lecture topic. Well, I don't get an opportunity to do my thing anymore. They can just deal with it!

Dr. Einstein responds politely. "That is quite interesting, dear Bones. We have a problem that requires a solution. How do we find the correct entrance to the tunnel? Does anyone wish to comment?"

Angus fields the question posed by our genius. "I remember a few stories Red Biggers told about the terrible things that happened in that area of Poland. When he visited Poland, he heard about Riese Project, which means giant, a monster created by evil men. The local men who helped build the tunnels disappeared, supposedly to build tunnels in other areas for the Nazis." His tone turns somber as he continues the story. "They never returned. Red's great-uncle was one of those men. He left behind a wife and five children, and his family never heard another word from him. There were many other men like him. There was also a concentration camp nearby, and prisoners did the hard physical work. It was an enormous undertaking. Thousands were in the concentration camp. Many vanished as if the tunnels swallowed them." He pauses for a moment in respect for the dead.

"Red said he heard they never connected some of the tunnels. That creates a puzzle with no directions, and many pieces don't fit. We have quite a task before us unless we can find that map. We can do it without the map if we had more people involved, but because of the danger, a damn Demon no less, we cannot include mortals. I guess the tunnel to the Castle is the logical location for the Machine since the Nazis planned to use the Castle as their area headquarters."

I sense a change in the air as we digest that information. We go all resolute and bulldog-ish. I see Sir Winston pushing out his lips and chomping down hard on his cigar and the famous scowl that made Hitler blanch evident on his face. David's jaw has tightened, and his face is a chiseled, gorgeous alabaster mask. Dr. Einstein is furiously wiping the glasses he no longer needs and trying to light his pipe. My head is held high. My shoulders are squared. My stomach is tucked in tight. Sophie is showing teeth and grimacing. We are ready to battle! Bring it on! Angus and Abigor have not gotten the hang yet of tempered steel's deathly cold inflexibility. They will learn.

Sir Winston says, "It is time to move forward with our first task. I suggest David and Angus pay a midnight visit to MI5 and search everywhere they might hide the map. Albert will research to determine if he can learn more about the Doomsday Machine. Even preposterous rumors are a place to begin. We must learn what was possible with highly classified German technology at that time. I suggest Bones and Abigor work on that. I shall talk to old friends on this side and the other side of the shadowy veil. Wait, Abigor, your greatest value to our team is your ability to infiltrate the demon world. They seem to be particularly well-informed about everything detrimental to our well-being. Please make contact with the wicked thugs and gather pertinent intel." The Great Statesman crosses his legs and begins to relax. We have a plan.

Abigor salutes, message received.

Sir Winston Churchill was not done. He pressed us forward toward duty and triumph because there were no other options for this old warhorse. "Every day, you may make progress. Yet there is stretched out before you an ever-lengthening, ever-improving path. You know you will never get to the end of the journey. But this, so far from discouraging, only adds to the joy and glory of the climb. We have begun the climb, gentlemen, Sophie and Bones. The British people did not weaken during fifty-seven consecutive nights of bombing during the War. We were outraged at their audacity and brutality. But we fought back, galvanized and indomitable. We won. We will win this battle, too, with all due respect to the good Admiral."

We are guided and inspired in our missions by Churchill. In Sir Winston's lifetime, other political leaders were not as cognizant of his astonishing ability for prescience and foresight. Prime Minister Stanley Baldwin was as responsible for the milquetoast response to Hitler's aggression as the much-maligned Prime Minister Neville Chamberlain. Baldwin said of Winston. 'I am going to say that when Winston was born lots of fairies swooped down on his cradle with gifts—imagination, eloquence, industry, ability, and then came a fairy who said no one person has a right to so many gifts. With all these gifts, he was denied judgment and wisdom.' Baldwin and other imprudent politicians viewed Winston through this unrealistic lens and dismissed his urgent alarms about Hitler without cause. A lesson for the ages.

Dr. Einstein, who has finished wiping his glasses, says, "I have not been idle, and I anticipated your request, Winston. As you know, many of the top scientific minds working for Hitler were recruited by the United States after the War. They were brilliant men and women who brought their knowledge with them. The operation was called Paper Clip. Over 300 such scientists were brought to America and given visas and prestigious positions. One such scientist was the brilliant Dr. Wernher Freiherr von Braun, who had been the lead on the V-2 rocket program in Germany. He helped develop the first manned spacecraft. Much of this was kept secret from the American people until 1998, when a disclosure law required the CIA to release documents about Nazi collaborators. A few of the scientists had been deeply involved in the Nazi movement. There is an extensive treasure trove of information in that released material. We may have to examine those files to learn more about Nazi technical advancements in the 1940s. I am tracing where that material is kept."

Sir Winston is excited to hear this. "Albert, excellent work. We anticipate hearing more from you about these records as your research progresses. I once said, The United States can always be relied upon to do the right thing—after first exhausting all possible alternatives. Obviously, I was right." The Great man lightened the severity of his statement with a grin.

"Albert, shall we visit the National Archives? We have German records from WWII. Unfortunately, many documents were returned to the German people in 1950, 1956, and 1958. We shall also want to hop over to the German Foreign Ministry Archives. If nothing else, we may uncover something that points us in a promising direction." Dr. Einstein waves his hand to show his approval.

I tell the guys, "I feel rushed to begin my research. Each heartbeat and each breath remind me that time is passing, and we are at a distinct disadvantage. Their plans are unfolding. We need information before we can even get our pants on. I am going to order a snack and work in the study. Good luck with your tasks, guys."

I have loved research since I worked on my dissertation. I retire to our richly appointed study in our luxurious suite provided by the ever-generous Beyond. We decorated and furnished the study to meet our needs and tastes. It has the feeling of an English Men's Club of the 1920s. Rich oriental rugs soften the dark hardwood floor in deep reds and heather hues. A massive oxblood red Chesterfield sofa complements the four opulent cocoa leather club chairs. The reading lamps give a lovely glow to the cozy room. Naturally, the lampshades have lush fringe tempering the light. My favorite feature is the large stone fireplace. It is gas, so I just push a button, and the faux logs fire up, adding warmth to the room. I sit in a cozy chair next to an oak library table to spread out my paperwork if I am successful in my research. I can print documents and give copies to our team members to read at their own pace. Before I came in, I put out an SOS to Fatima in room service for a great pot of coffee, a tuna salad sandwich with sweet potato fries, and a generous slice of buttermilk pie. Research is exhausting, and I need a full tank. It is time for dinner. I wish Angus could still share meals with me. Sigh.

David has taught me to sneak into dark-channel communication networks without being detected. If they noticed my nose in their business, it could end my research with a suddenness that would be stunning and probably fatal. We have all sorts of cutting-edge security provided by Miles' MI5 IT guys. Hopefully, they are not like traitorous

Wentworth. Channels communicate dark data from compromised entities or entities that purposely bolster the New Global Agenda organization and its nefarious plans. The top three are called TotalDark, FreedomStop, and Intriguedata. Thesaurus and Rubicon were the gold standard CIA spook channels back in the day. Until the Washington Post unmasked them. I can hack into dark media without IT knowledge because of my super MI5 nerds. Their software does the techy stuff, and I try to read the exchanges. Sometimes the data is encrypted, and I am locked out.

I have been at this for about three hours, and it is time for my next snack. Fortunately, Fatima brought two pieces of buttermilk pie. The dear woman knows me. I have noticed one odd thing that intrigues me. I keep seeing the name Seth. He appears to be a big deal in dark channel communication. Seth sounds innocuous enough, but I don't believe that is true. Let's call it therapist's intuition. From what I have determined, he works with an international organization. The information is hard to understand. I doubt Seth is his name; it is probably a code to hide his identity.

One communication says, "Seth is moving into position to strike on a biblical level. He brings the hefty NGA group with him." Another communication says, "We will move when Seth says to move from numerous positions." And lastly, I see the name again. "Seth is the lead. The top lead, make no mistake about that. He does not forgive mistakes." The wording is vague but threatening, and I have only learned that we must determine more about Seth. They, whoever they are, mentioned his name in several communications about incoming disasters. Naturally, Seth could also be a team or an organization. Since they use the pronoun 'he,' I am going with he is a dangerous and hostile man.

I will ask David and Angus if they are familiar with the code name Seth. I think that Seth is a hefty player in the dark community. I wonder about the Neo-Nazis and their worldwide network of psychopaths and Antisocials. Could they be involved in this? Sophie has been in the study with me, enjoying a nap. She looks up and barks at me as I ask myself that question. I take that to mean I am on the right track. Sophie and I agree we need to look into this shadowy Seth.

I want to share one paragraph with the gang. "One of the consequences of the CIA alliance with Gen org is evident today in a resurgent fascist movement in Europe. That can be traced to its ideological lineage back to Hitler's Reich. Supposedly, through Gehlen operatives who cooperated with US intelligence. "I don't understand what it means, but it sounds relevant. Suddenly, I notice I am shivering. I look at Sophie for a plausible explanation, and she has returned to sleep. Drat!

Darkness is swirling as a vague picture slowly emerges from the depths of the dark internet vortex.

Chapter Eight

Seth and the Monster

Darkness is unrelenting and sinister. The sun has turned its face away from this place. The air smells foul with a hint of decay, fungus, mold, and things better left unidentified. Dampness permeates everything in the tunnel. Seth is the name he uses now, a tall, lithe man who must duck in places to avoid hanging rock formations. His thin frame and pale skin make him appear to be a casting director's favorite for the Broadway play Oliver Twist as the undertaker, Mr. Sowerberry. Or maybe a dapper corpse. He is younger than Mr. Sowerberry; with gray eyes and reddish-brown hair, one might suspect he is from Ireland. One would be mistaken. He dressed for a foray into the revolting tunnels under Owl Mountain, jeans, a black turtleneck, a Ralph Lauren denim jacket, and Brunello Cucinelli Boots. Seth carries a large silver flash-light. Seth is accustomed to extravagance. He is supremely adaptable and just as comfortable here in the crumbling tunnel as he would be on the cover of Gentlemen's Quarterly. He is not an unattractive man. Lithe and graceful would describe him well.

Seth has come here to meet with Aaii. He has no concerns about the Demon King or his safety. Though Seth is in human form, he is protected by the highest of powers. He has never met Aaii before, so this should be amusing. Seth was told the Demon is seen in mythology as an imposing figure dressed for battle, riding a pale horse. Seth wears a silver ring with a secret inscription on his right hand. His ring is vital when calling on unpredictable entities.

After walking in the fetid tunnel for about thirty minutes, he reaches a large, circular area carved into the mountain. Six massive crystal chandeliers hang from the jagged rock ceiling. He wonders idly about the power source for the ostentatious chandeliers. Of course, Aaii is a Demon. He doesn't need ConEd or Duke Energy. What a tidy savings, no high energy bills every month. Three golden benches sit in front of gigantic double doors that reach upward to the high ceiling. The Demon undoubtedly stole these treasures from an ancient Cathedral or castle. The doors are dark, scarred wood with hammered, heavy, silver hinges and other hardware. He understands now. Aaii does everything with in-your-face New York style. One of the gigantic doors slowly opens, hinges screaming in objection. He wonders if he should mention a bit of WD-40 oil would quiet the doors. Nah. Much to his surprise, a four-foot-tall oddity stands there, dressed like a doorkeeper in a red velvet coat and black trousers. It has a fox's head and a man's body. Seth isn't sure if this is a costume for effect or if the guy has an identity crisis. Seth is perfectly at peace with either one. Truthfully, in New York, he has seen more bizarre creatures in Central Park.

The Doorman, or whatever he is, motions for Seth to follow him. Seth assumes a fox does not talk. They go through the door into a grand room reminiscent of Buckingham Palace or Versailles. The 20-foot walls are silver and tan with gold carved leaf relief encompassing the spectacular space. There are dozens of enormous gold-framed portraits of royalty gracing the walls. He wonders where the Demon stole these valuable pieces of art. Shades of the Nazis stealing art treasures during WW2, not that he minds the Nazis' thefts. A rich red and cream antique Persian rug covers the marble floor. Evidently, the Demon is passionate about chandeliers; four immense crystal chandeliers provide soft lighting in this luxurious space. Hundreds of dangling, sparkling crystals create dazzling patterns on the dark ceiling. He notices that some of the patterns are swaying. Why is there movement if the crystals are deathly still?

In the center of the space are two carved gold chairs with red velvet cushions and a black onyx table, lighted by two heavy ornate silver candlesticks. The piece de resistance is a regal gilded wood throne perfect for an illustrious sovereign. Preposterously, on the immense elaborate throne sits the Demon he came to meet. Yes, he looks terrible, yet comely like a tall Brad Pitt with longish hair. Seth doesn't know if human is his usual appearance, but he now appears human. He is dressed as a knight from the 1500s on his way to a spirited jousting match. Demon points at the fox doorman with an opulent jewel-encrusted scepter. The doorman silently glides out of the room.

Demon points and nods his blonde head toward one of the gold chairs, and Seth takes that to mean he should sit there. He is beginning to wonder if Aaii can speak. If not, they are in for a brain-numbing meeting. Seth bows slightly. Yes, he gently mocks his host and then sits with his head high and chin out. After all, he is wearing Ralph Lauren. He will not be outclassed by a demon who is obviously stuck in the wrong century and whose idea of proper attire is a clanking tin suit. Seth takes a moment to study the monster while pretending to tie his boot. The "knight" had the padded tunic and mail coat so popular when knights tended to stab each other in the chest with long pointed sticks. Mail trousers worn over leggings completed the rugged, manly look. His visor and helmet sit on the table as if he might be summoned to battle any minute.

Seth waits, thinking it would be impolite to speak before his host speaks. Finally, after what seems to be a disconcertingly long time, Aaii says, "We finally meet, Seth. I was foretold of your visit weeks ago. I believe we are of one mind about what must happen to reach our mutual goals. I want to create a one-world dictatorship because humans are incapable of governing themselves. You see the wars, the poverty, and the hatred. I enjoy power and believe you share that Deadly Sin." He laughs a booming enthusiastic laugh that vibrates the stone walls and bounces off the crystals of the chandeliers. Vibrations are not pleasant for Seth, who responds with a sickly grin. Seth can't place 'passion for power' in the seven deadly sins: pride, greed, lust, envy, gluttony, wrath, and sloth. He doesn't mention that error.

Aaii continues, "I care nothing for humanity, and I would not grieve if the great lizards replaced them. I think the destruction of the dinosaurs was an absurd idea, and I said so at the time. We should keep the large fascinating lizards and not encourage the propagation of mammals; it will not end well. I spoke quite forcefully." He draws himself up to his full height and throws out his manly mail-covered chest to show his pride at being correct all those eons ago.

Seth is getting more confused by the minute. He must ask, "Are you saying the dinosaurs were killed on purpose, and whoever was calling the shots could have avoided the mass extermination? I thought an asteroid killed the toothy giant lizards."

The Demon looks at Seth as if to say, you poor stupid, pitiful being, whatever the Hell you are. He coughs and suggests, "Shall we get to business? I have a jousting match in two hours. Let us be straightforward. We want ultimate power over the world. You and your colleagues have the leaders of many countries under your thumbs, and I have influential people under my spell. They asked me for wealth and position. I gave those things to them. My bill came due, and they are mine for eternity. When the day comes, they will burn in flames, and I shall laugh as I watch."

Seth is beginning to realize Aaii has a dark side. Uh, he is a demon.

Aaii continues, seeking more information. "We are working on bringing Hitler back. He can capture the support of the masses as he did before. I understand you have an update on that for me. In many ways, Hitler was silly and moved too fast, or he could have ruled the world decades ago. He took various toxic drugs that dulled his senses. In his defense, he had the ill luck to have as a foe a most brilliant and accomplished leader, Winston Churchill.

"As you know, the Nazis would have destroyed the despised Churchill, but he was protected. We know not by whom or what. What can you tell me about Hitler and the plans to clone him and accelerate the growth process?"

"Yes, I see your surprise, Seth. My associates have tutored me in these things. I own many Ivy League College Professors and found them quite useful." The Demon did not mention his plan B. If they could not control humankind, he would destroy them using the Doomsday Machine resting right here in his clutches. Also, he did not mention the other machine, the magic machine. It is a secret he holds close to his mail chest. Aaii settles back on his hard and painfully uncomfortable throne to listen to Seth. If one wears armor, comfort is not a priority. Amusingly, Aaii doesn't know where the magic machine is hidden. More disturbing, he doesn't know if it exists.

Seth is pleased the Demon was clear about his plans. Seth reassures him, "I agree with your goals. Power is my drug of choice, and I will have it one way or another. The NGA has been meeting secretly for many years, and we are well advanced in our plans. First, we must create chaos, and nations will collapse. Millions of people will give up their freedom for ideology, financial incentives, and security. People are very gullible and believe our deceitful, diabolical politicians and bureaucrats. The chaos has begun, and the world is greatly unsettled. A few stubborn and foolish humans stand and fight, but not nearly enough to stop the tsunami that rushes toward them even as we speak.

"As you may know, Dr. Mengele is dead, and Franz is dying. Franz brought Mengele's journal and the viable cells for Hitler, Goebbels, and Himmler to the scientists working with Mengele, and they are now safely in France. Afterward, he went to Austria to meet another group of scientists, and that is where he was captured. We do not know details about the tenacious gang that caught him. We know they had been pursuing Dr. Mengele for months, and one is supposed to be the despised Churchill and another Einstein. The good doctor thought the doppelgängers were silly theater to frighten them. I am not convinced that is true. At least two others are involved, an American woman and a younger guy always dressed in a bomber jacket. They have tried, rather successfully, to foil Mengele's plans for months. Blood is on their hands for the deaths of Mengele, Franz soon, and Hans. At one point, they imprisoned Mengele and Franz in the London Sewers. We had to break them out of their cell at significant risk to our team. Our entire plan rested on the good doctor's shoulders."

We killed a few Met Police crime scene techs, oh, and a coroner. The deaths were unintended—we used a bomb to cleanse the crime scene. The Met team members killed or injured simply wandered in at the wrong time." Seth shrugged his shoulders to show his dismissal of the victims. Aaii ponders the depth of their stupidity. He decides they are clumsy, incompetent dolts and once again mourns for his lost lizards. Seth continues his story, "Our Neo-Nazi team in London took care of that. We have had numerous meetings about the annoying pests who hounded Dr. Mengele and are working on a plan. Another unidentified man was also part of their team, and Franz shot him the night Mengele died. I will keep you informed about our progress. We intend to remove the intolerable nuisances permanently." He winks at the Demon. Aaii wants to kill Seth for his impertinence, but oy vey he cannot.

"The journal and viable cells, irreplaceable items, are in the hands of the brilliantly talented Dr. Herman Wagner. He worked as Mengele's second in command in the medical unit at Auschwitz. We were unaware of it, but he was also treated with the Youth Drug. There are rumors, likely true, that Dr. Wagner is a psychopathic killer who found himself in the perfect environment for his personality and, shall we say, his proclivities. He has always been our plan B, and we have kept him apprised of Dr. Mengele's work up until the night the good doctor died of an ill-timed but not unexpected heart episode. Now, Dr. Wagner has everything he needs, including talented researchers to clone the three men and accelerate the maturation process. This process was improved when we, uh, appropriated Dr. Suggs from the research laboratory in Innsbruck, Austria. He and his colleagues had done remarkable work in extending life."

Aaii has been listening and finally hears something of interest to him. He interjects. "Seth, I am gratified to hear Dr. Wagner is doing whatever is necessary to further our interests. He has courage. Most humans are weak and pitiful." Seth agrees about Wagner but is unsure what to do with this observation on humans, so he nods and moves on.

Seth's enthusiasm is growing as he shares these marvelous achievements with Aaii. "Wagner also works to resolve the aging heart glitch in Dr. Mengele's human life extension formula. Scientists believe we can extend human life to 120 or even 150 years. Our problem is a fundamental loss of resilience even if we eliminate the usual suspects, such as cancer and heart disease, as in our Youth Drug. Naturally, we must also consider life quality, including endurance, appearance, and general wellness. Once we perfect our Youth Drug, billions of dollars will be our reward. We have one great advantage we have found no side effects due to the drug. We know that Franz had a complete Youth Drug failure because the drug simply stopped working. He returned to his chronological age in a matter of minutes. Our scientists were monitoring him and are working on that malfunction. They have suggested that the human body has a ceiling, and Franz may have reached that ceiling." Again, he shrugged.

Seth is warming to his subject. "Dr. Wagner, as I said, ever the problem solver, has, uh, appropriated Dr. Suggs, a professor of epidemiology and biostatistics, from the Innsbruck research facility to complement our team. More literal individuals might use the unpleasant word, kidnapped." Aaii frowns to confirm that humans can be judgmental.

"Dr. Wagner has communicated with the researchers who worked with Dr. Mengele in London. The team in France will soon join the researchers in London. Dr. Wagner told me the acceleration process should take about six months after the cloning process to achieve full adulthood. Now we turn to you. We are hopeful you can assist us in returning the three Nazis to their natural passionate, brilliant, indomitable personalities. Franz told us he heard the Demon Abigor assert he could accomplish this magic before he disappeared. Is this true? Can you return them to their natural personalities, the essential essence of who they were in life? This step is crucial for our purposes."

The Demon had listened attentively. Aaii almost imperceptibly nods his head in response to Seth's question. Seth does not understand that the Demon has little interest in the human youth formulas or billions of dollars. There may be no humans left alive to be concerned about aging.

Unseen, a brooding shadow listens intently.

The patterns on the ceiling continue to swirl.

Chapter Nine

The Machine Document and the Hourglass

Sophie and I see Abigor when we enter our pleasant, sunny sitting room at the Savoy. Abigor sits in our Scottish plaid chair, staring toward the large window overlooking the street as if concentrating on something of vital significance. I sit across from him and ask if he has learned anything to help us in our mission.

He gradually turns in my direction and finally acknowledges me. "Oh, greetings, Bones. I was lost in thought. I wish I could answer thy question, yet I am not sure if I have learned much. I hast been listening in to the dark Demon Stream of Consciousness. It is hard to explain to a human. Pray pardon me. Demons' thoughts cometh together in a stream we can tap into at will. If one demon knows something, we all know unless it is blocked. The thoughts can run together, and it can be hard to separate who thought what. When we block thoughts, some bits might still come through. My thoughts no longer go into the stream." He says this with evident joy.

Intrigued, I have to ask Abigor questions, "Wow. Your Stream of Consciousness sounds like the vague things clairvoyants say, their vague impressions from the spirit world. 'Yes, I saw your dearly departed husband. He said something about your new red dress, or it may have been your pet squirrel. Do you have a red dress?' I always assumed they were misguided or cons. Of course, I have seen and heard much since then that makes me doubt my logical, science-based brain. Sorry, I digressed. Can you tap into the demon's thoughts from anywhere? With effort, can you trace a thought to a particular demon? This subject is fascinating!"

Abigor smiles and looks at me fondly as he says, "I am glad thou art enjoying this, dear Bones. It pleases me to see thee joyous. When I met thee as a Demon, I felt a connection to thee." The former Demon looks at me with warmth, and do I also see affection? Hmmm, this could be a problem, but I choose to ignore it. No doubt, I am indulging in a silly flight of fancy.

Abigor tries to explain the stream of consciousness in terms I will understand, "No, it is not always possible to "hear" the exact thoughts or pinpoint a particular demon. Yes, I can do it from anywhere if I have the quiet to concentrate. My success can vary from time to time. Think of an old radio. Sometimes it is crystal clear while other times, static from atmospheric conditions interfere with sound transmission." Seeing my surprise and interest, he quickly schools me. "Yes, I know about radios. Who do thee think pointed Guglielmo Marconi in the right direction? I hate to admit it. I foresaw the malignant force media would become." I concur. He should feel guilty about unleashing the media on us.

"I am sorry, dear Bones. I digressed too. I may recognize a demon's "voice" if I am familiar with it. Today I heard frightening things and knoweth not what they mean or if they are relevant to our mission. I sensed or felt a tunnel. I heard great destruction, magicians, much death, a group of evil men, twisted malignant power, and a smidgen about dinosaurs—the magnitude of the evil wast overpowering and nauseating. I do not know what dinosaurs meant. Perchance it is a code or metaphor? "He reaches out and lays his hand on mine to comfort me. I gently move my hand away. Maybe this is proper behavior for demons, but so is turning people into frogs. Still, I must remember he is adjusting.

I am concerned about his experience in the dark stream and need help understanding it. "How can you determine if this pertains to our mission? The tunnel concerns me and ties in with evil men, twisted malignant power, death, and destruction. Whether related or not to our mission, it isn't comforting and should receive more attention. I can't quite fit the dinosaurs in either." His impressions from the stream are a little too close to what we already know to be a coincidence. He has my total attention.

Abigor sighs deeply, "I can only keep tapping into the stream and desire to findeth a link. We have naught solid facts to follow at the moment." He looks at me with awareness, "I am beginning to sound like our esteemed Dr. Einstein." We take a minute to chuckle about that, my only concession to a more personal connection. We need light-hearted moments to retain our sanity, assuming we are still sane. Abigor frowns as he continues, "I know my speech is annoying to thee, and I am trying to be more 21st Century. My success varies, dear Bones." I am almost getting used to Abigor speaking in broken, sometimes inaccurate Shakespearean English. I notice his efforts to clamber into this century.

Sir Winston and Dr. Einstein burst into our midst as excited as schoolboys about something. Sir Winston's cornflower blue eyes twinkle as when his hounds have the scent. Tally-ho! Einstein's dusky eyes are calm, yet I see a new intensity. I jump up and give them hugs of welcome, eager to hear their news. Sir Winston sits down and reaches for his cigar and snifter, waiting for him magically on the massive coffee table. Abigor gives the gentlemen a smart salute. Sophie nods her head while she remains comfortably stretched out on the sofa.

Naturally, the enthusiastic Sir Winston is the first to speak. "We have exciting news, Bones, Abigor, and Sophie. We have been looking through records in our National Archives and the Military Archives in Potsdam. We saw only a minuscule percentage of all the records from the German War effort. Much was undoubtedly destroyed as the allies moved toward Berlin on April 30, 1945. However, after viewing mountains of material, we found this." Triumphantly, Sir Winston holds up two dog-eared, worn pieces of paper stapled together at the top. I take the documents from him for a closer examination. Apparently, whoever typed this did so on a well-used typewriter. The letters are not level and vary in size. The "e" and "T" are lighter than the other letters.

Sir Winston carries on, "We scoured through the documents to find references to Owl Mountain, Riese, Wunderwaffe, anything that might refer to a superweapon. We hit paydirt with Riese and focused our attention on those documents. If necessary, we will return to research Wunderwaffe later. There are hundreds of thousands of documents on the war. But, when we narrowed it to secret weapons under development by the Third Reich in 1945, we found something quite fascinating, dear Bones and Abigor. It was only two pages, hand-typed and lacking in detail, but its gist says a weapon code name Riese was under construction in the tunnels Hitler had excavated in the Owl Mountains. There was a rush to finish the tunnels as quickly as possible. Thousands of laborers were used and discarded by those monsters. Some of the tunnels are flooded now." He ends on a sad note. We never hear the atrocities Hitler and his goons committed without feeling deep and enduring sadness. As I look around, I see sadness fighting against their rage.

Sir Winston coughs, strikes a match, and concentrates on the paydirt payoff. "On the second page is a rough diagram of an enormous machine with numerous knobs, levers, and gauges sitting in a vault carved into the solid rock tunnel. Massive metal doors covered in rock protect the entrance from detection. According to the document, 'this machine uses redaction- and has the technology to -redaction. The dimensions are 12 feet by 14 feet, requiring a power source of -redaction.

When engaged, it can activate -redaction- around the world.' We were frustrated by the secretive nature of the document."

Peeved by the redactions but still buoyed by what they had found, Sir Winston hammers the bottom line. "Still, we were delighted to make such an incredible discovery in our first effort. Even the heavily redacted areas which hide the exact fundamental nature of the discovery may prove revealing." As Sir Winston gives us the good and bad news, David and Angus return. I look for indications of their success, such as a smile, a jaunty stride, or a cheery wave. Nope, not this time!

David sits beside me, puts his arm around my shoulders, and winks at me, and Angus continues to stand. His hands are in his pockets, and it sounds like he is jingling change. Does he carry change?

Sir Winston waves his cigar in delight as he greets David and Angus. "Welcome back, my boy. So pleased to see you. Albert and I share our splendid discovery with Bones, Abigor, and Sophie. Dear Bones, would you mind making copies of this document for everyone? Please be cautious. It is quite fragile." I go to the study to make copies, a little concerned about damaging the original document. Soon, pages copied, I return with no ill effect. As soon as I pass around the copies, I grab a cup of coffee and turn my attention back to the Great Man.

Sir Winston chomps down on his cigar, nods at Einstein, and continues, "Albert, you have been quiet. Please give us your thoughts on our discovery and its implications for the success of our mission."

Dr. Einstein puffs on his unlit pipe and glances at Churchill, "I am gratified that we have a point to begin learning about this, uh Doomsday Machine. My first thought as a scientist is, does this actual machine exist? We do not have a machine. We have two pieces of 77-year-old yellowed 8 X 11 paper. Yes, we have made progress in collecting data that may give us a peek into the function of the Owl Mountain secret, or it may not." I notice the speaker's mood affects my mood. I was excited when Sir Winston was speaking. Now, my balloon is deflated. No wonder Churchill inspired millions of hopeless people to fight on when winning the War was an unlikely fool's dream.

Einstein, entranced by logical facts, smooths his wild eyebrows and presses on. "If the information in the document is accurate, we still know very little. Factually, it says a large machine with levers and knobs is hidden behind two massive doors. Whatever that fuel might be, it could potentially activate something unspecified worldwide if it had fuel. I suggest we search for other documentation supporting this and giving us more data. I have nothing more to add." I understand. A genius needs facts.

David looks concerned, his eyebrows traveling toward each other. He takes this opportunity to comment. "This is interesting, gentlemen. I am impressed that you found a solid clue so quickly. If we can determine who wrote this, we may be able to go further. Let's check for fingerprints. As far as we know, these documents have been stored away from extreme temperatures and sources of degradation. It may be possible but unlikely to find a fingerprint. Of course, even if we found one, we would not know if the fingerprint belonged to the writer. Prints could belong to the typist or even someone who read the documents. Naturally, we would need that person's fingerprints on record to compare, which is another problem. Still, I think it is worth a try. I suggest Angus and I go to the laboratory at MI5 and do the testing ourselves. We want to keep the paper secret until we know who we can trust at MI5. Because of the paper's age and fragility, we must process the document carefully. What do you think, Angus?" Angus, who is still standing, looks distracted. I wonder what has caught his attention.

Angus waves his hand in agreement and adds his expertise, "Exactly, David. It is worth a try. Even if we find nothing, we are no worse off. If time permits, I suggest using ninhydrin since it is porous paper.

Perhaps 1,8 diazafluoren-9-one is another choice. It will turn the fingerprints purple, and we can photograph them to study at high resolution. Naturally, there are fingerprint records for members of the government and military. We could check those data banks. Most are computerized by now. It would be impossible unless we could use an MI5 computer or the Met's computer." Looking for fingerprints does not sound like a promising path to me. Yes, I admit we are willing to believe almost anything that might suggest the slightest hope in our current wretched position, but I am still a realist.

The room begins to shudder as if it were at the epicenter of a gigantic magnitude eight earthquake. The lights alternately dim and brighten. I grab onto my coffee cup as it tries to shimmy around the coffee table. We are in a state of high alert. Suddenly, Druid is in the middle of the room. I forget in between his visits how truly imposing Druid is.

Druid booms at us in rage, "What are you doing, spirits? Why do you drown in foot-dragging and indecisiveness? Did I not put this document where you would find it? Time is running out! Hear me! You must move with all haste to find this fearsome beast before monsters unleash its destructive power on the planet." Druid looks at me. "I have saved this human twice. Do not put her life in danger again! Hark! You have two tangled missions. You ignore Wagner and their diabolical scheme. You must seek out Suggs!" Druid focuses his intense stare on Abigor. "Go soon, get the weapon, and bring him here!" The air in the room whips around like a mini-tornado. Druid is gone, and a foot-high hourglass in a metal frame sits in his place. The sand is running through at an alarming rate. OH HELL! Wait, focus. Who is the weapon?

Well, that was jolting. Everyone at once is expressing alarm, annoyance, disdain, shock, or consternation at the Druid terror attack. I lean forward to get a better look at the ancient hourglass. It is stunningly beautiful in its silver frame with red jewels. Darn, I hope I can keep it.

Druid got our attention! Sophie snarls in indignation.

David is angry with the giant. "What does that colossus thug think he is doing? Do we not have enough to do without his egocentric, self-indulging, narcissistic theatrics?" I don't bother mentioning all three of his adjectives mean approximately the same thing. Now is not the time. Big Soph is looking at us, wondering if we will ever get moving. She sighs.

Sir Winston takes a deep breath and cautions us, "Let's be calm, gentleman and Bones, and discuss what Druid told us. He may be theatrical, as David says. No, I think Biblical might be a better description. Nevertheless, he is also accurate when he warns us. As I watch the sand running through the hourglass, I am overwhelmed by the magnitude of our mission. We will not falter; I propose we move forward with all possible haste, as Druid suggests. Let's hand out assignments. As Druid said, MOVE!" Druid has a way of energizing a crowd.

Sir Winston continues where he left off before the terror attack. "We can assume the document is accurate, or Druid would not have made it available. We must determine what to do to learn more. When we have thoroughly prepared ourselves, we will make a plan and hand out assignments. We will not be rushed into chaos. We will proceed with deliberate purpose and move with precision.

"For now, we will discuss David and Angus' midnight reconnaissance mission at MI5, looking for the Red Biggers file and the map on Owl Mountain. What did you find, gentlemen? Red Biggers' name keeps coming up. He plays a shadowy part in our mission."

David's lips are pursed. He is annoyed as failure does not suit him, "We looked everywhere, even ridiculous places, where they might hide a highly classified document. We planned to go back tomorrow night and keep looking. "He pauses as if something just occurred to him, "Hmmm, I just happened to think of the safe in my old office." He considers hopefully and says, "The safe might still be there. At least we don't have to fingerprint the Machine document. It is authentic."

David takes out his small notebook and makes a notation. Though his memory is impressive, as a good officer, he still takes notes. He puts away the notebook and resumes. "We looked in the personnel files in the HR computer, and the classified personnel files and Red Biggers' file is in neither place. We will look at the paper files in the basement. Since time is slipping away, we will return tonight. Also, we ran into Miles working late in his office. We reminded him we needed his help with our assignment and asked if he had heard anything from his superiors. He said he is optimistic and hopes to answer within 48 hours. We need their manpower and equipment to tackle the tunnels. Yes, we must move quickly, but we must also consider the big picture. Speed without preparation is poor planning."

Looking at me, concerned, David asks, "Bones, have you eaten? You look pale."

I am thinking, ok, the world might end at any minute, and my dear David is concerned about my eating habits. I don't say that. Instead, I reply. "I am fine, David. I ate while I was working in the study. Using your suggestions, I want to share what I found when deep diving into the dark network. I saw the name Seth three times, and the information connected with that name was disturbing. I wonder if you have heard of an underground character with that name or code name?"

Angus, who had finally sat down in a club chair, looked up, surprised. "Yes, Bones, I have heard the name. After I retired, I played cards with some of the active agents at MI5. We got together once a month, ate pizza, and vented about the job and crazy politicians. I could keep connected to the old agency and maintain my relationships with the agents. I remember them discussing a bloody tiresome bloke with the code name Seth. They tried everything to trace him down on the net with the best IT blokes and hackers, though they would deny they had hackers. He was involved in everything deviant, and they were convinced he was a danger to national security, but he was stubbornly elusive. One agent said it was as if he could become invisible. The bloody sewer rat had quite a nasty reputation. Were I still alive and 80 years old, I could go to those agents, especially the agent who said he was invisible, and ask probing questions. If it comes to that, David and I could question him. I am quite confident he would not recognize me in my role as the new George Clarke. It sounds as if you suspect he is involved in our investigation. What makes you think that?" We don't have time to explore my discovery now, and I don't have an answer to Angus' question. Yes, the elusive Seth is an itch in the middle of my back I cannot reach. In response to Angus, I raise my hands in an I-don't-have-a-clue gesture.

David jumps to his feet and shouts, "Angus, let us return to MI5 at once and turn it upside down! I wish Druid would point out those files for us while he is doing nothing else of value. We might as well get something out of it. Also, we can search for intelligence on the mysterious Seth." David grabs his bomber jacket and heads to the door, followed by Angus. Sir Winston salutes them and "sips" from his brandy snifter.

Dr. Einstein frowns. He is not in his comfort zone. No, not at all.

Abigor asks if they need his help in searching. David motions toward the door, and the three, uh, men run through the door. They don't bother opening it first; manners be damned, full steam ahead! Their body language says wrathful and resolute. Bring it on!

Sir Winston turns to Dr. Einstein and asks if he needs a light. The scientist shrugs and continues to fight his pipe. Sir Winston suggests, "Albert, we must concentrate on the various issues involved. If you do not mind, I will enumerate those primary issues. First, we must find the weapon if it exists. We have numerous reasons to believe it does exist. Admittedly, we have no indisputable facts. Yet, we know from many reliable sources that Hitler, the damnable scoundrel, worked toward such a catastrophic weapon. He knew he was losing the war and wanted to cause as much damage to the Allies as possible. As despicable as Hitler was, Albert, I do not believe he would have paused even momentarily if his fellow countrymen were also devastated by his horrid machine. We know the man, and we know his state of desperation, his drug use, and his anomalous wickedness.

"Many resources have indicated we can find the elusive monstrous weapon in Owl Mountain. There are a few tunnels into the center of the mountain. Some sources tell us the bugger is probably in one of the tunnels excavated under Castle Ksiaz. We want more information on Red Biggers. My intuition tells me he is a central character in this mystery. I have lived a long life, Albert, by following my intuition." Albert sagely nodded in agreement, as did Sophie.

"As you know, he was a member of SOE and, as such, he was fearless and capable. He had a personal interest in the area due to family connections. He may have learned threatening information on his own since the government, according to Angus, would not allow an exploratory mission to the tunnels. Also, Druid is correct. We have concentrated on the tunnel and ignored the other piece of our mission, Dr. Wagner. Since we are waiting for Miles's assistance, we have a slight opening in our schedule to devote to Dr. Wagner and his vile team. And another thing, I am puzzled by what Druid said to Abigor about a weapon. We must ask Abigor when he returns." Churchill strolls to the bar to pour another snifter of brandy. I wonder what happened to the first brandy.

Dr. Einstein is running on supposition overload now. He grumbles. "Winston, nothing has changed for me. We are in the dark, and new theories, counter-theories, and names keep popping up. We are approaching chaos, and I want time to consider what I have heard and formulate a direction for myself in this mission. I have an idea; I will work on that. If you, Bones, and Sophie will excuse me, I shall retire to my laboratory for quiet so that I can concentrate." I feel sorry for poor Dr. Einstein. We are not the personality types with whom he has been accustomed to working. We are, perhaps, a tad too action-oriented. Sophie looks up and grumbles in apparent sympathy with Dr. Einstein.

I listened to the Great Man and the Genius and tried to see the big picture in my mind. I wonder where Seth, the Demon of Owl Mountain, Dr. Wagner, NGA, and the Neo-Nazis fit in. Indeed, we know the Neo-Nazis and Dr. Wagner are part of the same sordid team. Are they all in cahoots in this dangerous game where humans are the enemy and likely the unsuspecting prey? I hope David and Angus find the map and Red Biggers's file. I cannot sit still any longer. I decide to take a run and allow my brain to process everything I have heard. At home, I did my best thinking while cutting grass with my little motorless lawn mower. Here, a run will have to do. I change into black running pants, a t-shirt, and red New Balance runners.

I am ready for some exercise and alone time to analyze everything I have heard today.

Chapter Ten

The Eye Patch

Dressed for a good run, I loop in Sir Winston, who is pondering the Miracle of Dunkirk or something, "If I may interrupt for a minute, I need exercise. I will be back in an hour or so. Is there anything I can do to help before I leave?"

He is so absorbed in his thoughts and world-class processing that it takes him a minute to notice me and respond to my question. Sir Winston smiles warmly at me and replies, "Excellent idea, dear Bones. Exercise is so important to your health. Be cautious and stay aware of your surroundings as I always counsel you. Danger is all around you, be prepared for it." He waves to me and does the famous victory sign, and I sign back.

The former Prime Minister carries on as I walk into the hall and mosey toward our private elevator. I am excited to begin my run since I have not been consistently exercising lately. I constantly remind clients that exercise is the best remedy for stress. I need to take my advice. The ride down to the lobby was uneventful, meaning no one tried to kill or cripple me, which was just what I had hoped it would be. The lobby is teeming with people for some reason as I weave my way through the human traffic cones. My, my, do I see Prime Minister Boris Johnson talking with journalists? No wonder the lobby is so swamped. I wonder if Churchill knows about Johnson's telly promo. He might want to say tootle pip! He is not a Johnson fan.

As I approach the impressive entrance doors to the hotel, I see a man walking a few feet in front of me. He stands out, medium height, muscular, with red hair. When he suddenly turns his head around to look straight at me, I am staggered to see he is wearing an eye patch!

What the Hell! I start running toward him, and he moves much faster away though he is not running. He glides just as Sophie does when we run; what is that about? A group of journalists is blocking my path, and I must circumvent them to get to the door. I desperately search both directions after I slam out of the door past a gaping concierge to the sidewalk. I spot him off to my right, plowing a row through the crowd like a mighty John Deere tractor. He is pulling away from me, but I have no intention of losing him. We must talk!

Running along the path plowed through humanity by the tractor, I can keep him in sight. All I can think is you must catch him. You must catch him! Focusing on the fugitive, I slam into a mammoth man in a gray-striped suit who steps in my way. I bounce off him and land knees-first on the sidewalk. I splutter my apology, ignore my torn running pants and bleeding knees, and run. The fugitive is still within my sight, turning to the left down an alley. I sprint faster, and my bleeding knees rebuke me. I screech to a halt at the alley, dive in, and slam directly into my target. I lose balance, slide, hit my head against a building, and fall to my knees, again. Ouch! Ouch!

A gruff English accent says, "Let me help you up, pretty Bones. Your knees look bloody terrible. How is your head? That was a nasty whopping hit." My knees silently agree, as does my aching head. He grabs my hand and hefts me up.

I can only continue staring at him and struggle to say, "Are you really, uh, Red Biggers? You look like him." I cannot get my poor dazed brain around this new craziness. The hits keep coming.

He smiles indulgently at me, reaches out to steady me, and confirms, "Yes, I am Red, and it is nice to meet you, Bones. Druid sent me to help you and your team. He broke a few rules doing that, but he is quite the rebel. I wanted to talk with you first to find out where you are in the mission before confronting the entire team, which may never happen. Druid said this would be the best way to approach it. Do you know who Druid really is?" Still trying to process this new startling event and my knees, I miss his question.

I stutter, "Listen, I, I am not entirely certain who, who I am any, anymore." Breathe, breathe, Bones, you will be alright. Just breathe. You are tougher than this.

I try again with renewed oxygen, "You are Red Biggers, really, the Red Biggers? The real one from SOE?" I am gradually moving toward the ability to speak sensibly.

Red smiles at me gently, as one might with a not-too-bright child. "Pretty Bones, I understand your surprise. I didn't realize you would run into me and fall. Are you always this, uh, clumsy? No harm intended." Yes, actually, I am—no need to go into that.

I resume with something akin to babble. "No harm taken, Red. Uh, can we go somewhere that we can sit down? My knees are screaming for a break. I ran past the *Coffee Cup* a few blocks ago. Let's go there. I need coffee and a dozen or so pastries." That is the key to survival, tons of restorative caffeine and sugar. That is my personal, not professional, opinion. However, I have suggested caffeine for depression.

Red smiles and takes my arm to head back toward the *Coffee Cup*. I decided to save my questions. Sugar fortifies. I notice people move out of our way as if some sixth sense tells them to avoid the man with the eye patch and the woman with the bleeding knees. That makes perfect sense to me. The shop is a little narrow building with tall, silent, stalwart columns, white stucco on the first floor, and red brick on the second level. It looks so Dickensian. Maybe Tiny Tim is a server here. A few outside tables with white tablecloths give it an incongruent yet pleasant Parisian touch. For privacy, we decide to sit outside. Red is an old-fashioned gentleman warrior. He pulls my chair out for me.

Soon an older gray-haired lady with sparkling hazel eyes comes out to take our order. I immediately feel at home. She reminds me of my Mama Bessie, my fraternal grandmother. She looks at me. "Sweetie, what can I get for you today? You look exhausted. Let me suggest our Cappuccino with whipped cream, cinnamon, and your favorite, light as a cloud huge Southern biscuits with butter and honey." She ignores Red, which makes me question if she sees him. I am reluctant to ask. This is London, and they serve my grandmother's Southern Biscuits. I wonder how hard I hit my head? I touch it, and the bump is a tad tender. I go with her recommendations and give her a big hug. I hope Red has money—I didn't bring anything with me, not even my phone.

Red waits until the sweet grandmother lady goes back into the *Coffee Cup*. "Tell me, Bones, where are you in your investigation? What do you need? How can I help you?" His words are music to my ears! We desperately need Red's help.

I have to think about that before I can give an intelligent answer, "Red, we need you. Will you stay with us and help? We must know what is in Owl Mountain and where to find it. We assume it is under the Ksiaz Castle. I can see that poor, unsuspecting Castle blown into the mesosphere. We have numerous sources indicating a wicked weapon and possibly more in the tunnels, but there is too much ground to cover for the six of us. Then there is the Dr. Wagner group, whatever that encompasses, trying to rule the world with Hitler at the helm. We do not know how much they have progressed in their evil mega-maniacal plans. We feel pressured by time and Druid. He left an antique hourglass to spur us to immediate action. Watching the sand drain, grain by grain, is terrifying. He said when the sand is gone, so are we as a species. Can you help us? Angus and Sir Winston said you know the area and could lead us to the weapon." I take a minute to breathe after my breathless oratory.

"I will help you, Bones, but I am in a peculiar position. I was not in Beyond. I am trying to earn my way there. There were situations during the War that put me in an unpopular position with Beyond. You know their Prime Directive, do not kill a human unless it is to protect an innocent, and only if you have tried everything else. I understand you had a serious problem with the Directive and the Powers in Beyond when you hit Hans in the head with a long gun. Several times. With great passion."

I protest with extenuating circumstances, "Uh, Hans tried to scramble my brains first! He swung numerous times at me. Only then did I hit back with appropriate glee. Truthfully, I was lucky not to hear the booming sound of thunder warning me I had stomped all over the line that must not be crossed. The Powers at Beyond have no sense of humor. Retribution is swift, so I am told. Be very careful, Red. I had not been told about the Prime Directive when I was whopping up on Hans. I found out much later."

Sweet Granny returns with my delicious restorative drugs, sugar, and caffeine. I dig in with gusto as I listen to Red.

Red seems discouraged as he explains his predicament, "I crossed the Prime Directive line and ended up in uncomfortably hot water. No doubt you know I was a member of the Special Operations Executive, and our orders were to win. I followed those orders as long as I believed what I was doing was right.

"I have another chance. I will break even if I can save more innocents than the number of villains I killed. These men were true villains, bloody villains, not just soldiers. I did what I had to do, and if I spend eternity in, well, if I don't make it to Beyond, I will accept that. I would not change any of the choices I made. Our mission was to conduct espionage, sabotage, and reconnaissance in occupied Europe and other areas.

"Along with the usual fighting gear, we were issued RBD hunting knives for hunting and fighting. It wasn't pleasant." I saw deep pain in his good eye.

"Instructors taught us how to use the knife to stop noise. SOE lives depended on surprise attacks.

"Casually, we were known as Churchill's Secret Army. If the enemy captured us, we knew there would be no rescue. We were expendable. The government would have denied any knowledge of our existence. We were equipped with a poison capsule in case it was needed to save us from the savagery of our enemy. Our existence was a secret to only a few we could trust. Many regular military officers worked against us, thinking we were not gentlemanly enough. Can you imagine that, Bones? We were fighting a damn, friggin monster with an enormous mobile killing machine approaching 18.2 million men, and we weren't gentlemanly enough? Many top British military officers were bloody old aristocrats who had no idea how to fight a modern war! They would have used bloody Roberts Rules of Order!"

I nod encouragingly for him to continue. I understand his feelings of confusion and perhaps betrayal.

"Bones, all that is to explain why I cannot join your group. As instructors taught me in SOE Bootcamp, I can help in sneaky, sly, stealthy, and covert ways. I will be communicating with you, the only mortal. You are still imperfect and must earn your wings too. Most of the time, communication will not be in person. You can SOS me if there is an emergency. I cannot promise I will always be aware of your message." He puts his hand on my shoulder to show we are in this together.

I am confused and frustrated. "How do I SOS you? Do you realize the Titanic was the first ship to use the SOS signal? Right? That did not go well."

Red smiles, "Yes, I am aware of that. I knew Charles Lightoller, the senior surviving officer on the Titanic, and he was a good, resilient, and courageous man. You can send a text to me. That will work as well as anything if I am needed. Just type in Red. I will get it at some point. I will drop hints and suggestions using Post-It notes and other ways. I can tell you that the map to the tunnels was hidden in the old, obsolete basement safe in MI5. It is where David found the Mengele Code file in your first mission. Tell David to look behind the back panel. He will have to unscrew it. Also, the document Sir Winston found with the machine diagram is accurate. Guard it. I will see what I can find out about Dr. Wagner and his cartel."

It hit me. "What? Someone at MI5 hid the map where others could not find it. How do you know? Who hid it? We must know who we cannot trust. Wait! When was it hidden?"

I heard these words as if the wind were whispering to me. "Generally, look under the Castle. Trust no one."

I saw a 20-pound note float down on the table. Red Biggers was gone.

Thank God for the note. What would I tell Mama Bessie if I couldn't pay the bill and add a generous tip? I cram down a couple of the luscious Southern biscuits with lots of honey and butter. It's OK. I ran here, and I will run back.

Wait, what did Red say? Do you know who Druid "really" is?

I run back to the Savoy, knees still bemoaning their painful fate.

Chapter Eleven

The Map

I rush into the suite, panting and shouting, "Hurry, we must tell David!". Sir Winston, Sophie, and Dr. Einstein are the only ones there. Naturally, they are startled and stare questioningly at me.

I sit down next to Dr. Einstein and try to catch my breath. He must have finished his exile in his lab. All three are looking at my ragged, bleeding knees. Sophie sits on my other side and puts her sweet head in my lap.

Sir Winston exclaims, "Dear Bones, what has happened to you? Did that evil Demon attack you again? Did he hurt you? You look awful! Let me get brandy for you." He moves toward the perpetually well-stocked bar. Since none of us drink, a full bar is eccentric. They can't indulge, and I don't drink. My weakness is robust, death-defying coffee—and desserts.

Dr. Einstein is back to cleaning his glasses and doing his wrinkled forehead thing. Frowning, he asks. "Bones, tell us what has happened to you. You were simply going for a run, and you came back looking like you were hit by a motor car. Oh dear, were you run down by a motor car? I have told Winston many times that the traffic is horrible here. Did you get the tag number?" I hear Churchill groan. Dr. E has never had a driver's license, and Sir Winston is a hideously incompetent driver. He views a car as a weapon of mass destruction used to strike fear into pedestrians and other drivers. He hands the brandy to me. I don't drink, but what the Hell? I empty the snifter in one gulp.

I answer as quickly as I can under this double onslaught, "No, I was not attacked by a demon nor run down by a car. I fell a couple of times while trying to catch Red Biggers." That caught the great men by surprise. They are temporarily speechless and bewildered, and I thoroughly savor the rare moment. Sophie knew exactly what happened on my run. She would have been by my side if I had been in danger.

"When I was going through the hotel lobby, I saw a man who looked exactly like the description I had heard of Red Biggers. His appearance is rather distinctive. He was leaving the hotel, and I rushed out to catch him. After running several blocks, I finally caught up with him in an alley. He confirmed his identity, and we had a long chat. He said Druid sent him here to help us. Because of Beyond rules, he can only communicate with me. I am still wicked or something. We must contact David and tell him the map is behind the back panel in the old basement safe at MI5. The same safe where they kept the Mengele Code file. Oh, the general area of the Castle is where we will find the right tunnel."

I stopped so they could contact David; however, they do that. None of them have phones. However, they can call as if they have a phone. I don't know how they do that. Please don't ask me.

Sir Winston said, "We contacted David, and he will search the basement safe. He and Angus will return momentarily. They have terminated their search for Andy "Red" Biggers' file since we have acquired the man himself. They could not find fingerprints on the document, which was always an extreme long shot at best. Since they have not found the Biggers file, I fear some detestable twit destroyed it. All in all, it was a relatively satisfying conclusion for their visit to MI5. They will have the map in hand." The former Prime Minister snips off the end of a fresh Cuban cigar and settles back to enjoy it. Mission accomplished.

I resume reporting on my adventure. "Red said he is earning his way to Beyond because he trampled all over the Prime Directive while serving in SOE during the War. Druid sent him to us, but Beyond's obscure, annoying rules limit Red's participation. I am to send him an SOS by text when he is needed. As a note of interest, he knew Charles Lightoller from the Titanic. Anyway, if he has a hint for us, he will leave a message for me. Evidently, he does not text out. He also said the map is relatively accurate, as is the document you found in the National Archives, including the diagram. I asked him to see if he could find anything on Dr. Wagner and his merry group. The more I think about it, the more I am convinced Dr. Wagner, the Neo-Nazis, and NGA are working together. It simply makes logical sense." Dr. Einstein and Sir Winston do not question my hypothesis.

Sophie has been taking in every word as she sits in her Sphinx mode on the sofa. The guys sit in silence, pondering the most recent information. I decide to take a lovely hot shower to wash the street dirt away and then put an antibiotic ointment on my knees. My torn running pants go into the trash. Refreshed with new clothes, black linen pants, a purple turtleneck, and a black blazer, I am ready to join the geniuses again.

Dr. Einstein is reliving 1920 or something. He asks, "Why would Red Biggers tell us where the map to the tunnels is located and not simply tell us exactly how to locate the tunnel and the machine? Perhaps, he could even tell us how to deactivate the monster. Then we would not need the map. Does this make sense to anyone?" He looks questioningly at me since I am the only one who speaks to Red.

I do my best to explain since I am not entirely certain either. "From what Red told me, he is restricted from helping us directly by rules from Beyond. Before he can be more direct, he must atone for the sins he committed during the war, according to Beyond. Red cannot be a part of our team. Fortunately, he is allowed to give us hints and stealthily point us in the right general direction. OK, here is some conjecture—that is what I think, but I really don't know." Dr. Einstein's firm grip on logical reasoning makes this indirect communication a difficult sell. I get it!

I suddenly remember that Red said something about Druid. What did he say? Oh, I remember. I blurt out, "Red said something puzzling about Druid. He asked, do you know who Druid really is? He did not explain, and I did not follow up since we talked about many startling topics. That question just went right past me. Do you know what he meant by that?" I look from one to the other, hoping for an explanation.

Sir Winston spends time searching for his silver pocket watch, which his father gave him. Suddenly, the exact time is crucial. He exchanges a glance with Dr. Einstein. Finally, he says, "Dear Bones, there are some things to which we are not privy. We will be informed by the Powers in Beyond when the time is right. No, I do not have an explanation for you. Red evidently knows something we do not know. I would assume Druid told him. Indeed, no one in Beyond would have given that information to Red." They seem eager to change the subject, and soon, they will have an excellent excuse.

As we discuss the illogical and disturbing, a ruby red note floats down into my lap. Sophie watches it in flight with great interest. I read the message aloud. "I hope to join you soon. In the meantime, you have a direction, BE READY TO MOVE! The time to gather information is coming to an end." It is signed Red. He is beginning to sound like Druid, just not quite as booming. No wonder they are buds.

Reading his note and looking at the antique hourglass provokes our sense of urgency. I break out in a cold sweat while Sophie shakes her head and lets out a low, deep-throated, menacing howl. The gentlemen look determined, locked, and loaded. We are blissfully unaware of the ghastly future that awaits us.

Horrors, old and new, are in the dark tunnels.

Chapter Twelve

The Wicked Machine

Aaii relishes thinking about his conversation with Seth and the splendid jousting match with Bart the Swine afterward. Of course, he wins the Jousting match, and Bart will feel his lance's painful effects for many days.

The Shadow silently watches.

Seth is a fool so consumed with the seductive allure of power he does not think rationally. He never questioned my goals. Why would I want control? I have all the power anyone could possess. I am from the fires of Hell. Perhaps, he missed that little clue. I will play his game because his group, NGA, is Part One of my plan. It shall be amusing to see Hitler and his deviates rule the earth. He almost accomplished it last time. He has the talent.

Nonetheless, he must work on his desires and temptations. He is motivated by ego, hate, and love of control, and he turns to drugs to cope with the immense anxiety one experiences in conquering the world. I shall help him stay focused on goals and use reason and logic. I shall not be his second in command. No, I shall be his master. Controlling Hitler will be entertaining.

Seth does not understand the power of the machine I possess. Probably because I did not share that bit of information with him, he also does not comprehend the magic of the other device designed by the geniuses Drs Rosen and Goldmann. It is hilarious! I have the power to destroy much of the world. I could quickly reduce the planet to steaming, smoking rubble, and wiping out all life. They might stop the destruction using Drs Rosen and Goldmann's magical device, the E=MC2 Converter. Won't it be hilarious when they learn the truth about the Fantastic machine? Admittedly, it has one or two inconsequential disadvantages for anyone who chooses to use it. Finding it would be their first challenge. They will hear they must go to the Dark World to find it. The idiot "Churchill" gang doesn't know the Rosen and Goldmann machine exists but not in Owl Mountain. Demon laughs until tears roll down his red cheeks. *Yet, they may open the gate to the Dark World for me.* The Demon Scowls. *The insufferable meddling fool Stallings learned something about my rouse. He pits himself against me in helping the Abigor and the woman. Damn! I have no power over a righteous spirit!* The Demon's false handsome face begins to crack and peel; a forked tongue flicks out.

I must have the Sunstone Compass to enter the Dark World, and I do not possess it. I am the only one who knows about a train filled with treasures that left Wroclaw and Walbrazych in 1945. The treasures came in train cars to the tunnels here in Poland and have sat undisturbed for 70 years. After years of searching all the tunnels, I have found nothing! The treasures must be in the Dark World! Why else would I remain here? I believe the valuables from the Amber Room in St. Petersburg wait for me, and I shall have those amber walls once I possess the Compass. Hitler made a pact with Satan to open the entrance to the Dark World and secret away his gold and treasure. Hitler did Satan's work in this world. A profitable bargain for both. It did not end well for Hitler—never trust Satan.

I am the only one who knows about the location of train cars now. The Demon sniggers. The horrible grating sound makes the Shadow cringe. *The Compass is mine! I know where it can be found and who possesses it. The legend of the Dark World is my ace card and will further complicate the Churchill gang's progress. The Demon I sent to that stupid woman said the self-righteous traitor Abigor, and the woman have the compass and the passwords. She annoys me, and she will die. We shall visit her when she is alone and defenseless. I am working on a plan to remove her from the protection of the annoying mutt. Other demons say the dog is enormously powerful, more powerful than any entity we have seen, and very protective of the woman. Fortunately, the mutt cannot destroy me, but it might be able to send lesser demons back to Hell. No one suspects I have a reason for entering the Dark World. Alexander the Great would understand.*

Aaii leaves his gaudy throne and ambles to the servant bell pull, an embroidered tapestry with a brass ring pull to the right of the double doors. If it actually were a bell pull, it would be attached to a pulley system going to the kitchen. A bell with a cute little hammer would alert servants to attend Aaii. One, he doesn't have a kitchen, and two, the bell pull doesn't call his servant, Fox. He pulls the cord, and a large portion of the wall disappears. No, I don't know where the wall goes or why he uses a pull. My guess? He is quirky. He walks through the opening into a small tunnel lit by burning torches. There is little room for movement in the tight tunnel. He is fortunate he doesn't suffer from bouts of claustrophobia.

A few hundred feet down the tunnel passage, he hits his gold signet ring against the wall, and it opens into a large 30 X 30 room. At the far end sits a massive machine with levers and knobs. The Demon turns knobs and pushes levers, and the metal giant wakes with red and white lights flashing, whirling, and blinking randomly. He looks at the control panel checking readouts on the gauges. He is pleased with the machine's performance and its cataclysmic potential. His deadly Plan B is delightfully entertaining. He rolls it around in his mind, savoring the delicious idea. For now, he will be reluctantly satisfied with Hitler conquering humankind. When Aaii decides to take that final drastic step to close the book on five million years of human history, he will gloat at having outwitted everyone. He is the only one "alive" who knows how this machine functions and its destructive capability. There are many rumors about the Doomsday Machine, and none are accurate. Most stories allude to atomic energy and mushroom clouds. They point to a bomb like those used in Nagasaki and Hiroshima during WWII. All the stories are incredibly flawed. This machine uses the earth and its unique construction against itself. He laughs merrily as he thinks about his enemies' stupidity and his power.

The Demon is quite prideful and practically drowning in self-congratulatory nonsense. Drunk on pride, Aaii doesn't notice a large shadow darkening the wall next to the door. Conversely, the shadow is paying meticulous attention to Aaii's every move.

Several members of the Third Reich and various scientists were involved in the project. They knew its secrets. Brilliant men and women designed and built the sophisticated weapon. They have been dead for many years because of the war, and the Demon killed the ones the war missed. In all, he murdered thirty-five people in cold blood. There was one other also, Red Biggers, an operative with SOE. As the machine was being constructed, he sleuthed around, trying to learn about it. He knew where it was hidden and may have intuited its tremendous capability. The Demon is prudent. He always says to err on the side of caution. He had Biggers killed by a Nazi spy working in MI5. The spy used the CIAs heart attack drug. He doesn't have to worry about Biggers going to Beyond and coming back as a potent problem since, at the moment, Red and Beyond are not on speaking terms. Without the enhanced powers, Red is relatively harmless. The killer spy shredded Beyond's Prime Directive. The Demon knows Biggers' numerous sins and dangerous knowledge, so he ordered his MI5 plant to kill the spy. Truthfully, maybe he did peek to be sure the lethal CIA additive was in Red's cuppa. The CIA comes in handy.

The Demon schemes. *I must throw the enemy into confusion and disarray. For whatever incomprehensible reason, the enemy is quite fond of the woman. She is a pet, I suppose. My deadly bear trap, my lure, uses only the finest organic peanut butter and the sharpest teeth. First, we must lure her away from the Savory and her powerful protectors. Luckily, she has a new playmate, my old enemy Red Biggers. Indeed, If she thinks Biggers is reaching out to her, she will take the bait and walk into the gaping mouth of my trap, and it will SLAM, SHUT with deadly finality. She is not an intelligent woman.* The monster grins ludicrously, exposing savage pointed canine teeth as he does a premature victory dance.

The Shadow watches.

The Shadow knows what evil lurks in the heart of the Demon, and he knows many secrets. Shadow says softly to himself, "Demon, your time is coming." He makes a pistol with his right hand and points his finger at the Demon. "Bang"

Chapter Thirteen

Seth and the NGA

Seth has a pricey yet quirky office with all the accouterments necessary for an eccentric executive living in New York City. He has an appallingly expensive, enormous burl desk with a glass top that sparkles in the artificial light. There is nothing on his desk to tell us anything about him. His white desk chair sits behind the vast desk. The chair is soft as pudding leather and ergonomically designed to fit him perfectly. Behind his chair stands a combination bookcase and bar with glass doors and spacious shelves to display his photographs of famous people and prestigious awards. Is that Albert Speer, sans uniform, wearing a casual sweater and pants, standing next to a German Shepard? My, my, there is Goebbels in a well-tailored black suit and fedora hat smiling into the camera. Almost certainly, few people would recognize either of them without their signature Nazi uniforms.

To the right of his desk is his sitting area featuring two white Chic Set sofas designed by wildly popular Lonzo Columbo for a distinctive look. Seth can alter the arrangement with little effort, and these unique pieces add much pizzazz for a trifling $160,000 each. His burl coffee table matches the desk and perfectly complements the plush white leather sofas. Naturally, the artworks are modern, impressionistic, and from the day's most fashionable, trendy artists. Each piece is unique in its subject matter. Seth’s taste leans toward the avant-garde morbid, with many works portraying death and dying. The large oil behind one sofa depicts an open coffin with a sign on the bottom which reads, “waiting for you.” One must admire his ghoulish wit. When newcomers visit his office, he takes them on a fascinating tour of the artworks divulging artists’ names, how much he paid for each one, and how much it has increased in value. Most visitors are more interested in the "why" than invested dollars.

Plush, wild graphic rugs greatly annoy the gleaming traditional teak floor. Seth enjoys the "best" life has to offer if it comes with a price tag. One might notice no photos of a wife, children, or friends, not even a beloved poodle. One might also wonder if Seth is loved. One would be right to wonder.

Seth is preparing for a meeting with other senior members of the New Global Agenda. Annette Simmons-Wright, Juan Diez, Emerson North, and Julian Chan. This will be their final planning meeting before moving to the next stage with their reprehensible plans. They had hoped Dr. Mengele would honor them with his illustrious presence today. Regrettably, the good doctor is probably at this very moment roasting in Hell since he rebuffed his last opportunity to repent for his many sins. Mengele is quite dead and thus not available for speaking engagements. Due to this awkward circumstance, they invited his colleague, Dr. Herman Wagner. Disappointingly, he told Seth he was working furiously with his scientists to achieve their goals. They have made significant progress and should soon have three cloned nuclei and a usable Youth Formula ready for distribution. Instead of being here in person, he would send an enlightening and electrifying report for their meeting.

Seth's willowy executive assistant, Heather, strides into the room in her 5-inch heels and silently slides a sealed folder across his desk. Heather is a tall blonde in her late forties who compulsively wears black clothing and shoes. Victorian funeral jewelry is her passion. A few of these treasures have locks of hair made into jewelry. It was trendy during Victorian times to include hair belonging once worn by the dearly departed in lockets and rings. She is quite the sentimentalist, as were the Victorians. If she were not so deathly pale, she might be considered handsome.

Seth asks the ever-efficient Heather if everything is ready for the meeting at 4:00. She nods, licks her blood-red lips, and slinks back into her office. Seth is excited; they are finally at a point where they can make a significant difference in the world. Probably not a popular difference, but a difference all the same. Once they have released the Mengele Youth Formula to the world's elites, billionaires will begin to wrestle with each other to finance their diabolical projects. Dr. Wagner has nearly finished putting the final touches on the Youth Formula. His report is in the sealed folder on Seth's desk. Seth will open it when they are all assembled in a few minutes. Antonio's Italian Garden, the trendiest restaurant in NYC, will cater for the meeting with their usual panache; their coffee and little delicacies are incomparable delights. His favorite liquor store sent over three bottles of their best bubbly Armand de Brignac *Ace of Spades*. Seth is glowing with pride. Everything is perfect.

Heather shepherds their guests into the room, leaving every guest wondering how she walks in those heels. Seth doesn't appreciate guests wandering in harum-scarum; they must enter his office as a group. He turns his sophisticated attention to Annette first. She is a sturdy middle-aged woman who holds the line against graying hair with a dark brown tint. She wears a navy-blue suit that complements her ruddy complexion. Her sensible shoes and round horn-rimmed glasses hint at profound intelligence. She is an undersecretary with the State Department in Washington, which is extremely useful for the NGA.

Juan is an anchor on a major media network and hosts an evening news show interpreting innuendo for viewers and spinning the "news" to make it NGA-friendly. Juan is a handsome African-American man in his late thirties, tall, with short hair, a well-trimmed beard and mustache. His expensive, gray-striped wool suit accentuates his broad shoulders. He wears a small American flag pinned to his lapel to suggest patriotism to those unaware of the words engraved on the back.

Juan shakes hands effusively with Annette. Smiling broadly at her, he says, "Annette, dear woman, it has been too long. How is the ever-bubbling narcissism in Washington? Is there anything I should know for my news show this evening? I always appreciate your little nuggets of vitriol and brutal insights." Annette laughs at the irony; Juan's capacity for vanity is legendary. Annette is sans nuggets today, but she feeds rubbish to him regularly. They, in turn, reward her with favorable coverage, totally fantasy-based press, and regular monetary gifts. Annette is an ambitious and psychopathic woman. She read that only one percent of the population is psychopathic. She considers the diagnosis a badge of honor, which she wears with pride—more insight than usual for a psychopath.

Seth strides over to Emerson to shake his hand and gush about his gray silk suit with a matching pearl gray tie. The perfect complement to his stylish suit. He gushes effusively, "Emerson, my man, how is your golf game these days? Have you beaten your partner Chuck yet? He is a savage on the links! Your bank is doing extremely well, I understand." He smiles his best white, canine-heavy toothy smile for the millionaire banker. Emerson is 60ish with beautifully cut white hair and hard as sapphires startling blue eyes. He is a small man carrying a few extra pounds under that expensive Prada jacket. He smiles back at Seth, "It is always a pleasure to see you, Seth. I have been looking forward to meeting Dr. Wagner in person. I am amazed at the news of his incredibly brilliant projects." He looks around the room as if seeking Dr. Wagner's manly frame, perhaps hiding under the desk.

Seth coughs, straightens his tie, and says, "I have some disappointing news, Emerson. Dr. Wagner is nearing the culmination of both of our vital projects, and he could not step away to join us today. The good doctor felt terrible about missing our meeting; he sent a report I will share as soon as we are seated." Emerson is noticeably upset by this abrupt change in the agenda. His hard eyes pierce Seth to the bone. He does not appreciate nor tolerate last-minute changes. He is not a man with whom one trifles if one wishes to grow old gracefully. There are suspicious rumors about Emerson, none of which have been investigated with vigor or prosecuted. Emerson is not a serious consideration for Seth. Seth is what he is, which is not what he seems to be. He smirks—his little secret.

Heather and a server from Antonio's bring in two big carts with food, several silver carafes of coffee, champagne with glasses, and water bottles. Heather and the servers hand out white bone China dishes and sterling silverware to Seth and his supercilious guests. Soon everyone is seated on the shamefully expensive sofas, ready to partake of their luscious repast.

Seth turns to Julian Chan, who has been in a heated conversation with Annette. Seth asks, "How is it going in China now? I see some unexpected changes in governments and situations have created unique opportunities for your investment and political groups. I congratulate you on your good luck."

Chan smiles at Seth's naive statement and responds. "You are most kind, Seth. Truthfully, these happenings were unexpected for much of the world. I was not surprised because we created chaos for our benefit. Surely, you must realize these fortunate occurrences were not mere coincidences?" He smiled at Seth and bowed slightly. Seth had heard rumors suggesting Julian's associates were involved in the recent outbreak of a new version of the Black Death, causing a steep drop in the economies of several countries. The New Black Death is not nearly as lethal as its predecessor that emerged in the 1300s lingering for centuries and wiping out a third of Europe. It returned with a vengeance in

1665 in London when 70,000 residents died. Since it is a different world in sanitation and medical technology, the New Black Death is somewhat concerning but not the lethal sentence it had been the first time around. A fear factor arose because of the ominous name Black Death, which threw many countries into a needless panic. Medical expenses soared outrageously, and fearful individuals locked themselves in their homes and would not come out to go to work, school, shop, church, or get medical attention. Suicide rates soared dramatically. The wealthy moved to areas with a lower concentration of cases. A couple of the more greedy Pharmaceutical companies prospered with billions of dollars flooding into their bulging accounts. Julian demanded his cut. Not satisfied with that devastation, Julian's hackers using mobile emulators, broke banks in the US and Europe, draining companies of substantial financial assets. Banks and credit unions lost billions of dollars in a matter of days. Seth and Julian shared a bone-chilling chuckle and clinked glasses of champagne. Both of them are on the boards of greedy pharmaceutical companies. As Chan's colleagues reached further into the muck for scum, they drew out more diabolical and highly talented hackers.

If the Shadow were standing unseen in the corner of this room, he would witness a surreal scene of dangerous neurotic, narcissistic people who pass for normal, prosperous individuals if one doesn't look too closely. He would notice everyone is wearing a little American flag on their lapels, even Chan. The Shadow would be white-hot, incredibly furious, and vengeful, burning like the fires of Hell. Across the room, Juan looks into one corner and asks Annette if she sees something peculiar. He points his manicured hand in that direction. He sees a shadow on the wall, but there is nothing solid to cast a shadow. Never a discerning woman, Annette looks, sees nothing of interest, then takes another sip of her champagne and returns to her conversation with Emerson.

It took extraordinary strength none of us can imagine to stay Druid's hand from destroying everyone in the room. Slaying them is not his assignment and would only postpone their evil plans. He knows many others around the world are involved in this abomination. Druid promises himself each person in this room will see him and his mighty sword the next time they meet. They may not survive that encounter. Suddenly, a cold wind blows through the room. Juan, sensitive to external stimuli, feels a dangerous threat and shivers.

Everyone else is focused on Seth, who is opening the sealed folder on his desk. He swings around with a flourish, like a magician about to pull a rabbit from a silk top hat. He then puts on the trendy, costly designer glasses he doesn't need. The report is a brief, concise three pages. Seth reads in a low baritone:

> From: Dr. Herman Wagner
>
> To: The NGA Committee
>
> Progress on the Mengele Youth Formula and Hitler Cloning Projects
>
> After receiving the viable cells from Adolph Hitler, Heinrich Himmler, and Joseph Goebbels, along with Dr. Mengele's journal, I am pleased to report that we have made tremendous progress. I have been kept informed about the work Dr. Mengele and his associates were doing. He knew relentless and aggressive foes were pursuing him. Dr. Mengele was concerned he and his small group might be captured or killed by their pursuers and wanted to ensure his work would continue. He would send a report to me each week here in France. He chose France for our lab to avoid easy detection.

Dr. Mengele was a brilliant scientist and planned for all eventualities. Franz brought the cells and the journal to our group at significant risk and danger to himself. He then returned to Austria to gain the cooperation of scientists with whom he had previously worked. Franz did not know we had already appropriated Dr. Suggs. To be perfectly truthful, it was a hostile takeover.

We are working on the heart glitch. Because of our experiences with Hans and Dr. Mengele, we know an aging heart is not an immediate problem. Both men were over a hundred years when they suffered heart attacks. The aging process can cause changes in the heart and blood vessels. As the heart ages, it cannot beat as fast during physical activity or times of stress. By stretching when the heart pumps blood, elastin helps cushion the fluctuations in pressure inside the artery. Like rubber, it is highly tolerant of repetitive stretching and relaxation. Regrettably, similar to rubber, it will eventually wear out.

If we cannot resolve the issue in the Youth Formula, which I believe we will in time, we can replace the elastin in the heart as it reaches the upper limit of age provided by the Youth Formula. Since everyone treated is dead or dying, other than the Hit Team and myself, we have a few years to perfect the elastin. Currently, my heart is strong and youthful—we do not know the condition of the Hit Team. They are obsessively secretive.

Fortuitously, we will collect another enormous fee when providing the elastin patch. One area of concern in the past is that the Formula has been administered only to men in the prime of life, and it promoted long life and wellness. No other adverse symptoms have been reported, and Dr. Mengele recently enhanced the Formula to accelerate the healing process from an injury. I understand he achieved this with massive quantities of Vitamin C, MSM, Selenium, Cobalamin, and another element I do not know. The secret ingredient was not in Mengele's notes—it is part of the current formula. We must have solved that mystery before creating the subsequent batch. We have analyzed the enhancements formula, but thus far, we have been unsuccessful in identifying the last element.

I don't know what would happen if older men or women were treated with the Formula. This question brings up another issue. We have never injected women with the Youth Formula. We have no data on women subjects. Dr. Mengele did not address this in his notes, and Franz said Herr Doctor never mentioned women subjects to him. We will begin to experiment with women in the next few weeks. We have started bringing in elderly homeless men whom no one will miss. Fortunately, there is an abundant supply of these subjects in France.

Next, we are in the process of cloning the viable cells of our illustrious leaders. As you know, reproductive cloning is copying an entire organism from a somatic cell nuclear transfer. The DNA is identical in the original and the clone. You may not know cloning humans is very challenging and requires extreme care. Spindle proteins are very close to the cell nucleus, and removal of the nucleus can damage the spindle proteins needed for cell division. If this happens, our only viable cells will be destroyed. Also, primate cells are sensitive to dyes and ultraviolet light. Through many years of single-minded research, Herr Doctor overcame these challenging barriers and complexities to design a plan to clone a human without damaging the nucleus or spindle proteins. We will be following his detailed instructions precisely. We should have the cells ready to multiply in a few weeks.

I am delighted to have this incredibly encouraging update for you, and I look forward to hearing your thoughts.

Respectfully, Dr. Herman Wagner

Clinical Director, Mengele Projects

Everyone in the room started shouting at once. The excitement was palpable. The ambitious project to clone Hitler has been on a long journey beginning in the days after WWII. They were understandably elated to be the individuals leading the committee as their plans for world dominance became a reality.

Emerson jumped up, waved his arms wildly, and yelled, "Quiet! Let us discuss these developments and our immediate plans. We cannot cackle like chickens. I will begin—first a very positive report. If the results are as good as the report suggests, I am extremely grateful for Dr. Mengele and Dr. Wagner's fine work. The challenges can be likened to climbing Mt. Everest in a snowstorm, which I have done, by the way. Damn nasty business!! Julian, what are your thoughts?" Emerson looks at Julian, sitting on the edge of the sofa, trying not to hyperventilate.

Julian is encouraged as he contemplates the optimistic report. "I am astounded! We have been planning and waiting for this for so long that I cannot believe it is now within our grasp. Still, I do not want my hopes to soar without certifiable results to support the extraordinary words. I don't know Dr. Wagner and remain skeptical until proven wrong. When I have doubts, I dispatch another expert to evaluate the work in most situations. In this case, there is no one else, which disturbs me greatly." Julian scowls at them to show his doubt and displeasure. He is torn between his emotions and his cognitive ability.

Annette has left her seat on the sofa to walk around the room as she processes the news. "Gentlemen, I agree with Julian and Emerson. The report is much more positive than we could have ever imagined or hoped. For that, I am extremely excited and look forward to a new world. Yet, based on this report, I am reluctant to create new plans other than precursory ones. We should have a preliminary plan before we leave here today. I suggest we each work on a list of people in our organization who will want to take the injection. What if we need more scientists? A list of top scientists in the appropriate fields is a necessary precaution. I would like to hear from Seth about his discussion with the, uh, Demon. His part is vital to our success with the cloned leaders. I understand he has made certain promises. By the way, what is his name? I feel foolish saying, Demon." The others nod in agreement; they feel silly too. The Shadow, who was present while Seth read the report, shakes in silent rage.

Seth leans forward, whispering, "His name is (He holds a piece of paper with the word Aaii written on it.). He is in the top hierarchy of Hell and a member of the Trinity. It is said to be bad luck to say his name." He looks furtively around the room, perhaps expecting to see the Aaii gulping his expensive champagne. "I shall use the word Demon from now on. His power is frightening and thrilling. I met with him in his Owl Mountains dungeon recently. It is a majestically appointed dungeon, but a dungeon all the same. He wants to be part of our movement for the same reasons we do—power and dominance. He was quite hospitable and forthcoming. We had talked before about his inclusion in our organization. He can give us what we need to make Hitler the dictator over the entire world. According to Dr. Wagner, we can clone the three Nazis, but that is not the desired final product. We must have Hitler, Himmler, and Goebbels as they were in life, not cheap, robotic imitations. The Demon has said he will perform this modest service for us. We knew it was possible because Franz heard Abigor assure Dr. Mengele that he could perform this magic. Then Abigor changed sides and joined the enemy, the shocking coward. I sought out and found a demon through demonologists with whom I am friends. It took a large expedition and a huge expenditure, but we found him. He agreed to talk with me, and here we are. In addition, I must mention he has a weapon, a machine developed during WWII by Hitler's scientists with tremendous power. He did not share this information with me. I have heard the rumors. I hope he tells me more next time we meet. Who would like to attend that meeting?"

Seth looks around the room at each person. Julian, Juan, Emerson, and Annette vigorously shook their heads, creating quite a disturbance in wind currents. A mini windstorm was blowing the curtains. Or perhaps that was the Shadow. Yes, he is still there.

It appears Seth has no takers. Seth thinks, what a bunch of pompous, pretentious cowards.

However, he smiles and nods. They have no idea what Seth is, nor will they find out until it is too late.

The Committee members gather up their tattered dignity, wrap it around themselves for comfort, and continue making preliminary plans.

A shadow moves unseen and unheard in the room—a furious shadow.

Chapter Fourteen

Demons Abound

We are in waiting mode as Miles negotiates with his superiors. Waiting is painfully uncomfortable for all of us. We can no longer fully trust MI5, but our Team agrees that Miles is solid and has our complete confidence. Still, we have given him minimal details since he might share our information with others. We have asked him to provide agents to help us search the tunnels. The map now in our possession has not entered the conversation, and we will not divulge the general location of the tunnel we seek, only that it is in the area of the Castle. We regret the need for subterfuge, but our reliable intel suggests we are faced with at least one mole in MI5. Nonetheless, this is the hand we were dealt. We may need specialized equipment and warm bodies to help us once we arrive.

We have not seen the area, but we know some tunnels are flooded, and there are many interconnections. We want to explore the main tunnel and all the unflooded connections. Exploration will be highly time-consuming, and our time to act is in short supply. The Demon might have hidden other weapons, and we don't want to miss anything. Naturally, the humans will not be allowed in the inner chambers as the Demon, or his nasty cohorts would slaughter them without compunction. Abigor is the only one who has any idea what we may face when we reach the inner chambers, and even he doesn't know with certainty.

In the meantime, as Sir Winton says, we cannot just "rest on our oars" as we wait to hear from Miles and acquire Abigor's secret weapon. Abigor tells us he has a plan to secure his "secret" weapon, whatever configuration it might be. He is annoyingly mute, and our time is precious. We will invest it in working on Dr. Mengele/Dr.

Wagner side of our mission. According to our resident Giant, we must contact Dr. Suggs. It is getting late, and we are all gathered in our suite to discuss our next moves. We are better informed now and can plan for the next few hours of purposeful activity.

Sir Winston, anxious to get started, stares at each one of us to press his points. He begins the meeting, "Team, we know our mission is divided into two parts. Stop Dr. Mengele's ruthless associates as we tried to stop him, find the Doomsday Machine, and deactivate it. We progressed on the former because Dr. Mengele no longer breathes his foul breath into our air. We will return to that aspect of our mission when we can proceed with the Doomsday Weapon. Yes, we will be dealing with a dangerous tunnel situation and a mighty demon who may or may not be alone. Abigor told us that Aaii could call legions to help him if he wished. That is unlikely, but he will probably not be alone. We cannot guess numbers. We have asked Miles to help us search the area and nearby tunnels. David, please tell us about your conversation with Miles?"

David has been discussing this with Angus. He stops and replies, "Yes, we arrived late at MI5 searching for the map, though it is not as specific as we thought. Since Red contacted us, we have abandoned the search for his file. He should be able to provide the information we sought. Luckily, we ran into Miles working late in his office. He looked exhausted. Was that your impression, Angus?" Angus waves his hand vigorously in accord.

David, looking concerned, continues, "He was pale and lethargic. After asking about his health, which Miles dismissed, I reminded him about our mission and its urgency. Naturally, he has no specifics about the mission. He does know it is in the Owl Mountains in Poland. It is outside the country, so his cooperation gets complicated. He said he had approached his superiors with a believable story and would have an answer within 48 hours. He is optimistic they will agree. With Miles and his team, our job can be more thorough and less labor-intensive for us. Of course, one might ask, why not just pop over to Poland and take a look for ourselves? I will let Abigor explain as he explained it to me." We are all eager to hear this. Angus pauses in his pacing. Once again, Dr. Einstein, the dear man, searches around on the floor for his superfluous glasses.

Abigor stands up to address David's question. "Verily, it would seem sensible to go to the tunnel now that we hast a map. As I told David, that is impossible. We must maintain secrecy as long as possible. If we cast about there, Aaii will know immediately and suspect our intentions. He is of a suspicious mindset. He has longer to prepare his demons against us." Drat! We are reluctant to drop what sounded like such an excellent action idea. Truthfully, we want to get to the tunnels and kick demon arse now! Reason restrains us.

Sir Winton sits forward, obviously disappointed, and grudgingly admits defeat. "Abigor, I understand your caution. You are correct. We cannot give Aaii time to prepare. That question is settled. Let me ask another question. Druid said you would seek a weapon, and he called the weapon a -he-." Please explain what this means. It is incomprehensible to me." That question has us on the edges of our chairs, except for Angus, who likes to pace.

Abigor is not meeting our eyes. He is obviously uncomfortable with the direct question, "I am sorry, Sir Winston. I am not at liberty to answer thy query. Thou will have an answer soon, and I think thou will agree with my decision." Surprisingly, Sir Winston let the question go for now with just a slight raise of his eyebrows. The Great Man lights a cigar and fumes.

Sir Winston, David, Dr. Einstein, and Angus decide to begin our Dr. Mengele mission by a pop over to Austria to talk to Dr. Suggs.

Perhaps, he knows the whereabouts of Dr. Mengele's ghoulish associates. They hope to find the scientists who possess the Youth Drug and the cells for cloning. Besides, Druid had pointed them in that direction. We don't know if Franz made his way to another Team—if one exists. He did hint at that possibility. Dr. Suggs may have heard rumors or even gossip; scientists talk too. Hey, we are desperate, and it would be more than we have now.

Before Franz went into a coma, he hinted that such a team existed in another country, and they had the journal and the cells. Franz was in and out of consciousness, but the dying man mumbled about it numerous times. Was Franz merely rambling, or were there nuggets of truth in those ramblings? We have to try to find out. The only place to start is Austria and Dr. Suggs.

David is excited to have something, anything, to investigate. He suggests, "I think we agree we must act, and this is what we have now. As we know, pull one string, and all sorts of things fall out. Dr. Suggs is remarkably knowledgeable and still furious with Dr. Mengele and Franz. I think he feels manipulated, which he was, and used by the monsters for highly unethical research. He would probably love to have his revenge. I call that motivation. If everyone is in accord, we shall leave immediately. Abigor, Bones, and Sophie will remain here in case we get a break on MI5 assistance. Now that we know the approximate location of the tunnel to the Doomsday Machine, we are waiting for permission from Miles' superiors and Abigor and his mysterious weapon." David looks pointedly at Abigor before he continues, "It has only been a few hours since we found the map with Red's invaluable help. We can't expect an answer from Miles immediately; bureaucrats move slower than stalagmites. Also, they do not know the entire story, and we cannot share it with all its craziness. The absolute need for secrecy puts us at a disadvantage in asking for their heavyweight help. It would be quite expensive, and Miles will have to sell it with only a quick peek behind the curtain. When we return from Austria, we must complete our planning for tackling the tunnel with Miles and MI5 or alone. We cannot push the mission off longer than that."

Sir Winston is sipping his brandy and does a high five (He is getting so 21st Century savvy.) in agreement with David. "I am grateful that we have a place to begin. Dr. Suggs' laboratory in Austria is an excellent resource for all the superb reasons David enumerated. However, I would be more at ease if we had other sources. What do you think, Albert? I see you have been considering this quagmire." Sophie is paying close attention and shows her teeth and gums in agreement. Her opinion holds great weight with us.

Dr. Einstein looks up, realizes we are in the room, and searches for his pipe and tobacco. He finally says, "I agree with you, Winston. We are running out of time. I feel it in every fiber of my body. Not everything we understand is cognitive. We were given a sixth sense for excellent reasons. I sense the need for immediacy, and it spurs me forcefully forward. We must use our time well. I will return to a few research facilities I visited last year, searching for Dr. Mengele and his thugs. One facility in France inexplicably intrigued me when I visited there. I shall begin in France. The lead researcher was Dr. Herman Wagner. Spears told us the name Wagner had come up when he questioned Mengele's scientists. I was not at all satisfied with that man. No, indeed, I suspect he hides something—I am almost certain of it. You and the others go ahead to Austria, and I shall meet you here when I finish my sojourn to fashionable France. Leaving Bones, Abigor, and Sophie here to await information from Miles is wise. For obvious reasons, I am uncomfortable leaving Bones alone again." David is frowning. He is unconvinced the idea is so dandy. Abigor looks innocently around the room. I expect him to start whistling at any moment. David blames Abigor for my recent grapples with a fire-wielding demon determined to torch me.

Speaking of fire, David is smoldering. He says through clenched teeth, "Abigor, I will give you one more chance to protect Bones while I am away. I am violently opposed to this final chance, but Sir Winston interceded on your behalf. You and I will tangle if anything happens to Bones, even a broken fingernail. I promise you will not enjoy it. I can't destroy you, but I can make you wish I could destroy you." David punctuates these brutal words with a look meant to turn Abigor to stone. It did not seem to work though it would have been entertaining to see.

After the guys leave, Abigor, Soph, and I settle down to do some good old-fashioned brainstorming. I order a snack from room service to fortify me for the mental exertion. A couple of ham sandwiches with a tasty lobster salad should do nicely. A pot of coffee will make my brain neurons function at high speed.

We sit with legal pads and pens instead of tablets and cell phones. OK, we are old-fashioned. Abigor is eons old. Catching up on technology takes time. We are still working on his 21st Century English. Our focus is on handling our part of the strike on the tunnels. There are a couple of possibilities. We may be alone, with just our team members, or Miles may receive permission to help us. With equipment and numerous agents, it would be easier to search the tunnels thoroughly. We suspect someone at MI5 is not our friend, and we don't know how high up the food chain this person may be. I hope Red will give up more information so we will not work completely blind. The rules he plays by are impossible to understand, which puts us, well, me, in danger. I throw this out for Abigor's consideration. "It appears there are two possible scenarios: we are on our own or not as we attack the Demon and his Doomsday Machine. No, it frightens me to think of it, but there is a third scenario. Whoever might be a plant at MI5, and we do not know if there is only one person, may attempt to prevent us from locating the Machine. I don't know how that would play out, but we cannot dismiss the possibility." I am beginning to sweat.

As I say this, I think of Sir Winston's speech to the House of Commons at the beginning of WWII. "We shall never surrender. And if, which I –I do not for a moment believe, this island or a large part of it were . . . subjugated and starving, then our Empire beyond the seas, armed and guarded by the British Fleet, would carry on the struggle, until, in God's good time, the New World with all its power and might steps forth to the rescue and liberation of the old." He made this famous speech on August 20, 1940. All was dark as Europe, one country after another, fell beneath the overpowering treads of the Nazi war machine. I have read the speech a dozen times, and tears still come to my eyes when I remember it. Churchill did not know if his island home would be fighting alone. Though he sounded confident, he knew the odds against them were devastating. We are in the same position now. Extraordinary powers beyond our ability to understand are poised against us, but we have no choice. We'll fight with help from MI5, or we'll fight alone. We *will* fight!

Big Soph looks concerned. This is unusual for her because nothing on earth can harm her. Abigor looks stern and determined as he answers, "I agree those are the possibilities we face, Bones. We can go directly to Poland and challenge the Demon Aaii in his hideous lair or wait for reinforcements. Remember, there is no guarantee that we shall overcome the forces of evil. I beg you, do not participate in this mission. I am confident David wouldst concur with me." He silently beseeches me with his eyes to hear his words.

Abigor composes himself and continues, "Aaii is dauntingly formidable, and we shalt need all of our powers and spiritual resources to overcome him and tackle the Doomsday Machine. We must eliminate

Aaii, find the Machine, and attempt to destroy it. We may be able to accomplish the task once we locate it. However, I have one troubling concern. Aaii is a great Demon with magical powers, and he may have used sorcery to protect the Machine or trigger it. If we art not careful, we may activate the machine by misstep. I have heard rumblings in the Demon Stream of Consciousness that the power is not in the steel monster per se but in what it might initiate, something similar to a domino effect. I see an image of mighty flames, then blind darkness." I feel chills. Cold shivers travel up my spine at his words that sound ominously prescient. I close my eyes. Yes, I see vaulting flames. Now, I know why it is called Doomsday. Do I see the fire of Hell? I had no idea how close I was.

As I pick at my sandwiches recently delivered to our suite and process our options with Abigor, a faded picture starts to peek through the darkness. After I eat and drink my coffee, I ask Abigor for his best guess for the capabilities and energy source of the Doomsday Machine. His face is like stone, as if he is preparing himself for an epic battle of biblical proportions.

In a tone that matches his sullen dour visage, Abigor shares an insight, "Bones, thou knowest I am eons old. I have seen much and done much in those thousands of years. Nothing has ever frightened me. Now, I am fearful for the world and all of humanity. Those poor souls art innocently going about their lives, not knowing they could be, and might very well be, dead in a matter of days. A horrific monster of death is rumbling toward them, and I feel helpless even with all of my immense powers. For the first time in my existence, I am truly humbled. As thou knowest, better than I, we are not guaranteed success on these missions." It hits me like an explosion. Abigor's heart has been stone-cold dead for eons. Abruptly it has revived and beats warm and vulnerable. Empathy will be quite the existential journey for our new angel. Priorities, for now, we must focus on our Armageddon.

Unaware of my epiphany, he continues his summary, "I think about what Admiral Stallings said, that we would lose this battle, and I wonder if he could be right. My darkest fear? It may be the last battle. This battle may be our last chance, as if we are replaying Revelation 12. I am sure thou knoweth it, Bones." I have no idea why my guys think I know the Bible word for word and verse by verse. I do not and have no idea what is in Revelation 12. Sir Winston and Angus made the same assumption about my biblical knowledge.

Abigor whispers, "The great dragon was thrown down, that ancient serpent, who is called the Devil and Satan . . . he was thrown down to earth . . ." That does sound familiar. Abigor looks at me gravely and says, "The fight between good and evil is happening again, and we are the only angels in the fight. Verily, I am the only angel." I understand his meaning, and I feel overwhelmed with a sense of doom. Again. How can we possibly win the war with one slightly tainted angel? I need confidence and hope. "Is there no one else to help us? No one? It does not sound as if Miles and MI5 can be of any help at all, even if they decide to join us. Not unless they have an extra priest or two."

Abigor appears emotionally shattered. He says, "There is one other, but I do not knoweth if we can count on his assistance. Also, as I hast said, we need yet another to confront Aaii. As grim as this sounds, dear Bones, I must be honest with thee. We cannot prevail with only the members of our Team." I can see the fear in his emerald eyes. That frightens me. He is an angel. What chance can I possibly have as a mere human?

"What? Who is this other? Why have I not heard anything about this? Don't you think that would be outstanding information to share?"

I am getting exceptionally tired of impossible-to-understand rules and vexing secrets.

Abigor sees my annoyance and looks toward Sophie as if she has an answer. "As I have said, I am not at liberty to share that information with thee, Bones, uh, and Sophie. Remember, I report to one who limits what I can say and do. I promise you I am working on getting the help we need." I don't know about Abigor, but I believe we are outrageously outnumbered and outgunned. We need heavyweight warriors, and we need them now! Abigor has rules. The gang has rules. Red has rules. I have nothing but defiance, red high heels, and fury. Abigor whispers, "Michael and his angels fought against the dragon. Michael won." What? I swear to God I will slap him with all my might for what little good that will do. If nothing else, I will feel better.

I ask a question. Yet I am not at all certain I want to hear the answer. "Abigor, do you have any idea who might be on the other side lined up against us in this battle?" Even as the words leave my mouth, I want to turn away like a frightened child to avoid hearing more bad news.

Abigor doesn't look any happier about answering than I am about hearing the answer. "Lovely Bones, I will not disrespect you by sugar-coating the possibilities. Aaii may be alone. Still, remember he commands legions of demons in Hell. He could call on all of them. That number is at least in the hundreds, or he could invite just his lieutenants. I have no idea how many demons that would be, but I know they are vicious and experienced fighters. Aaii will know we are coming, and he shalt not feel threatened. I don't know how much he knows about our team. He shalt be overconfident. He is a demon. They, like psychopaths, are also narcissists. I pray we shalt subdue him before he realizes his error in judgment. We are not capable of killing him. He cannot destroy us. He can slaughter thee, which is why I do not want thee in that final battle. Be aware he can stop us from finding the machine. We will talk about how we might subdue him when the others return. I have a plan. Pray he is alone and foolish." I silently prayed.

We are focusing too much on the negative aspects. As Sir Winston warned another generation, Abigor quotes, 'If you will not fight for right when you can easily win without bloodshed; if you will not fight when your victory is sure and not too costly; you may come to the moment when you will have to fight with all the odds against you and only a precarious chance of survival. There may even be a worse case. You may have to fight when there is no hope of victory because it is better to perish than to live as slaves.' "

Abigor says what our Team knows to be true. He asserts, "As multitudes have done in the past, I look to Churchill for wisdom. In our case, I do not know if we have had an opportunity to win without a great loss, Bones. We entered the game late, and all the pieces have been in place for 80 years. We must play the cards as they were dealt. We are at this stage and must fight viciously for humanity with scant hope of winning. Our team has formidable spiritual and brute force brawn and inimitable resources. All of us, except you, dear Bones, can fight on for eternity, and we are duty-bound to do so." Yes, they are immortal, and I am not. I don't think humanity has eternity to wait while they wage this battle, and I feel powerless. I will not tell Abigor, but I plan to be there to fight and accept the consequences. I will not cower in a corner, making safety my priority. There are worse things than dying. Failing my team is one of those things. Sophie hangs her head as tears run down her beloved face.

As we await the others, Abigor and I listen to soft Beethoven and Chopin in the background and grapple with the situation in which we find ourselves. All is peace and solitude in our opulent suite above a sleeping London. If only Londoners knew their survival is in the hands of four spirits, one newly transformed angel, an ancient entity of tremendous power who looks like a Great Dane, and an American psychotherapist. The giant Druid suddenly shatters our peace. Damn him. He never knocks.

Giant scolds, "What are you doing? Did I not tell you time is slipping away with each beat of your heart? Look at the hourglass! Abigor, seek out your secret weapon at once. Bones, you are in grave danger. There is a plot unfolding. Believe no one and stay close to Sophie." Big Soph stands beside me—an unmovable rock.

"Ask Dr. Suggs. He has answers. He knows." Sophie is yawning at Druid. She is intimidated by no one. She nods her great head to acknowledge her grasp of his message. She already knew. Both Abigor and I look at the antique hourglass at the exact moment. The sand is running faster, and there is little left. I gasp. How did I lose track of the hourglass? What can we do without knowing if Miles and his men will help? Searching even a limited area is daunting. Honestly, what help would MI5 be against a demon?

Druid whirls around and disappears. His booming voice still echoed in the quiet room.

A red piece of paper flutters in the draft of Druid's departure, and I pick it up when it lands in my lap. It says, "Things are moving much faster than I anticipated. They, both human and not human, are united and lethal. Move to finish your preparations with all possible speed. You must go, Bones. You must play your part. No one on this earth can take your place. I will try to protect you, as will my compadre." It is signed Red. Well, David will not be happy about this. He fears for my safety and has sufficient reason to do so. I always knew I would have to be there.

Shaken but unwavering, Abigor, Sophie, and I wait for the team to return. What else can we do?

Chapter Fifteen

Planning the Mission

Dr. Einstein returns before David, Angus, and Sir Winston. Abigor and I are exhausted by our brainstorming and our various visitors bearing tales of gloom and doom. Sophie is exhausted from listening to us whine. Dr. Einstein, the most brilliant scientist of the 19th and 20th Centuries, notices nothing. He is not into Emotional IQ.

We decide to wait until the others return to share the lamentable news from Druid and Red.

Dr. Einstein comes over to the sofa and hugs me. He salutes Abigor and Sophie. He fiddles with his pipe, runs his hands through his wild hair, and clues us in on his journey. "I have much to share with you after my trip to the research facility in Montfort l' Amaury. It is just a few kilometers from Paris. I asked questions around the village before I approached the facility to gather information on its history and any gossip circulating about the scientists. I spent quite a few hundred euros at the local bar L'Atelier Bouteille. The villagers were thirsty, and I was pleased to buy the rounds. They were open and generous with their remarks, but they knew little.

"The Facility is called Long Life or, in French, Longue Vie, located about five kilometers from the picturesque village. A tall stone wall covered in tangled wild vines surrounds the property. I would assume the wall is almost certainly centuries old. As you know, the Romans were there for nearly five hundred years. The industrious Roman soldiers built many charming buildings, walls, churches, and bridges in the area." The genius takes a puff on his cold pipe and resumes.

"I was blessed with answers while digging for gossip and rumors. I learned the scientists had been there since 2019. Before that, it was a religious retreat. Their current literature states they work to extend life by studying animals with unusually long life spans, such as elephants and bats of the Myotis brandtii species. Luckily for the bats, they have a long life span equivalent to 280 years in humans and age very slowly. Two variables that seem to play a part in their longevity are low reproductive rate and hibernation. What is the critical variable? We don't know, but it would be highly beneficial to answer that question." I can see his powerful brain doing the equations. Then he proceeds to discourage me, a mere human.

"We are beset by sagging skin, gray hair, stiff joints, and various diseases in the human aging process. Our organs begin to enervate. The heart is a good example." Reminding me of those pesky realities certainly does nothing to lift my gloomy mood.

The good doctor continues with all things geriatric, "However, to our benefit, we live twice as long as one of our closest cousins, the chimpanzee. We seek the evolutionary, metabolic, and cellular tricks responsible for long-lived species. Silverback Gorillas are approximately twenty times stronger than humans. With all their prodigious strength, they are relatively short-lived. It is fascinating information to consider, Bones." Reluctantly, Dr. Einstein leaves the life expectancy of bats. I wonder if he perceives our impatience. Nah.

"The Longue Vie literature is quite Albert Schweitzer in tone and content. By the way, he was an excellent scientist and dear friend. Their literature is where the resemblance to Albert appears to end. The grounds look more like a prison than a research facility dedicated to helping humanity. Guards are at the gates, and they are armed. It is subtle, not to attract attention, but they are prepared for a minor war. I surmise at least twenty security guards are on duty around the clock. The security guards live in the village, so they have learned to be discreet. There is a dark rumor that one loquacious guard, Claude Dupont, died suddenly without apparent explanation for his demise. Villagers suggest he was imprudently chatty when drinking with friends. That may have been Claude's fatal flaw. His family asked probing questions and then suddenly left the village. The local police have nothing to investigate. Alone this gossip tells us nothing but adds to the other information I learned about Dr. Wagner and his facility. It makes me wonder about the good doctor." These tidbits certainly raise my "bad guy" antenna.

Abigor crosses himself as he hears these cruel truths. Sophie growls to show her violent disdain.

Dr. Einstein jogs my memory when he asks, "Bones, do you remember the research facility in Innsbruck? These research facilities typically lack intense security other than perhaps electronic security. Wagner's security measures would be more appropriate for safeguarding the Crown Jewels." Dr. Einstein continues without waiting for my answer.

"The villagers I spoke with knew nothing about the scientists. It appears they live on the grounds. I had to ask myself, why? I am inquisitive, as you know, and I doubt this research facility is legitimate. That is not within the bounds of probability." He stops and looks to us for confirmation. We agree with thumbs up. "None of the villagers knew anything about the Director, Dr. Wagner. He doesn't go into the lovely village just a few kilometers away to eat delicious French dinners. No, he does not. Why? I find his behavior extremely curious."

Shrugging off this incongruity, he moves on. "I called to make an appointment with Dr. Wagner, ostensibly to discuss his field, extending human life. I implied I was writing an article for a prestigious journal. Truthfully, I have been working on an article for about 90 years now, but not on extending life. My article is *Ather Relativitatstheorie*. You would find it fascinating, dear Bones." I wouldn't hurt the sweet man's feelings for anything, but he vastly overestimates my interest in physics. Abigor squints at us. His bewilderment is painfully apparent. I suppose he didn't take physics in Demon's School.

"If Dr. Wagner were a serious scientist responsible for financing a large facility, he would have leaped at an opportunity to be profiled in a journal article in *Clinical Interventions in Aging*. Academic recognition brings donors, and all researchers need contributions to continue and expand their work. Again, I ask the question, why was Dr. Wagner indifferent? He was simply not concerned. I know this because he told me he didn't have time for interviews. Then he hung up on me! Evidently, he still uses a real phone. I can still hear the bang!" He finished indignantly!

As Dr. Einstein recounts this peculiar and boorish behavior, Sir Winston, David, and Angus return. David pulls me to my feet, swings me around, and kisses my lips with a passion that makes me dizzy. I like it! I take it they had a triumphant day.

After greeting us, Sir Winston looks for his silver matchbox, finds it in his jacket pocket, drops it, and settles down with his cigar. I pick the matchbox up and hand it to him. He is excited to hear about the good doctor's excellent adventure. "Dear Albert, it sounds like you have some pertinent information for our group. I am delighted to hear it. Please tell us what you learned on your excursion to France. Then we will recount our, shall we say, extraordinary experience in Innsbruck. I think you will find it fits in nicely with your investigation."

Dr. Einstein recounts everything he told us. There are a few probing questions from Angus and David. David wants to know if he ever got inside the wall. "No, David, I had seen and heard enough to know this was not a legitimate research facility. I walked around the wall to check the number of guards and gates. Numerous Sentries guard all the gates except one in the far back of the property. Naturally, that would only matter to Bones. The rest of us can enter wherever we wish." David quickly said Bones would not go to the facility under any imaginable circumstances nor into the demon tunnel. The poor dear man, I shall leave him to his soothing thoughts for as long as possible. Red insisted I must be in the creepy tunnel, No one could take my place, and I think I should bring the Sunstone Compass. Whoever wrote this script included Abigor and me. As they ask in the Marines, do you want to live forever? That question, asked more emphatically, was attributed to Sergeant Major Daniel Daly in 1918 at the Battle of Belleau Wood. My kind of Marine! So, Sergeant Major, I am reporting for Doomsday Tunnel and France duty!

Angus asked Dr. Einstein if he noticed security dogs. He asks this question with me in mind, and David gives him a dirty look. Our Genius looks at Angus and ignores David. "They did not include dogs in their security, and I was at the facility several times at various times of the night and day. I also noticed the guards looked bored and distracted." Our genius painted a detailed picture for us. So, satisfied with Dr. E's news on the Dr. Wagner drama in France, we move on to Sir Winston's report.

Sir Winston began, "I never worry about action, only inaction. We have moved steadily forward in our knowledge in the last few hours. Thank you, Albert, for your exceptionally informative report on Dr. Wagner and his dubious facility. We shall determine what else we can learn about Dr. Wagner from Spears's splendid data systems. He may, by chance, have a questionable history. David, would you call Spears and put that request into motion?" David immediately leaves the room to call Spears at the Met.

Sir Winston salutes our theoretical physicist and tackles his Innsbruck story. "We arrived without announcing our visit. We were not confident we would be warmly embraced. It was possible our previous shootout at their facility could have negatively influenced their perceptions of us. Last time, we were there to capture Dr. Mengele, Franz, and Hans. Those guttersnipes started the gunplay. Undoubtedly, since the Austrian scientists were inexperienced in our death-defying experiences, they might have been slightly concerned when the bullets began to fly. Yes, quite inconvenient." Sir Winston is having entirely too much fun telling this story. He is grinning from ear to ear.

Warming up to his exploits, he continues. "When we arrived, we asked to see Dr. Suggs. We said we were there concerning an investigation. Their receptionist took us in to speak to Dr. Diya Ahuja. She is the assistant director of the facility. She is relatively new, so we were relieved not to have an association that brought up distressing memories. I was impressed by Dr. Ahuja, a middle-aged lady with thick dark hair, tall and robust. I suppose the best descriptive word is intense. She reminded me of an intelligent panther with glasses."

"Naturally, she was surprised we were seeking information for an investigation. After we introduced ourselves with various, uh, fictional names, she was anxious to talk to us. Although she seemed troubled and stumbled on her words, this is her story verbatim. ' "We recently had a tragic, yes, tragic, and inexplicable occurrence. Our Director, Dr. Suggs, left to go home one evening after work and did not come in at his usual time the following day. Dr. Suggs is very regular in his habits. He is always in his office by 8:00 am, sipping coffee and reading his emails. He did not arrive then, and we heard absolutely nothing from him. We called his phone, and it immediately went to voice mail. His family was out of town on holiday. Dr. Scott, our lead in the lab, and I went to Dr. Suggs' house to reassure ourselves he was not hurt or ill. The front door was open when we arrived. We walked in and called his name. When we received no answer, we went into every room in his house. We checked his garage and the backyard. There was no sign of him. His car was in the garage, where he always kept it.' "

" 'We knew it was time to call the local constable. We were mystified and beginning to become fearful. The constable came with several officers and mounted an investigation. They were quite thorough and asked us to contact everyone at the facility to determine if anyone had heard from him. Over the next few days, they interviewed everyone who knew him. His family was also in the dark and terribly worried as they had not heard a word from him. Dr. Suggs has been married for twenty years and has two teenage children. He is devoted to his family. People don't just disappear, at least no one I know. Gentlemen, does your visit have anything to do with Dr. Suggs? It has been two weeks, and we still have no information. It is as if Scotty beamed him up.' " Interesting reference, I thought. Ah, a Star Trek fan. I think I like her. The former prime minister has a prodigious memory and can quote long epic poems decades after reading them. Repeating this conversation was a piece of cake.

Churchill turns to David, who says he and Angus don't know anything more about the mysterious disappearance of the renowned doctor. Sir Winton asked them to go to the constable's office in Innsbruck and look at the doctor's missing person file. It is late evening now, and we doubt Innsbruck is a beehive of crime. Few officers are in the office at this time of night. Since David and Angus will duck into invisibility, they can review the records at their leisure without troubling the nice constables. If possible, they will copy files that might be useful to us. The guys will only be gone for a short time. This Innsbruck trip is a cinch assignment.

Dr. Einstein shakes his head in disbelief. "Winston, it is beyond the realm of possibility that Dr. Suggs' mysterious disappearance is a coincidence. We have a research facility guarded like Fort Knox, then a prominent scientist in the field of human life extension disappears. I don't think it is too fanciful to wonder if the two are part of the same malevolent plan." He shook his head in disbelief.

I thought this was the time to share the messages from Red and Druid. Both messages were relatively short. The main points were the same. We must act without delay implementing our tunnel plans and seek out Dr. Suggs, and I must be there in the tunnel with the compass. We all looked at the hourglass as we talked. I failed to mention that Druid said I was in danger. Truthfully, I always expect some lunatic will try to tie me to a railroad track or something equally unpleasant.

Sir Winston acknowledges my intel with a wave. "This is alarming news, Bones. We have two missions that are related yet separate in their locations. We have seven members on our team. Red and Druid are staunch allies, but we cannot include them in our strategic plans. Mysterious guidelines govern their behaviors. We can only pray they will be there when needed."

He searches for his handkerchief in his jacket pockets and then looks around the room. "At the beginning of WWII, our response time was alarmingly short, and the situation worsened by the minute. Yet, the focus was simple. We must defeat Hitler before he conquered all of Europe. After subjugating Europe, we knew the Corporal would come after us on our Island home. Because of feckless appeasement policies, we had not prepared for war. We did not have the necessary equipment, trained men, or weapons. Those were unbelievably dark days." He dabs his eyes.

"We face dark days now. In our current situation, we must decide which mission to complete first. We have too few team members to achieve both objectives simultaneously. Druid and Red said that we must immediately journey to the tunnel. I believe that task is quite urgent. The other mission will wait until we stop the monster machine. If the Doomsday Machine should activate, no scientists, viable cells, NGA, or Mengele Journal will remain to concern us. The Demon, according to Red, is in league with NGA humans. They probably have no idea that he controls their future with his weapon. We must immobilize the NGA fanatics before they complete their totalitarian plans, but Aaii is our first target. Do you agree, Albert?" Dr. Einstein, the dear man, is wandering around the room looking for the glasses he is wearing. Hearing his name recaptures his attention.

Einstein pushes his manic mane back, adjusts his newly found rogue glasses, picks up his unlit pipe, and responds. "Going by what Druid said, and he has never been mistaken, we must confront the Demon, destroy or neutralize the Machine, and do it without delay. I don't know what Red means about Bones and the compass. Why is her inclusion necessary? Our journey is exceptionally perilous. Understandably, we have never fought a demon with supernatural powers. I do not think a mortal could survive the unimaginably lethal weapons he will have at his disposal. He will use everything in his arsenal against us. Why would we sacrifice Bones? We must be honest. It would be a sacrifice. Fortunately, we have Abigor to advise us. We must hear from Abigor now to develop a plan for facing Aaii in battle." We all look to Abigor.

David and Angus return as Dr. Einstein is saying this. The proper English gentleman warrior, the unflappable David, screams at the top of his voice. "What do you mean we will sacrifice Bones? Have you lost your mind? What is wrong with you?" He looks from Einstein to Sir Winston, fury turning his face scarlet and contorting his handsome features into a death mask. "We will do no such thing as long as I can save her! If you continue to suggest this sacrifice, I shall take her to a place of safety, and you will never see her again! I will fight all of you! You will not win. I promise that!" David is shaking with fury. He is the most frightening entity I have ever seen, more terrifying than the demons. We are all stunned, taken aback by the primal force of his rage.

I love David with an intensity that is impossible to comprehend. I would do anything, anything, to save him from this pain. I never understood the true depth of David's love for me or mine for him until this moment. I am overwhelmed with gratitude that this remarkable man is mine. If I die at this minute, my life will have been worthwhile. Our love is stronger and more profound than even Elizabeth Barrett Browning could have understood. 'How do I love thee? Let me count the ways. I love thee to the depth and breadth and height my soul can reach . . .'

I run to David and throw my arms around him, holding him close to me. I know he can feel the frantic pounding of my heart. "David, my love, we are in this together. We have been since the day I first saw you. I gasped, my heart racing when you walked into my office in a little village in North Carolina. We will finish this mission together, whatever that means. I don't know why I was written into this script, but according to Red, I must be there in the tunnel. My duty is clear, as is yours. We love each other because of who we are. If we could run away from our duty, we would no longer be the two people who fell in love." I know David understands that we have no choice, yet he is torn between what he knows is right and his fears for me. My heart is breaking for him. I can feel it shatter into millions of piercing shards. David will do what is right as he always has, but his spiritual struggle is excruciating. Slowly, he begins to calm down and return to warrior mode. What a man!

Sir Winston embraces both of us. He whispers to David, "My dear boy, you are the finest British warrior I have ever met, and I have met many in my lengthy life. You know that every man in this room, and Sophie, of course, loves Bones. I would give anything to keep her safe other than my honor. Druid, Angus, and Sophie have saved her life at various times when she was in danger. Abigor attempted to save her, but she was too angry and aggressive to allow him that privilege." He grins like a schoolboy thinking about that furious battle. "Our missions have no guarantees, but we will do everything we can to keep Bones safe. She has been quite forceful and righteous in her own right too." The Great Man pats me on the head as he says this—my audacity delights him. I am overjoyed that the former Prime Minister considers me an extra daughter.

David turns to Sir Winston, resigned to reality, and says, "Yes, I know I can trust each of you with her life. We have a mission and must complete it to the best of our ability. Humankind, though they don't know it, poor souls depend on us. We shall create a plan that gives us the best opportunity to succeed. Honestly, we are not without tremendous talent, power, and ability. We can trust in ourselves and each other and our all-powerful resources. Someone said, 'A person often meets his destiny on the road he took to avoid it.' There is no road to avoidance. We go to the tunnel and attack the bloody Demon and his bloody metal monster. Oh, one other thing, Angus and I reviewed all the police files on Dr. Suggs. We found nothing of interest. The police are at an impasse with no leads to move forward. They hope for more information from the public. Unfortunately, hope is not a plan" He hugs me gently without the underlying desperation.

Sir Winston slaps David on the back, "Thank you, David and Angus." He turns his attention to Abigor, "It appears that you, sir, are our best resource to prepare us for whatever is thundering toward us like a herd of buffalo as we rush to stop it. Tell us first what we are likely to face."

Abigor is frowning, and serious, "Bones and I discussed this at great length whilst thou were working on thy tasks. I hast been listening to the Demon Stream of Consciousness. They are a prolific source of information. They cannot keep me out, nor can they hear my thoughts. When I engage, I see walls of soaring flames, conflagration devouring cities and killing multitudes. I see clouds of ashes and sense the odor of sulfur. In unbearable heat, one cannot breathe without choking. I can barely see around me. Can it be Hell? I assumed it was Hell into which I was looking. It was not. I do not know the Beast or its power source; I know the consequences are deadly and catastrophic." The look on the former Demon's face is abject despair.

"Sir Winston, you asked me what we shall face when we enter the tunnel. As I told Bones, there are three possibilities. We are fortunate that all demons are narcissistic and psychopathic. Aaii will overestimate his power, brilliance, and invincibility. Aaii will also believe we are less formidable than we are. At best, he will be alone because he perceives no threat from our team. He may have a favorite lieutenant with him. He may hath several lieutenants or call the legions of demons he leads in Hell. My best guess? He shalt be alone or accompanied by a few favorites."

Dr. Einstein asks, "How do we confront him and his friends when we arrive? What is our immediate strategy?" The eminent scientist lifts his wild eyebrows as he looks at Abigor.

Abigor stands to speak, and his crystalline eyes sparkle with light. "Dr. Einstein, if the numbers art few, we attack directly. As I discussed with Bones, our battle is Revelation 12 again. Instead of throwing them from Heaven to earth, we remove them from the tunnel. That would be a frontal attack. We clothe ourselves in God's armor: Helmet of Salvation, Breastplate of Righteousness, Belt of Truth, Sword of the Spirit, and Shield of Faith. We must spend time in prayer and return to a state of righteousness. I think we are probably close to that state now. I am an angel, so I am righteous by nature. The Word tells us to put on God's complete armor, which can resist the devil's attack. Literally, righteous means being right. The Father chooses such a person. Salvation means we believe in God's word and confess our sins. The breastplate is given to us by God for salvation. It protects our hearts and souls. The belt of truth is most important; the armor will not protect us without the truth and the light. The sword of the spirit is the Word of God. The shield is both offensive and defensive. Roman shields were as big as a modern door." He smiles now and quips, "Don't worry, our shields will not be that large. Faith believes what thou cannot see. I believe we shalt win this battle because good is more potent than evil. I cannot prove that to thee, but it makes me invincible. Since we must put on the armor of God, obviously, we do not wear it all the time." I am hopelessly lost in Abigor's explanation.

"We must wear all this armor to protect us from evil's flames, swords, and arrows. Evil can be defeated. We learned that in Revelation 12." I shake my head vigorously, hoping it will jog some brain cells. Nope.

Abigor looks at each one of us. "Each of you must spend time understanding the armor and its meaning to you. Confess your sins and accept God's Word. We must have our armor to win against the demons. We do not have the power to do it alone. Also, as I told Bones, we cannot conquer Aaii alone; we need a spiritual colossus. A demon fighter. I know where he lives, and I will bring him in soon. We can handle the lesser demons with the appropriate Holy gear."

To get back to your question, Dr. Einstein. We shalt tackle them in direct battle, disabling them one at a time. I will explain how to contain them when we are ready. I must plan for this in minute detail, and I will get into other weapons later. Our war is not about physical strength but spiritual power. Bones could be just as successful as Angus, or me, for that matter. Physically demons are monstrously strong. Spiritually they art weaklings."

I can see we are all a bit confused about what we are supposed to do to put on this armor. It doesn't sound concrete enough for me. I am most comfortable with clear directions I can follow linearly. The process worries me. How shall I know if I am doing it right?

Sir Winston is grave when he questions our former Demon, "Abigor, who is this person of whom you speak? The spiritual colossus? I believe we have a right to know who will join us." Sir Winston's jaw is jutting out, which is not a good sign.

Abigor shakes his head. "I cannot reveal his name without permission. Soon, I shalt be able to share with thee. He will be with us within hours. I shalt leave soon to fetch him. Be at peace, Sir." Sir Winston does not look as if he is at peace. He is doing grave damage to his cigar.

Angus responds, "I think I understand. I felt a tremendous surge in spirit after giving up my life to save Bones. I did it because it was the right thing to do. I felt a lightness and calm I had never felt before. I am now at peace with myself and with my spiritual growth. My armor is in place and just needs a little polishing before we tackle the Demon and his mates."

David looks as confused as I feel. "How do we know if we are doing it right? It sounds as if we must wear our armor appropriately to be our most mighty. How will I know when I am ready?" Dr. Einstein and Sir Winston nod in agreement. This procedure is entirely too iffy for us.

Abigor responds, "I must say something hurtful to you, David. I admire thee greatly, so I do not want to do this. Thou hast asked me a question I must answer thee truthfully. Earlier, when you were more worried about Bones than the mission, you did not have the armor of God. Do you understand that? Saving humanity is God's mission, and He gave that mission to us, his Holy warriors." Abigor looked pained to have to say these words. My beloved David hung his head as Abigor's sharp words slashed at him.

David looked at me and answered Abigor, "Yes, I understand. You are right, Abigor. All of my energy must go into accomplishing our mission. We cannot afford to fail, and by everything Holy, we shall not!" When he said those words, a dim light shone from within him. As if a candle glowed from within him. We were astounded. Again.

Abigor answered our unasked question, "That is how you will know. Thy armor wilt shine from within thee. Though it is said we wear it, that is not factually true. It becomes part of who we are, and we show righteousness with the truth and the *light.*" Well, at least now I have something to go on; either I am lit or not. I don't see the light around me. I must keep working on understanding the process. Darn!

Dr. Einstein waves as he moves toward his laboratory as we explore how to prepare ourselves for victory over the demons. Sir Winston calls to him, "Where are you going, Albert?" He thinks this is an odd time for the genius to wander off. We must be prepared by tomorrow.

Chapter Sixteen

Black Swans

When he returns, Dr. Einstein takes a minute to look through his notes on the study before sitting down, "Abigor said something that made me think of a study I participated in when I was at University. I am terrified that I may be right because if I am, our mission is more horrific than we could ever imagine, a perfect storm worldwide disaster, a Black Swan. If true, things would become so bad I wouldn't want to live on Earth. I must look at the probability before we leave tomorrow. I shall return in a few minutes, or it may take longer. Dearest God, I pray I am mistaken." The brilliant scientist staggers a little as he walks toward his laboratory. We gape at him in wonder. What can he mean? Einstein does not exaggerate.

Since we are running out of time, we must prepare everything for our trip to Owl Mountain tomorrow. Sir Winston asks David if he has transportation, weapons, and other equipment in place. David stands and paces around the room as he reads from a list. "We have scheduled a private jet to transport us to Owl Mountain. Thanks to friends in High Places." David raises his eyes to the ceiling with his cute little smirk.

"Sir Winston and I will assume the piloting duties. Our flight plan has been filed, and we are prepared for our flight. The closest town with an airstrip near Castle Ksiqz is Poznan Airport. We will be picking up our jet from NetJets at Heathrow. We have determined it is the most convenient way to fly, and we own a portion of the jet. We are, therefore, quite familiar with the plane. Since we don't require a flight attendant, I nixed that luxury. The flight will take approximately 3 hours. The jet will be waiting for us when we complete our mission. Bones will, of course, need an airplane to travel." Deep pain is momentarily etched on David's handsome face as he says those words. His control is remarkable.

David continues with his plans, "I have LED torches. Everyone except Dr. Einstein will carry .40 Glocks. We have two rapid-fire machine guns with 500 rounds for each one. Angus will carry one, and I will heft the other. Yes, we cannot harm the demons with firepower; however, we also know he could enlist local thugs. We have heavy-duty work boots, a ballistic vest, and a military kevlar helmet for Bones. Abigor has said we should all wear a blessed silver cross on a sterling chain around our necks. We will each carry an ancient glass vial of Holy Water on our person."

"I asked the guys in bomb control at the Met what we might need to disarm a massive bomb. I have no idea what is waiting for us, but we must have a mechanical kit to disarm it if required. We may not use our special powers as we would with the usual explosives. The creepy Demon may have rigged it, and we don't want to worsen the situation. Of course, the conjuring may block us from interfering with the machine. The Demon may have protected it with magic. Abigor will advise us on that.

"If the devil weapon was not rigged, the machine guns might come in handy. We are going in blind, so we can only do so much in preparation. We don't have the bomb robot. That would have been fun. Can we blow up the Machine? We will have to examine it when we get there. Dr. Einstein will help determine our path. Our time to operate would be extremely short if the monster rigged it. I have never felt so ill-prepared as I began a new task. God be with us and guide us in our mission."

Sir Winston looks solemn yet determined as he nods toward Abigor. "What can we do to prepare ourselves against a demon? We possess courage, tenacity, and strength of character. We always intend to win all battles we enter. We are not familiar with demons and have no experience with them. Therefore, we were blessed with our team member Abigor." The former Demon bows respectfully to our leader.

Abigor says, "My suggestion is to add a spiritual powerhouse to our team. Exorcism is a powerful ancient ritual. Sanctified Melchizedek priests or bishops can perform an exorcism, and recently the criteria were expanded to include other priests. Naturally, actual possession is rare. The priest must wear a white tunic with a purple stole. He uses Holy water, reads specific excerpts from the Bible, and makes the sign of the cross over the possessed person. The priest must be mighty in his faith to stand against a demon. In this case, we would want Aaii to leave the chamber so we can reach the machine. The ceremony for this is similar to a traditional exorcism. The priest must prepare himself spiritually before beginning. In the sacred ritual, he will say the Litany of Saints. Other priests may be involved in the process." We are gaping at him in disbelief. Are we going to use an exorcism, like in the movie? Didn't that priest die?

Dr. Einstein is aghast. He manages to splutter, "Excuse me, Abigor, I am afraid I must have misunderstood you. You are not suggesting we ask an exorcist to fight with us." Angus is rolling his eyes.

Abigor sees our collective expression of disbelief and sighs, "Please hear me. I know because I was once on the receiving end of an exorcism when I was still a vile Demon. Father Antonio Romano was the priest and a veritable boulder in his faith. He is not far from here in St Albans, 40 minutes from London by train. He is now at the Cathedral and Abbey and retired. Originally from Italy, he decided to retire in the London area because he worked closely with the Brits during WWII. You should know he is about 95 years old now. When I last saw him five years ago, he was as solid as a massive oak tree and as unlikely to fall. I mention him because we need a priest for this critical mission as an integral part of our team. It is crucial because we cannot afford to fail, no matter what the good Admiral says. Sadly, we would be adding another human; it shalt be a death-defying task for Father Romano and Bones." He nods gravely at me to show his sincere regret. David scowls back at him.

Bravely, Abigor carries on, "An exorcism may be the only way to defeat Aaii. I shalt take the 12:20 train to St. Albans and return with the good father within a few hours if I am successful in my entreaties. He will need a couple of hours to prepare himself, and then we can leave for Owl Mountain. Since David has a jet at our command, the good father can easily travel with us." We were all staring at Abigor, thinking the same thing. Exorcism is a real thing? We will adjust, and I suppose Abigor should know about exorcisms. We must trust him as the expert on all things weird and demonic.

Sir Winston interjects in surprise, "Is this the weapon you spoke of, Abigor? I have heard that name before, Father Antonio Romano. Yes, he could move around freely as a priest during the War. The Padre helped us learn German troop movements and logistics. Of course, he was quite young when I met him. We only met once, but I felt his devotion to God. Padre wore it with grace and humility. He was a slight man with dark hair and startlingly intelligent gray eyes behind thick spectacles. Nothing about him forewarned the enemy of danger, yet he was passionate about defeating the Nazi devils. Father Antonio accepted many incredibly perilous assignments. He was an exceptional man, a legend in the Allies' military circles. Truthfully, I am concerned about his advanced age," Churchill grins, thinking of his advanced years. "Will he still be physically and intellectually capable of performing an exorcism? I would never question his spiritual strength. I cannot even conceive what intellectual prowess and unwavering willpower a spiritual battle with a demon would demand. We shall only have one opportunity to defeat Aaii."

Abigor nods, acknowledging the great man's legitimate concerns, "Yes, I was given permission to reveal my weapon to you—it is Father Antonio. Our time is short, and our list of skilled exorcists is even shorter. I am fearful we cannot overcome Aaii without an exorcism. I shalt leave now. Angus, would you accompany me to St. Albans if I need help with this Godly man? I do not know his physical condition. However, I affirm that his spirit is steadfast. We shalt learn more when we see him. I believe I am led to seek him out." Angus jumped up and grabbed his jacket, and they left without further discussion. Though our group is concerned for Father Antonio's safety, it will be up to him to decide whether he wants to join us for what may be his final mission. I break out in a sweat, thinking about everything that could go wrong. I need strong, thick coffee and perhaps some cheesecake.

Chapter Seventeen

Father Antonio and Schwache Erde

Within seconds of leaving the Savoy, Abigor and Angus are standing outside St. Albans Cathedral, awed by the massive ancient structure that whispers comforting words of peace and salvation. In a reverent tone, Abigor divulges what he knows about this hallowed place, "I know this is a place of miracles. The Lord healed the sick, and other miracles occurred within these venerable walls. The Cathedral was built in 1115 under Abbott Richard d'Albini, and for centuries, the Holy structure played a significant role in the matters of the day. Discussions within these walls forewent King John signing the Magna Carta in 1215.

The monks produced exceptional manuscripts on religion, science, music, and the classics. My visits here were few; I won't dwell on those visits. It is hurtful for me to say I was the enemy.

"Most historic buildings were destroyed, as was the shrine to St. Albans. The holy relics disappeared. I saw the destruction. Today it still haunts me, and it haunts this magnificent Cathedral. It is a sad building, and I feel its sadness. It has seen too much sin in humankind. I think that is one reason Father Antonio chose this place. It needed a loving friend." The sheer size of the structure is overwhelming. The nave at 85 meters is the longest in all of England. Despite all the sadness she has endured since the 12th Century, she is a proud structure. She moves graciously forward into the 21st Century with hope and a generous soul. The spirit of God is shining brightly in her.

We cannot underestimate the importance of St. Albans, the man, in understanding this structure and its inner core of courage and faith. He lived sometime during the 3rd or 4th Centuries. Legend says St. Albans sacrificed himself to save a priest he had befriended. He told marauding Roman soldiers he was the priest they were searching for when they confronted him. After a brief hearing, he was condemned to death by decapitation. An unlucky soldier carried out the sentence, and a well sprang up where the good man's head lay. The executioner died immediately after the beheading and fell lifeless beside Albans. These are legends, many scoff and label the legends fantasy. Abigor was there and witnessed the tragic events in person. He swears the stories are true. I wasn't there, so I shall accept his word.

After their short train trip, Abigor and Angus walk through the west door into the narthex. Both genuflect and cross themselves before approaching the altar. They were overwhelmed by the solemnity and peace emanating from the narthex. A hallowed fragrance made the air sweet to breathe. Without consulting, each moved into a pew, kneeled, and prayed for guidance and spiritual prowess. They prayed for the success of their mission and humanity. When they arose, they saw a very old man wearing the traditional black cassock of the priesthood, standing mere feet from them. He appeared as Sir Winston had described him, yet many years had passed, and his hair was the purest white. He was bent like a tree that had weathered strong wind currents. His glasses had thickened as decades of study had taken their toll.

They waited for him to speak out of respect for his robes and years. Finally, Father Antonio addressed Abigor, "I believe we have met before, have we not?" He said these words with an edge of anger. Abigor nodded. "Ahhh, I thought so. I seldom forget a demon with whom I have battled. Why are you here, Demon?"

Abigor remembered that battle for the soul of John Carpenter, a choirboy at the Cathedral. The boy and some of his adventurous friends had experimented with an ancient Ouija Board, one of them found in his grandparent's attic. They were seeking chills and excitement. They got more than they bargained for when a demon entered the door they had foolishly opened. Abigor was confident he had another soul to add to his belt. He chose John to possess. As the days passed, John changed. He shouted blasphemies, insulted his friends, and was frequently ill. Sometimes he would fall into heavy sleep from which it was hard to wake him. His pleasant, cheerful manner became sullen and combative. John spoke in strange languages he could not possibly know.

Father Antonio, who knew and liked John, was approached by John's distraught parents, who begged him to perform an exorcism. His parents had previously consulted physicians and psychologists. These professionals had no explanation for John's unusual behavior, and there was no diagnosis code in the DSM for his bizarre behavior. His frightened parents were desperate and did not know where else to turn for guidance. Father Antonio agreed to an exorcism, and late one stormy night, the ancient ceremony began. Abigor found himself in a deadly duel with a determined priest. Lightning struck against the windows, and thunder exploded as the two combatants struggled for young John's soul.

Abigor did not understand and had never heard the Texas Rangers' motto, 'No man in the wrong can stand up against a fellow that's in the right and keeps on a-comin.' The Rangers' motto was a critical deficit in his education. The priest began the attack by saying the Lord's Prayer, Hail Mary, and the Athanasian Creed. These ancient Holy words were his piercing weapons. "In the name of Jesus Christ, our God and Lord, strengthened by the intercession of the Immaculate Virgin Mary, Mother of God, of the Blessed Michael the Archangel . . ." The Demon and the priest engaged in a staggering battle of good versus evil, like battles waged between this world and the other since time immemorial. The priest fell heavily to his knees in agonizing pain time and time again. He would shake his head to clear it, gasp in air, and slowly lift his bruised and bloody body off the floor. The Padre was violently thrown against the walls and across the room. Abigor could see the racking pain and weariness incised deeply into Father Antonio's face. The Demon savored his victory. Yet, every time the priest fell, he rose more spiritually robust, battered but withstanding each physical blow. He would pull himself back up, tighten his sash, stagger forward and continue to fight, strengthened by his unwavering faith in God and the promise of eternal salvation on his lips. With sheer grit and faith, Father Antonio literally dragged John back from a crumbling precipice just before it collapsed into the flames. Abigor was none too tenderly thrown back into Hell by the triumphant priest. Abigor wisely decided he did not want to challenge that spiritually indomitable holy man again. Ever. And yet here he is, unshaken in his belief that Father Antonio is the priest he needs to add spiritual heft to his Team when they engage Aaii.

Abigor assured the good man that he was no longer a demon and had been saved and returned to his heavenly home by the intervention of a Godly woman. The priest crossed himself. The truth shines brightly. Abigor introduced Angus without mentioning that Angus was quite dead. A mere trifling detail at this point.

Father Antonio, trying to ease the effects of gravity on his bent frame, sat in the pew in front of Angus and Abigor and asked again, "Why are you here? I was told that someone was coming, and your request would be world-shattering and perilous. What do you need from me? I have fought many battles with the evil in this world. As you see before you, I am elderly, and my strength is not as it once was. The passing of days has ebbed it away."

Where does one start in answering such a question? Angus said, "Father Antonio, the world and all its inhabitants are in grave danger from the evil that walks among us. Abigor sincerely believes we need you to help us defeat that evil. You are correct, Father. What we will ask of you is incredibly dangerous. I must be truthful; you might not survive the mission." The priest moves closer to Angus and squints at him through thick glasses. My son, has anyone told you that you look like an American actor? What is his name, oh, Dirty Harry?" Angus smiles his crooked Dirty Harry smile.

Trying to get the conversation back on track, Abigor said, "Father, I have the utmost respect for thee. Thou easily defeated me once. We are on the same side now. We need an exorcist to help us banish a demon. We must reach and destroy a devastating weapon that might be capable of obliterating the earth as we know it. I know how that sounds, but there art sufficient reasons for believing thus. There is no one else to whom we could turn, and thee, thank God, are a short train ride from our headquarters. Time is running through the hourglass at an alarming rate. Will thee help us?"

Father Antonio looked entirely at peace when he answered. "I was told I must perform one more exorcism. It is my duty to obey. God does not make polite requests; He tells us what He expects from us. I am a very old man, and my days are numbered. I am not worried about myself. I have led a righteous life and shall joyfully go home when He calls me. I have a small bag packed with the items I was told I would need to battle this evil. I have been in prayer since I received the message. I am ready." He read from the Bible in front of him, "John 14:27 Peace I leave with you, my peace I give to you. Not as the world gives do I give to you. Let not your hearts be troubled, neither let them be afraid." The angel and the ghost closed their eyes in silent prayer.

"I have no fear, my sons. I will get my bag, and we shall depart for the train station. God be with us. My body is humbled, yet my spirit defies, and we shall defeat the dark forces with Archangel Michael's help." His words took Angus by surprise. The Archangel Michael?

The two humans and the angel genuflected again, crossed themselves, and walked into the unknown, fortified by nothing other than their faith.

They were a curious trio heading to the train station in the middle of the night: a priest, a former demon, and a dead, retired MI5 agent. The priest usually traveled around the village on his old, heavy-duty pink Schwinn bike. He will leave his bike close by at a friend's house. Cretins steal bicycles; however, his 50-year-old battered pink bike is unlikely to be at the top of their most-wanted list.

Humans subconsciously want to help our heroes, and, in fact, this is part of their winning arsenal. Their questions are answered with a smile; their motives are not questioned, and they are sent on their way with a hardy cheerio. Our travelers could ride the train for the 20-minute trip at no charge. Ticket inspectors pass them by and go on to the next passenger. They gave 50 pounds to an older woman who could not find her ticket so they would not be guilty of breaking one of the Ten Commandments.

David picked them up in the Rolls when they reached the Covent Station. It was the first time Father Antonio had ridden in a Rolls Royce. It is only an 8-minute walk to the Savoy, but the team did not want to tire the aged parson. Big Soph came along for the ride to help him feel at ease. He quickly decided the Rolls was better than his pink Schwinn. Terrifying to depend on a 95-year-old man to save the world, Abigor had little hope that humanity would survive without Father Antonio. He can still hear Admiral Stallings's final words ringing in his ears. Abigor was looking forward to telling the excellent admiral he was dead wrong.

When the guys return to the hotel, Sir Winston, Sophie, and I are waiting for them. I had ordered a pot of tea and a few biscuits in case our guest was hungry. I also ordered a couple of hearty ham and cheddar cheese sandwiches with chips if the good padre happens to be famished. He may have missed his evening tea.

Dr. Einstein had not yet emerged from his laboratory. The tension is building. What did our brilliant scientist see that we did not? Would this new twist further complicate our already outrageously impossible lives? Almost certainly, it would.

Since the padre joined us, I am thrilled to have someone to drink tea and eat biscuits with me. I give him a warm, Dear-God-we-need-you, welcoming hug and pour his tea. Sophie stays close to him.

The Team discusses the plan for tomorrow and our roles in our strategy. We told Father Antonio about the Sunstone Compass. He had no idea what that meant or why the compass and I must be there. He has never heard of the Sunstone. We want to wait for Dr. Einstein before we discuss our strategic plan in detail. He will be playing an essential part.

After we finished tea, Dr. Einstein came out of his laboratory looking alarmingly wild, even for him. His pipe is in his shirt pocket, and smoke circles above him. His glasses hang from one ear. His eyes are wide. He sits down on the sofa, holds one of the throw cushions close to his chest, and tries to calm himself. After a few minutes, he manages to speak, "I must share some shocking information with you. It is terrible, absolutely terrible. I think I know what the Doomsday Machine does. Regrettably, I don't see how it does it. It resonated with me when Bones and Abigor described what he saw on the demon stream of consciousness. Did I tell you I took a class in geology as an undergraduate at the Federal Polytechnic School in Zurich in 1900? Our professor, Dr. Eric Snell, was researching his brilliant theory about what would happen if the most devastating geographic feature on earth were to explode at once. He suggested that the tremendous destructive potential of earthquakes and volcanos could be triggered at the earth's magma level. As everyone knows, the planet is made of layers, the lithosphere, the asthenosphere, the mesosphere, the outer core, and the inner core. Tectonic plates are large pieces of the lithosphere that move around under the earth's surface. When everything functions as it should, there is a balance, and we survive. Occasionally, an earthquake will occur, or a volcano will erupt. Typically, these are of short duration, and then we return to normal. Though these geographical monsters might cause significant damage locally when they act up, we have not been annihilated!"

Warming to the science, he explains further, "We may think of the planet as solid, and it is not. There is constant movement, and much of it is fluid. For example, the seven major tectonic plates move because of heat from radioactive processes. Sometimes they move toward each other, and sometimes they move away. The outer layer of the earth is the crust. It is about 25 miles thick under the continents. The temperature can vary from highs of about 1600 F to 4000 F. The asthenosphere is the part of the mantle that flows and moves the plates. The movement, high temperatures, and pressure are continuous and, in some areas, extreme. There is a relationship between earthquakes and volcanoes. Please excuse me. I don't want to get too technical." We are all thinking that train had left the station. Poor Father Antonio looks stunned by all the scientific-technical details the doctor throws at us, yet we are accustomed to Dr. Einstein's lectures. We duck.

Oblivious, the dear doctor continues, "Any questions so far, gentlemen and Bones? Excellent, I thought you would catch on quickly." We never catch on quickly, and Dr. Einstein never recognizes our complete confusion. Looking up at us, the genius abruptly pauses. "I am sorry. Do I know this priest?" We introduce the scientist to our resident Priest. He welcomes the Holy man aboard with warmth and sincerity, then continues, "When a plate is driven under another plate, there is the possibility of earthquake activity or a volcanic eruption. Quite often, an earthquake precedes an eruption. The time in between can vary greatly. What if, just what if, as Professor Snell theorized, one could create a chain reaction of earthquakes, volcanic eruptions, one after the other by introducing intense, disruptive energy into the somewhat stable equation?" The doctor looks at us as if one of us might have the answer. Nope, it failed again.

Sir Winston and David are getting frustrated with this scientific lecture when we are supposed to be preparing for our epic battle tomorrow. We must cross-check our plans to ensure we have not missed anything important. We still don't have a thorough strategy with a timeline. As the former Prime Minister lectures, "If you don't have a timeline, it is a wish, not a plan."

David is looking at his watch. I wink at him—he winks back and adds his sexy grin.

Sir Winston clears his throat, takes a sip of brandy, and says, "Albert, dear friend, I appreciate the depth and breadth of your knowledge concerning the earth's layers, volcanos, and earthquakes. Nonetheless, shouldn't we be preparing for our mission tomorrow? Our time is, as we have said numerous times, running out. I feel as anxious as I felt while waiting for the Dynamo ships and boats to set sail, knowing our time was slipping away and we needed a miracle." We all check out the hourglass and suffer a heart-stopping jolt. Little sand is left.

Dr. Einstein is determined to stay on course. "You don't understand, Winston. We cannot invade the tunnel tomorrow. I think the

Nazis designed the Doomsday Machine to do what I have just said to create a domino effect of earthquakes and volcano eruptions worldwide. Do you know what that would mean to planet earth?" He stares at us. We look back intently and squinch our eyes, none of us the wiser. Basically, we assume it would be counter to humankind's well-being.

He sails forth with a severe grimace, "Let me tell you what that would mean. If even just the supervolcanoes erupted, the eruptions would throw thousands of tons of volcanic ash, rock, and gas into the atmosphere and upon the earth. If all the live volcanos in the world, approximately 1500, erupted, the atmosphere could not support this onslaught of toxic material. Volcanic gases, hydrochloric acid, hydrogen fluoride, hydrogen sulfide, and sulfur dioxide would contaminate the air. The earth would be covered with a thick layer of ash. Acid rain would kill all vegetation on earth and poison the groundwater. The temperatures would rise; humans and animals could not breathe. A layer of ash and smoke would cut off sunlight. Temperatures would then plummet. There would be no escaping from the devastation. Flames, the flames Abigor saw in his vision, would engulf the entire world. It would become a dead planet. I doubt any species would survive. Our species certainly would be eliminated." The Genius says this with complete composure.

Shocked, David demands clarification, "What are you saying, Dr. Einstein? The Nazis developed a machine that could control volcanoes and earthquakes to such a degree they could activate them? Surely, that is impossible. What kind of energy source would have that much power, and where would it strike to create the domino effect you mentioned? I have heard rumors about a Russian device called SUR that might fire up an array of high-powered antennas and inject a large dose of microwaves into the high atmosphere. Supposedly, their goal is to disrupt weather and possibly create earthquakes on a small scale. So this information is not entirely bizarre." I must disagree with David. All of this is highly bizarre to me!

Dr. Einstein exhales and continues, "Excellent questions, David! You touched on the heart of the issue, and I do not have a hypothesis about the energy source. I must study this in more depth. Dr. Snell called the weak spot "Schwache Erde." He believed that if a disrupting force manipulated this weak spot, it could trigger the worldwide catastrophe we are discussing. Professor Snell knew the approximate location of the weak spot. He believed it was where two huge tectonic plates came together. I must find his research study and identify the location. I may not be able to do that by tomorrow morning—I shall try. I am virtually certain this is what the Demon is planning. The scenes Abigor saw on the demon stream of consciousness likely came from the vile Aaii. It is the only hypothesis that makes logical sense and fits the facts as we know them. Since Snell was German, Nazis would have had access to this research. His study was at the University of Zurich. Possibly, someone close to Hitler read his work and shared it with the madman staring at a final humiliating defeat. Hitler would have had no reservations about destroying the planet. He was unstable. I am sure Bones would agree with me on that." I nod my head in agreement. Yes, Hitler was unstable, and his volatile behavior was exacerbated by drugs, possibly morphine, crystal meth, and cocaine, administered by his quack doctor.

Dr. E continues with growing passion, "Aaii does not care about the planet or its inhabitants either. We must stop him! To do that, we must find the weak spot in the earth's tectonic layer and determine how the Doomsday Machine's disruptive force functions to activate the immense power in the tectonic layers. That is the simplicity of the idea. The uncontrollable power is in the ground; the device simply disrupts it. We will leave the energy source for later."

We were hit with another impossible mission when we thought we had made progress in creating a workable plan. Dr. Einstein said he would leave for Zurich and the University at once. He will return as soon as possible. At least, we might have the answer to one question, where is the weak spot? Assuming we can find and control the Machine, we will likely need to know the targeted coordinates. We will try to recalibrate or offset it to strike another less sensitive area if nothing else. It would be perilous but not the total Black Swan Tsunami we are now facing. My brain is swimming with the loose threads we must clip to forestall the horrendous fate waiting to pounce.

Poor Father Antonio isn't accustomed to our life of dizzying, as David would say, beastly predicaments. It is like being on a merry-go-round of wild, vicious creatures nipping and clawing at us while we valiantly try to stay astride. Poor dear padre was under the erroneous impression that all we had to do was conquer one annoying demon plotting to demolish our beloved planet. Au contraire that would be a piece of cake, as the 1930s English Air Force pilots used to say. Then we still have the mad scientists who have Mengele's journal, viable cells, and perhaps Dr. Suggs. Elite psychopaths beset us as they attempt to enslave all inhabitants of the planet with a cloned Hitler at the helm. These dire and unsettling calamities will have to be pushed to a back burner until we resolve the whole incinerate-the-planet problem.

I pour another cup of coffee for the confused yet spiritually rock-solid priest and offer him biscuits. Hey, at least that is something I can control.

Chapter Eighteen

Seth and the Demon: Act 2

As Seth makes his way through the moldy, foul-smelling, blood-chilling tunnel, he thinks about his four colleagues who were swash-buckling and Billy Bad in their meeting. Yet, they shrank back in terror when he asked if they wanted to meet a demon. As Seth remembers their faces, he laughs. He saw genuine fear in their eyes. They were weak when confronted with the possibility of actual in-your-face danger. These people, Annette Simmons-Wright, Juan Diez, Emerson North, and Julian Chan, are planning to handcuff the planet to a totalitarian regime run by a newly reimaged and packaged Hitler? Yet, they cower at the very idea of meeting Aaii. Truthfully, he set them up with a prevarication. Of course, he could say the Demon's name. He did not have to write it. What a bunch of mushy revolutionaries—he wonders, not for the first time if they are the right people for this world-crushing project. By force of circumstances, committee members should be daring gatecrashers, predatory lions, volcano surfers, and life's paratroopers.

He may kill them.

He pulls his Canada Goose puffer jacket closer around him and shivers. His kitten-soft Burberry scarf caresses his neck.

The Committee and their totalitarian, communist ilk plan to retain the controlling power firmly in their grasp. They imagine Hitler as a necessary evil to attract the masses they require for their movement. They are not alone in their ambitious plans. Numerous other Stalin, Mao, Kim Jong Un, Pol Pot, Castro, Idi Amin wannabes from around the planet will join them in enslaving the people. They are constructing an elaborate trap. They believe the charismatic, fascinatingly dynamic

Hitler, as bait, will lure victims. Then snap! Trap clamps down on their necks with a terrifying finality

Goebbels packaged and promoted Hitler as a preternatural figure during his rise to infamy. He was supposed to embody the proud German spirit—Kampfgeist. Will he still be the same master of passionate oratory mesmerizing the masses with his theatrical performances? Hitler had crowned himself the "world's greatest actor." For him, it was all a grand drama in which Hitler made himself the dazzling star performer. All that glitters is not gold—it could be a gold poison dart frog.

Are humans less credulous now? That is a question to be answered with time. Luckily, the Committee and their ilk will not be troubled by the drunkard Winston Churchill. He is long dead and unavailable to shred their dictatorial plans. One stouthearted, 65-year-old man armed with only a gold-tipped cane and a Havana cigar reduced Herr Fuhrer's plan for world domination to a smoldering heap.

He laughs again. Dictators are always cowards and fools. Why else do they secure the military or paramilitary forces first? Popular leaders do not protect themselves from their followers.

Unbeknownst to Seth, Abigor, the former Demon, made a bargain with Hitler in the early days of his ascent to power in the German State. They agreed to trade a trifle, an intangible, Hitler's soul, for unprecedented, virtually unstoppable military triumphs. Der Fuhrer learned there are no guarantees, not even from demons. The incredibly steadfast Winston Churchill had not been factored into their Faustian bargain. The two leaders never met, but Hitler despised the British Bulldog as the burrowing, poison barb in his side. He lambasted Churchill as a "drunkard," "lunatic," "paralytic," and "world arsonist." World leaders had taught Hitler to expect capitulation, appeasement, and weak-kneed pacification. Then, Heaven help him, Adolf encountered Churchill, an intuitive man who observed Hitler's behavior and ignored his hollow words. Churchill understood that Hitler was a pathological liar with psychopathic and narcissistic tendencies. At that point, Churchill drew a line in the sand. He might as well have etched it deeply in solid marble. It was unmovable. Churchill did not flinch as constant blows rained down on his head from both "friends" and foes alike. He became more entrenched in his point-blank, unwavering strategy, "we shall never surrender" with each blow. In true narcissistic style, Hitler called Churchill "the real father of this war." Seth knows Hitler will be pleased that his old enemy is long dead and gone.

Seth is looking forward to meeting with the bizarre Demon, Aaii, who still indulges in medieval jousting. As Seth rounds the last corner, he is greeted by the Fox Doorman dressed in his festive formal uniform. He is also sporting a jaunty black top hat today. Fox opens the door to the ostentatious inner chamber, and Seth is again overwhelmed by the royal opulence and priceless art pieces. Aaii perches on his ancient carved throne in full, probably terribly uncomfortable jousting garb—he greets his guest Seth, "What a delight to see you again. I realize that visiting here is not easy travel for you. Please be seated, and perhaps you would like something to drink. I have a fully stocked bar for visitors. I believe the last visitor before you was in 1955." Demon saw nothing particularly notable about his skeletal social schedule.

Shuddering, Seth quickly said, "You are kind, Aaii, but I am not thirsty at the moment. I want to continue our conversation from last we met. I promised to keep you informed about our movement's progress. I have excellent news for you today. We could not be more excited about our progress on both fronts, Dr. Wagner and his team's brilliant research accomplishments and NGA's extraordinary preparedness for introducing our new world leader, Adolph Hitler. Naturally, we shall change his name. And, the mustache—a mere swipe of the blade—gone."

Since our meeting, I have talked with the executive committee of NGA, Annette Simmons-Wright, Juan Diez, Emerson North, and Julian Chan. They are moving forward in each of their areas of responsibility. We have structured our assignments and calendars to know where we are in our individual and collective goals.

Seeing he has Aaii's attention, Seth continues, "I visited Dr. Wagner at his laboratory in France last week, and he is on schedule to clone the viable cells this week if all goes as he plans. Since he added Dr. Suggs to his team, his work has progressed remarkably well. A minor point, Dr. Suggs is quite concerned about his family's safety. Wagner has assured him that their safety will benefit from his employment with our organization.

"Wagner has a remarkable team of researchers in the acceleration of the aging process. As one would guess, these professionals are rare, and he was fortunate to acquire them. They will be invaluable in accelerating maturation when we clone the three Nazis. We have no desire for toddlers. Wagner's immediate goals are to clone the cells and bring in the acceleration team for the next phase, aging them quickly. Most of the research on the aging process comes from research done in childhood Progeria, Hutchinson-Gilford syndrome." Noting the mystified look on the Demon's face, Seth elaborates, "As you may know, these children look normal at birth but fail to thrive. The syndrome causes hair loss, aged-looking skin, joint issues, subcutaneous fat loss, and heart disease. They are often fated to die young of a heart attack or stroke. Their condition does not impair intellectual ability; this is vital for our purposes. Progeria is rare, so it does not attract the massive donations of most childhood diseases. Experts are not numerous. There has been recent growth in both interest in Progeria and research studies and publications. Naturally, the focus of the research is to moderate and ultimately stop the fatal aging progress of the disease. Scientists have made definitive connections between Progeria, heart disease, and normal aging. However, first, they must understand why accelerated aging occurs. The protein that causes Progeria is present in everyone's cells. Thus, as our scientists readily appreciated early on, understanding this disease may also help us understand normal human aging. This data may serve Dr. Wagner in our Youth Drug research. We still have that nagging heart glitch to resolve."

"Dr. Wagner's third phase, supervised by our Youth Drug Team, will be halting the aging process at the ages of the Nazis at their deaths. Hitler was fifty-six, Goebbels was forty-seven, and Himmler was forty-four. He is considering adjusting Hitler's age down a few years. Naturally, there has been tremendous interest in slowing the aging process; studies and publications abound. Our talented team of scientists has been working on this for years. Our Youth Drug team will oversee the third phase."

Seth heartily continues, hoping to bring Aaii on board, "We have had some exciting developments recently. Researchers have learned much about the reasons for the acceleration in Progeria. We have an IT hack in a couple of the most prestigious studies to stay abreast of developments. We have learned the LMNA gene is the culprit. It instructs the lamin A protein needed for a well-structured nuclear envelope. Without the nuclear envelope, cells die prematurely. The eminent Dr. Wagner has been studying this information in minute detail." Seth pulls out his notes from Dr. Wagner. Seth puts on his trendy glasses and reads, "He and his team have begun a full-scale research study involving disruption of phosphorylated lamin function at enhancers as it contributes to Progeria." Seth puts his notes away and continues, "Understanding why aging occurs and how to mitigate it is a goldmine. Remember, Wagner has vast funds and resources, plus no smothering ethical standards. He can complete studies in record time." Aaii is becoming more bored by the minute. He checks his fingernails. Yep, still there. He Inspects his chain mail chest plate, stockings, and helmet. He is staring off into space now. Seth knows he must rev up his pace.

Seth continues, "Dr. Wagner's work with lamin A has been nothing less than ground-breaking, really revolutionary. They have tweaked lamin A to remove the deadly, less desirable traits and retain the age acceleration component. This is the interesting point; if the envelope is defective, the cell ages prematurely. Dr. Wagner and the team will manipulate the envelope to control accelerated aging. Wagner is confident in this innovative therapy, and they will age the three cloned leaders to adult level in just a couple of months without detrimental effects. I won't bore you with details." The Demon clearly shows he is already bored to death, and that needle is swiftly approaching the red zone.

Seth is speaking faster to finish before Aaii turns nasty. "When they reach that goal in their progression Dr. Suggs' team will suspend the aging process and add the Youth Drug to enhance their strength and ability to heal. The scientists will use gene therapy to replace the defective lamin A with the functional protein. Gene therapy is not as fantastic as it sounds. Scientists and physicians use gene manipulation quite often now. Look at the Covid19 gene mRNA therapy used around the world. Wagner's team and Dr. Suggs have been ingenious in bringing us to this highly successful, cutting-edge solution.

"We will discuss my colleagues' roles in NGA when we have concluded step one of the cloning process. I will mention they are making lists of the wealthiest people in the world. These individuals have the means to buy age regression, our Youth Drug. However, Youth Drug has never been tried on elderly subjects. We don't know if subjects will regress to an earlier physical age, feel more youthful and stronger, and have increased energy, immune response, and stamina. We are working toward the first possibility." Seth failed to mention he is contemplating killing his entire executive committee. Why bring negativity into the celebration of triumphs? He smugly continues, "Our monetary return from that part of our research should be in the billions of dollars. Do you have questions, concerns, or suggestions?" Aaii did show mild interest at the mention of "in the billions of dollars." Still, the Demon is sorry he invited babbling Seth to visit him. Naturally, they are not on the same page since Aaii has been terminologically inexact about his plan B—he lied by omission. If Seth and his colleagues do not conclude these projects in a reasonable timeframe, they will learn about his Plan B. He is wondering if it would not be better to destroy the world now, with the upside being he would not have to endure another brain-numbing Seth progress report. Why does Aaii not simply obliterate Seth? He doesn't because he cannot, and that realization is jarringly disturbing. What can it mean?

Finally, Aaii replies, "Fascinating information, Seth. You seem to have covered every detail of the plan and our current and projected progress at least once. I am particularly interested in meeting our timeline. Next time we meet, I will have contacted all of my executives in positions of highest authority from around the globe. These men and women are indebted to me until doomsday. They have surrendered their independence in exchange for fame, beauty, success, or fortune."

"They will do as I tell them. I find humans in politics are a particularly fertile field for my harvest sickle. You and your executive committee should have your completed, detailed plans, including the leaders, locations, and specific tasks, in place and perfected when Hitler reaches adulthood. I will then embed three with their uniquely talented personalities. Goebbels will be invaluable in selling this new Hitler to the masses. He is undoubtedly a genius at disinformation and misinformation. Please return when the cloning is complete, and the cloned leaders are approaching adulthood. I will do my magic as promised. They are crucial in implementing our NGA indoctrination plans."

Seth is no more transparent than the jousting Demon. He knows a weapon is here and wants to test the water with Aaii. The weapon is a sensitive subject to approach, but Seth plows on, "That is our complete and exhaustive plan thus far. I have been entirely transparent with you. Is there anything else I should know about your plans to coordinate with us?"

The Demon looks as innocent as possible for a handsome monster in armor. Aaii considers the question before replying, "Seth, I think you already know everything you need to know." His smile would melt all the earth's glaciers, including the massive million-year-old Antarctic glaciers.

Fox moves silently into the purloined room and stops in front of Seth. Aaii waves a warm goodbye as he puts his helmet on. Dismissed, Seth rises from the brutally uncomfortable antique chair, and Fox leads him to the ornate doors, opens them, and slams them as soon as Seth's boots clear the sill. Seth waved back to a closed door, and now he disappeared into the damp tunnel as literally and figuratively "in the dark" as when he arrived. Indignant, he wrestles his Bunyanesque flashlight from his puffer pocket and retraces his footsteps.

The Demon looks at Fox and says, "What the Hell is Seth?"

Chapter Nineteen

The Vision

David and Angus decide to visit the Innsbruck Police to monitor the Constables' progress on Dr. Suggs's disappearance. Aware of the gold nuggets often found in chatter, David and Angus will hang out for a while, listening to the constable chit-chat on the case. As a former South Carolina State Constable, I know one learns more from casual locker room conversations than from reading the case file. Not everything goes into the official file. The "gang" will have opinions and good old-fashioned cop intuition to share, and frequently chatter leads to a break. If indicated, they will become visible and consult with the constables posing as MI5 agents (the alive kind), lending a friendly helping hand to fellow officers. If they can find the elusive Dr. Suggs, they may also collar the other Mengele research team. Locating him is not urgent at the moment, with the whole blow-up-the-earth thing consuming our lives. However, while waiting for Dr. Einstein to return, they might as well work on this aspect of the mission. David and Angus have spent their lives dedicated to Law Enforcement and intelligence; naturally, they like to dip their toes into those familiar waters when the opportunity presents itself. What fun they would have leading Dr. Suggs' missing person investigation if only it were possible. I give them both a hug. David gets a fiery kiss that lasts longer than I had planned. In my defense, life is uncertain, have dessert first.

Abigor and I decide to crash the Navy College and chat with thc always fascinating Admiral Stallings. Usually, he is grudgingly willing to share a few cryptic, dark tips with us. We invite Sir Winston to visit his friend, Admiral Stallings. Sir Winston decides he will stay at our headquarters with Father Antonio and delve into our spiritual plan of attack. He hopes the Padre may have ideas that give us the desperately needed edge. Father Antonio has been faithfully battling evil for seventy-five years. He is our beloved demon stomper extraordinaire. When the Great Man finishes strategizing with Father Antonio, he will pop over to join us at the College.

Previously Admiral Stallings had warned us that our battle would be a calamity. We, naturally, were highly annoyed and alarmed by his gloomy prediction. We need specifics; how will the evil cretins defeat us? How did he arrive at that conclusion? Talking with Stallings is frustrating; he has more information than our team and spoons it out to us in disconnected bits and pieces. We are hopeful that the planets and stars have realigned in our favor and that his prognostication will shift. Our mission circumstances have been in constant flux since we began. We have many loudly clamoring tasks, such as conquering the tunnel devils and neutralizing the Doomsday Weapon's power.

Abigor told us what we might expect to face when challenging the Demon in his Owl Mountain dungeon, with or without possible reinforcements. We may encounter one nasty-tempered monster or several legions of ill-tempered nightmares fresh from the sweltering heat of Hell. Since I am not well-versed in all things Hell, I asked Abigor how many monsters are in a legion. He squinted at me, never a good thing, and reluctantly answered, "There are three to six thousand demons in a legion. Mercifully, the tunnel cannot be nearly large enough to hold that ridiculously high number of demons. They wear battle gear much like 2nd Century Roman soldiers, which may include a helmet, mail breastplate, gauntlets, manica for arms, and greaves for shins. They carry a deadly long sword called the gladius. Since mere mortals cannot harm them, the armor is purely pageantry and strutting pomposity. They tend to grandstand when they leave Hell for little excursions such as the Owl Mountain tunnel. We hast no idea if Aaii shalt call for reinforcements. That would complicate our plans, but we must prepare to defeat him no matter how many warriors he brings to the battlefield. The number is insignificant." I glare at him. My logical brain struggles to process that naive concept. OK, let me see if I have this right; if Aaii brings one warrior or 5000, we (the seven of us—counting the Padre) will be locked, loaded, and eager to rumble? Right? Hell no!

After we ground Aaii into the dirt along with his clinking, clanking band of Tin Soldiers, we may be peering into the steel face of a weapon of horrific destructive ability. A veritable Armageddon, the last epic struggle between righteousness and wickedness. We are the good guys. We are few but hell-bent on eliminating this Nazi monstrosity before our planet of 8 billion souls becomes a black hole in space. If Dr. Einstein is correct, only one place on earth can trigger the earthquakes and volcanoes that would incinerate us. Well, not us, me, Father Antonio, and humanity. The guys would remain hale and hardy.

I looked up the word Armageddon, and it means a mountain range. That fits our final battlefield in the Owl Mountains entirely too closely for my comfort.

Of course, then we must determine how to disarm, recalculate, or destroy the almost century-old weapon. Perhaps, we will be fortunate, and time has reduced it to a rusted, hulking, gray mass of junk. If we are not lucky, our mission is to render it impotent or at least less devastating. I suppose we could just blow up Owl Mountain. David and Angus have been examining the diagram of the Doomsday Machine that Dr. Einstein and Sir Winston found in the Military Archives. They hope to learn more about its construction and operation, a place to start. It is something, anything. I am beginning to sound desperate. (OK, let's move on and do something useful, Bones.)

Abigor and I will grab the #188 bus back to the venerable Old Navy College to visit our friend and oracle, Admiral Stallings. We are running to catch the bus, and I turn my ankle, slamming down on the uneven cobblestones on my hands and knees. Darn high heels! Luckily, I wear scuffed jeans, so my knees are good; I didn't scrape off the scab from my last clumsy fall when I chased Red. I can live with one scraped hand. Before I inelegantly dropped, I thought I saw a dark shadow in the trees, then it vanished. Darn, our bus is driving away! Abigor waves his hand. The bus comes to a screeching halt, and passengers slam back against their seats. We get on and sit down. Miraculously, bus #188 begins to roll again. The bus is teeming with vibrant life. Again I am reminded no one else on board is responsible for protecting the earth from merciless, bloodthirsty demons and Nazi death machines—no wonder they look happier than we do. Oblivion is blissful.

It is a perfect day. The azure sky is crystal clear, and yellow sunbeams paint the College grounds with a glow of perfection. I am untouched by the beauty surrounding me. My mind is racing; I want to hear what the enigmatic, always dispiriting Admiral can tell us. Yet, I fear his prediction has worsened since our last visit. I don't know what is more horrifying than our defeat and the end of the planet. Still, I believe in the Admiral's ability to predict an even more cataclysmic fate.

Abigor and I walk through the heavy oak entrance doors and move directly across the lobby to the spooky staircase. Today I am happy to have the physical exertion caused by the impossibly long flight of stairs. Pain helps to distract me. When we finally reach what is supposed to be the third floor, his office is in front of us. Today the number on the door is 1616. I am puzzled. Abigor is not and recognizes my perplexity. "In the Revelation to Saint John 16.16." Well, that certainly clears it up for me. Angels can be so annoying.

As usual, we stand outside the door for a few minutes, admiring wear patterns in the wood floor and flaws in the plaster walls until

Admiral Stallings directs us to enter his cabin. The door opens slowly, and we hear him say from across the room, "Come in, Abigor and Dr. Wyndot." I am delighted to see Thelma Dove sitting across from him. Two battered chairs wait beside her.

I greet them, "What a pleasure to see you, Ms. Dove, a delightfully unexpected treat. Good afternoon, Admiral Stallings."

Admiral Stallings, his eyebrows approaching one another, looking miffed, admonishes, "I must admit I am surprised. I thought I was quite clear at our last meeting. What do you want of me?" I glance at Thelma. Her mournful downcast eyes and pouting lips whisper melancholy. I know her story—her captivating eyes have witnessed too much inhumanity and barbarity. When the Nazis killed the Admiral, she joined Sir Winston's secret Special Operations Executive to aid the dwindling French Resistance fighters. Many of her French and English friends were killed fighting to free France from the jaws of Nazism. Of the forty-one women in the SOE-F Section, only half survived the War. The French Resistance fought while hidden in the shadows, trusting no one and dependent only on each other for survival. They were the prey, ruthlessly hunted and persecuted. Ferocious wolves were gobbling up France, and many Frenchmen collaborated or cooperated with the wolves hoping to survive. Resisters became lonely outcasts, abandoned and oft betrayed, in their beloved France.

I try to imagine how a smile would transform Thelma's lovely face. Perhaps she smiled before the War. Thelma says nothing, but she reaches out, takes my hand, and squeezes it. I am pleasantly surprised by her sudden affection.

Sir Winston pops into the room, startling everyone to his perverse delight. The Great Man chuckles, "Good afternoon, Admiral and Miss Dove. It is a great pleasure to see you, as always. I trust you do not mind if I join the conversation. We come to you today on a matter of grave urgency, and we wholeheartedly welcome your generous assistance. Our mission is coming to an abrupt conclusion. I will be frank; we need help, and our position is unsatisfactory. Many resolved enemies, known and unknown, are positioned against us. Circumstances force us to prepare an immediate plan to meet contingencies when many are still shrouded in darkness. We appeal to you for any assistance you can honorably give us, Jeffrey."

Abigor addresses Stallings, "Admiral, I concur with Sir Winston we art not in an advantageous position. Since we spoke to thee, our mission has evolved in various ways. We want thine thoughts on these alarming developments. When thou made thine haunting prediction, did thou have a vision of the tunnel and the battle? We could prepare if we knew, for example, how many fighters we would encounter. We can overwhelm Aaii with enough information—and luck. We have also enlisted the assistance of a spiritually powerful exorcist. I have battled with him in the past, and I have no desire to do it again. Did thou have a vision of the battle?"

I was bewildered when Thelma answered him. "No, Abigor, Jeffrey did not have a vision. I saw the horrific battle; the monsters shed human blood, and you were defeated. The Demon Aaii won and cast aside your holy warriors. The ghastly images sent me to my knees in prayer for your team."

"I understand the urgency, Sir Winston." Oddly, I can see Thelma's images, and those horrid images emotionally kick me in the stomach. Lightheaded, I have to sit down.

A sticky note floats into my lap. Ah, a text from Red reassures me, "Don't be afraid to face the devil himself, spunky Bones. We will protect you." The note is heartening. I think I like Red's notes. But who are "we"? No one appears to notice my airmail.

Abigor presses for more information, "Doth thou see the same vision now, Thelma? We must create a plan to be prepared." I am trying to calm my breathing. I am a psychotherapist. I can do this.

Sir Winston, standing behind Thelma, gently lays his hand on her shoulder. The tension in her muscles visibly eases. She straight, holds her head high and squares her shoulders. Thelma is a soldier and a fighter again. The transformation is incredible; she appears to gain strength from Sir Winston's touch.

Thelma says nothing, closes her eyes, and her breathing begins to slow, and she appears to go into a trance. She is frozen; only her eyelashes flicker. After several nail-biting minutes, Thelma opens her eyes. She seems confused at first and shakes her head. I finally found the courage to ask, "Did you see anything, Thelma? Has the battle scene changed?" Admiral Stallings is watching her intently. His eyes do not leave her face. Sir Winston's hand is still on her slim shoulder. He steels her spine with his powerful presence.

Abigor is standing, leaning toward her, and gently probes, "Thelma, what did thee see? Please, we must know." We all hold our breath as we wait for either devastating or hopeful words. I am afraid I will start hyperventilating, and my heart is pounding in my ears. I want to run from this room to avoid hearing what Thelma might tell us.

Thelma clears her throat and whispers, "I saw the terrible battle, the bloodshed. I heard screaming and curses. I saw smoke everywhere . . . flames . . . others who are not of your team. They were horrible . . . rage and brutality. The scene is . . . maybe Hell. I saw Sir Winston, David, and Abigor. The smoke . . . choking, how can anyone breathe? Oh, they don't breathe. Know this, the battle is raging . . . you hold the key, it flows in your blood . . . the key to the, uh, machine." Thelma has opened her eyes and looks directly at me when she says that final sentence. She wipes away tears. Though Thelma weeps, her face is set, muscles taut, and she is a good soldier. The admiral nods to her, and she rises, looks intently at each of us, and bestows an encouraging smile. Then she slips silently from the room. The door, in sympathy with Thelma, closes soundlessly behind her. We are, except Sir Winston, astounded by her remarkable spirit.

We look to the Admiral for guidance. We aren't sure how to interpret her vision. Admiral Stallings says, "You wanted to know if the picture had shifted, if you still had a chance to triumph in the Owl Mountain tunnel to Hell. When Thelma told me about her first vision, the battle was over, and you had lost. Her visions have always been accurate. Undoubtedly, something unknown to us has shifted, as did her vision. The celestial kaleidoscope is reshaping itself, and the shift has added weight to your side of the battle. We don't know how that will affect the final act. Thelma's new vision is a blessing. The die is not yet cast, and the mission has not yet ended in defeat. You have a chance, even if it is razor-thin. You, my dear friends, are caught between the devil and the deep blue sea. Victory is conceivable against tremendous odds. We must pray the odds to continue to move in your favor." We let out a collective sigh of relief. I can breathe again.

I see the dark shadow I saw when I fell. It is outside the single window in the Admiral's cabin. The window is much too high for anyone to be outside looking in. No one else appears to notice, and I decide not to mention it. The overwhelming challenges threatening our mission negatively impacted my senses. I saw two impossible images, Red's note, and the shadow. Darn, I suppose I could add the surreal seance as number three weird.

Well, we could say that our odds have improved from zero. I ask Admiral Stallings if he has an idea of what, if anything, might help us trim the odds. After chewing on his bottom lip for a few seconds, he warns, "You are aware of my limitations. I have explained that to you before. Sir Winston understands the ties that bind me." Sir Winston nods in somber agreement. "I have been considering the rules and my heartfelt desire to help you. Thelma is distraught about the battle, so I would also like to ease her concerns. It will not break anything if I tell Bones to keep the compass close while she is in the tunnel and not let it out of her control. I know I once told you to destroy the evil relic. That ship has sailed, and destroying it is no longer an option. Bones, hear me on this, do not fear the darkness. It cannot harm you. You are not alone. Your team has already discussed the Armor of God, Holy water, a silver cross, and prayer before entering the tunnel. The ancients knew how to weaken demons. I have studied ancient literature, and I have learned a few things. You have one strong advantage, the greatest leader the world has ever known. He runs a tight ship." He bows toward Sir Winston. Admiral Stallings pulls a piece of old yellowed parchment from a desk drawer and uses the Montblanc fountain pen on his desk to draw a design. It is a circle inside a square; written in the center is *Vade retro, Satan.* He explains, "These are ancient Holy words going back into the mist of time. Benedictine scribes first penned these words in 1415. Vade retro, Satan, means roughly go back, Satan. Regrettably, this design will not destroy demons but may weaken them and force them to leave the tunnel and return to Hell. The effect may not be permanent. You will be in deep water, work quickly and abandon that evil place. There are no guarantees. You must carry one of these drawings close to your heart." Our three team members look at the drawing skeptically, but we are not proud, considering how few demon-thrashing tools we have at our disposal.

Abigor reassures Stallings, "Thank you, Admiral, and also our sincere appreciation to thy lady. We will use the tools thou have given us to our best advantage. We are indebted to you as we undertake this Holy mission, perhaps our last. Be confident; we have no intention of losing, no matter the cost to us. We shalt fight!" I may get used to bad-arse angels.

Sir Winston slaps Abigor on the back with enthusiasm. To Stallings, he chides, "Jeffrey, I have found that sometimes rules are meant to be broken. I always choose the greater good. The SOE to which Thelma belonged broke almost all the gentlemanly rules of waging war at the time. It was my secret weapon, and I bless every member of the SOE."

Sir Winston reaches out to shake the Admiral's hand. "You have been quite generous, my old friend. I cannot express my profound admiration for your lady. She has always been a fearless warrior. She fought Hell for Abigor's soul and won." Abigor bows and crosses himself.

The Great man reminds us as he chomps on his cigar, "You know we shall do whatever is necessary. It is not enough to do our best; sometimes, we must do what's required. This is one of those times. If you learn anything else, please contact me immediately. I expect our current journey will end by late tomorrow night. Whatever happens, God help us."

The Admiral rises from his chair and embraces all three of us, making the sign of the cross. We walk to the open door and into the drafty hall. Naturally, we look at the numbers on the door before heading to the stairs. The number is now 413; Abigor quotes Philippians 4:13, "I can do all things . . .|" I cling to and tightly embrace those reassuring words. What else can I do?

Sir Winston turns toward us and proclaims, "I must return to the Savoy to see if Albert has returned. We shall discuss his journey to Zurich and his new information for us. As soon as you return, we will finalize our strategy for our Holy Crusade at Owl Mountain. We are not Knights Templar or Richard the Lionhearted, but we follow in their bold footsteps. May we be worthy." Before we can respond, Sir Winston pops out, leaving us standing there looking at air.

Abigor, the former Demon, is the only one who knows if these ancient symbols have power. I have to ask, "Will the Admiral's Holy design be effective against our Enemy?" Abigor responds, "He doth have confidence in its ability to protect us." Hmmm, I knew that.

Abigor slows down as we descend. He is going down the steep stairs faster than I can keep up. He says, "I have never seen that particular design. There are many designs and symbols, both evil and Holy. For example, the Sigil of Baphomet is the insignia of the Church of Satan. It is a Pentagram. In ancient times the pentagram was used as a Christian symbol representing the five wounds of Christ. Few people realize that today. Satanists stole the Holy Pentagram from us."

"I never saw this symbol as a demon. I have experienced the power of genuine symbology. Thus I art hopeful. Most modern symbols for Satan and witchcraft art nonsense for playing dress-up. The ancient symbols can be extraordinarily potent. One must be cautious."

I waited until we were on flat ground to answer. Breathing and descending are mutually exclusive. I take a deep breath and say, "We have several tools, some of which you have said have the spiritual power to protect us. Now we have this symbol recommended by the Admiral to add to our arsenal. I think the team will be encouraged by what we have learned today; we have not lost the battle yet. We go in prepared to meet whatever is in the tunnel. I feel more confident, not that I ever seriously believed we were dead before we had begun. Too many variables outside our knowledge and control can influence outcomes."

I hope Dr. Einstein is back from his trip to Zurich. If there is a weak spot in the earth's crust that can trigger earthquakes and volcanoes, we must identify its location. That will be our only solid defensive tactic. Make sure the monster machine cannot activate it. Easy? Right?

Abigor looks back at me and whispers, "Bones, I saw the shadow too. Thou didst not imagine it either time."

What?

Chapter Twenty

Traitors and Saints

Much of the MI5 campus is shrouded in darkness. Agents and staff have gone home or are on assignments. In the administrative suite, one office is draped in a deeper, more oppressive darkness. Inside two people are whispering words of duplicity and perhaps treason. They do not want to draw attention to their meeting. They should not be here together, and there would be unpleasant consequences if anyone saw them. The effects would be full-on godawful if they were overheard. It is possible that a recording device is installed and monitors every sound. If so, it is a closely guarded secret. Because of this chilling possibility, they whisper like two naughty children planning a raid on the kitchen.

They could have met off-campus, but one is scheduled to work here tonight. For emergencies, a skeleton staff is always on duty, and numerous essential personnel are on call. MI5's mission is to ensure national security and their workdays never end. The stout dictator of a rogue country could be coordinating a missile strike. Small groups of homegrown terrorists may radicalize new members, and cybersecurity is an interminable headache. These miscreants usually do not advertise their nefarious intent in advance for obvious reasons. The agency never sleeps.

One of the whisperers is a woman. Both are trusted high-ranking personnel. Their heads are close together as they speak in low, hushed voices.

The woman's speech is fast. She licks her lips as she reports, "The Committee insists that we act immediately. David's team is ready to tackle the Owl Mountain Tunnel, and we cannot allow that to happen.

They have made arrangements which indicate their journey to Poland will be soon. The NGA Executive Committee has instructed us to stop them no matter the cost. We have carte blanche to act, but it must be at once. We do not know their names besides David Smythe and George Clarke, but I was told there are six members. From what we could learn, there are five men and one woman with a gigantic, vicious canine in tow. David's Team is well-trained, lethal, and brutal. Their official classification is Armed and Extremely Dangerous; therefore, we must be cautious in approaching them. No one seems to know anything about the other four members. If indeed, that is an accurate count. We know both David Smythe and George Clarke are probably former intelligence officers. Our informants have said they may be staying at the Savoy. We do not have a room number. Our plans must be complete tonight."

The man looks around furtively as he replies, "I have heard two of the members are in their sixties or using high-end make-up and procedures to alter and age their appearances. I would assume it is the latter. Why would they have older men in such a vicious group?" he asks, half to himself while trying to puzzle it out.

He shares intel. "Of course, we cannot do anything until we verify their location. We have a photo of David leaving the Savoy with a dark-haired woman in her thirties. That does not mean the team lives at the Savoy, but it is a logical assumption it is their base. We have a two-person surveillance team outside the Savoy 24 hours a day. Also, they saw the woman leaving and returning with another man. He was tall, about her age, with blond hair. Both wore faded jeans and black t-shirts. She wore red high heels, rather peculiar but easy to spot. Naturally, we will need a ruse to search the Hotel. Annette is working on that now, and an NGA contact on the site is aiding them. The attack will happen tonight as soon as Annette shares the plan with our team of ten operatives from the London Neo-Nazi group. They have been on standby to carry out the assignment. The Nazis have encountered David's group before and claim they are merciless psychos."

They both chuckled at the word psycho. The woman laughed as she added, "Do you think the Neo-Nazis are getting soft? Still, they are supremely confident in themselves and their colleagues. After all, David's team size is absurdly inadequate for their tunnel mission or anything else. How troublesome can eliminating them be?" Her smile was deadly cold and smug.

As they enjoy the light-hearted moment together, they fail to see the dark shadow in the corner and, to their peril, do not sense its savage rage.

They sneak out of the executive suite one at a time and disappear into the shadows.

In another part of the ancient city, Sir Winston returns to the Savoy. He hopes Dr. Einstein will return soon with the vital information needed to begin the first stage of their tunnel mission, seek and destroy. They will leave quickly for Poland and are determined to make their mission successful. David and Angus have made all the travel arrangements and acquired the necessary equipment and protective gear for Bones and Father Antonio.

Father Antonio is sipping a cup of tea and praying for the success of their mission, guidance, and spiritual strength. He is no longer a young man, and that fact weighs heavily on his frail shoulders. He asks himself, am I still the rock of spiritual might I have been all these years? Yes, I am confident that has not changed. It has been many years since I fought and conquered demons. My spirit is strong, if not stronger, than ever, yet my body is fragile. Can this aged vessel withstand the tremendous power of my soul, especially when it bursts forth in battle? I am distinctly aware that this will be my final mission for God on this plane. Yes, I am at peace with that and eager to begin following my new path. I yearn to hear these words, "Well done, good and faithful servant; I will make you ruler over many things. Enter into the joy of the Lord." He looks up from his prayers and sees Sir Winston. Padre cheerfully greets the Great Man, "It is so good to see you, Sir Winston. I was getting a little lonely. I hope you were successful in completing your task. Thanks to dear Bones, I have had my afternoon tea; I am well-fed. Would you please sit down and chat with me? May I bring you a cup of tea?" The dear Padre does not understand the Great Man's drinking preferences.

Sir Winston is pleased to see the faithful priest, a legend in intelligence and military circles. He pats the Padre on the back and sits beside him on the sofa. Father Antonio is undoubtedly well known in the highways and byways of Hell. His rock-solid religious firepower makes the wicked denizens of Hell shudder with fear. Sir Winston's cigars and brandy snifter sit on the coffee table where Bones put them, awaiting his return. He grabs his silver matchbox and lights his cigar. He is ready to converse now.

He frowns as he replies to the Padre's question, "Father Antonio, I wish I could tell you if our tasks were successful, I will know in time. We were pleased to learn our mission in Owl Mountain is no longer considered a catastrophe waiting to unfold. We have an opportunity to win against rather long odds because fate shifted something. Thank God fate shifted in our favor, Padre—when you joined our team. We may win, and to be frank, I never seriously believed a demon and his evil ilk would best us. The deplorable guttersnipes! We are few, more now that we have added you and Abigor. Red and Druid are members in some mysterious way. I am convinced we are powerfully formidable." His jaw juts out in determination as it did so many decades ago when he stared across the English Channel at Hitler. Dear Sir Winston's steely stare discombobulated Hitler, and the loathsome monster blinked.

Remembering that era, Churchill recalls a vision of bomb explosions that electrified the night sky, venerable old structures reduced to rubble, and torn bodies in the wreckage. Everywhere he looked, the scene was covered with a thick layer of dirt and debris from the thousands of bombs showered on London. The bombing, "blitzkrieg," lasted for 57 consecutive nights killing over 30,000 people. The people were shocked, yet they called him to hit back harder than Hitler had hit them. His handkerchief was moist from the tears he shed with his gutsy East End Cockneys. The Great Man peers into the past and says now, as he said in July of 1941. "We ask no favours of the enemy. We seek from them no compunction. No, we will mete out to the Germans the measure, and more than the measure, that they have meted out to us. We shall never turn from our purpose, however grievous the cost." He looks at Father Antonio knowingly and says, "Nothing has changed. Bullies are always the same. They will do their worst, and we will do our best." Sophie gravely shakes her head as she sees those same exploding bombs. Yes, she was there. She was there when Rome fell in 410 to the Visigoth King Alaric and long before then. Soph is of the ages.

The door to the suite suddenly flies open, and Dr. Einstein blasts into the room as if catapulted from a cannon. He is in disarray, nearly bursting with excitement. In haste, he drops his pipe to reclaim it, and his glasses fall off. Sir Winston rushes over to help his friend, and they nearly collide. Wisely, Father Antonio has decided to stay seated safely out of the fray.

Sir Winston takes the brilliant scientist by the elbow and edges him toward one of the leather sofas. After he is seated, he stares at Sir Winston in befuddlement as he struggles to regain his usual stoic composure. About this time, David and Angus rush through the still open door, having sensed the maelstrom of emotions. Abigor and I are not far behind. Abigor pushes me out of the way until he can assess the unfolding situation. Clumsy as usual, I fall over a footstool. Everyone stands still, gauging the situation. They decide all is well and carry on. David pulls me off the floor and into his waiting embrace. I cling to him. All the planets align when I am in his arms. I need to fall over footstools more often.

After exchanging greetings and, where appropriate, hugs and kisses, we sit down and turn our undivided attention to the still-eager Dr. Einstein. David sits beside me with his arm around my shoulders. I called room service to order a sumptuous dinner for myself and Father Antonio. One cannot attend appropriately on an empty stomach. Bowls of seafood bisque and an assortment of sandwiches are on the way for the good Padre and me. Perhaps, a little cherry cheesecake too.

Sir Winston takes the reins and ventures, "Dear Albert, it is such a delight to see you. I trust your task was completed to your satisfaction. We have been endeavoring to complete our tasks. Bones, Abigor, and I have interesting news from Admiral Stallings and the lovely Thelma Dove. David and Angus popped over to visit the Innsbruck constables to search for Dr. Suggs' missing person case paperwork. So please, Albert, compose yourself and tell us about your journey to Zurich. We have been anticipating your return with growing curiosity." Churchill settles back, cigar in hand.

Dr. Einstein rearranges his faux reading glasses and exclaims, "I am so pleased to be back with you. I have much to share, and I know our time to act is measured in hours now. I found Dr. Eric Snell's publication. Remember, that was 1901, and we did not have computers to store research papers for effortless retrieval. I finally found it in the archives room at the University of Zurich for the natural sciences and medicine. Many research studies have been stored electronically, but not so with Dr. Snell's paper. I talked with several librarians about the study and asked for the list of researchers who had signed it out. Anyone reading an article kept in the archives room must sign in and sign out. The document is not allowed outside the library. The list has existed since 1902, but there was only one visitor until many years later. That was 1939, and his name was," He pauses for impact and then whispers, "Heinrich Himmler. He may have seen its potential. Later it would be especially relevant to his official duties."

In the 1940s, three people read the study. The last name on the list shocked me, Ernst Mesmueller! Of course, I knew his notorious reputation; we will discuss him momentarily. He viewed it on April 06, 1941. According to the access sheet, he had it from early that morning until late that evening when they closed. He returned the next day and kept the same schedule." None of us were familiar with the name other than Sir Winston. He was the only one who didn't look blank.

"I apologize, Bones and gentlemen. I must take a few minutes to explain the history behind visitors to this study. I lived it, but you are also familiar with the history of scientists in Nazi Germany. We all know Hitler hated Jews, but many of his most brilliant scientists were Jewish, much to his chagrin. When Hitler came to power, many Jewish scientists hurriedly relocated to less threatening countries. I was one of those scientists. We saw the writing on the wall. Hitler's dangerous ideas created a dearth of scientists for his many projects. His ludicrous inability to foresee the consequences of his sinister and unconscionable ideas and prejudices bogged down his creative and productive ability. Evil will not succeed. The Doomsday Machine was created too late in Hitler's reign to affect the war effort. Soon, all the people who had access to the monster machine were either jailed or dead."

"That Machine, our current mission, was conceived at a 75-acre facility near St Georgen in Austria. The facility created and tested weapons of mass destruction, and the head of the SS and Hitler's trusted ally, Heinrich Himmler, oversaw its development." We all sat up straight at the second mention of that terrible name and the context. The genius continued, aware of our horrified reaction, "Yah, of course, you recognized that name at once. He is one of the Nazi monsters the Mengele scientists planned to clone. I don't believe in coincidences. Himmler would have intimate knowledge about the Doomsday Machine. Perhaps that is why Hitler chose Himmler to be cloned. Like the Owl Mountain facility, it is located in tunnels excavated into the earth and rock. Again, a nearby concentration camp provided labor similar to Riese at Owl Mountain."

David looked up suddenly and nodded to Angus. "Didn't we hear about that after the War? I think we did, but like Owl Mountain, it was overlooked and forgotten. We were more interested in the threat from the Russians at the time." Angus agreed there was talk at the time.

Dr. E listens intently to the MI5 agents, then resumes his history lesson, "When the Nazis completed the facility, its first commander was General Ernst Mesmueller. He was a favorite of Hitler and a ruthless taskmaster when overseeing a project. I have heard stories about him I will not repeat. I don't want to cause nightmares needlessly. This was a very ambitious project, and considering how similar it is to Owl Mountain, I wonder if Mesmueller was involved in both projects. The General used thousands of prisoners from the nearby concentration camp to excavate. It was backbreaking work, and many of the poor prisoners did not survive."

Sir Winston pats Sophie's huge head thoughtfully as he interrupts again. "Albert, of course, I have heard about this facility, the weapons, and Mesmueller. I am afraid I do not see the significance to our mission other than historical." The rest of us nod in agreement hoping for enlightenment. Sophie tries to be polite. She listens as silent and unmoving as the Sphinx.

Dr. Einstein is annoyed with the interruptions. "Would you please allow me to return to the library list in Zurich? Again, the person who stayed for two days studying Professor Snell's research on volcanos was Ernst Mesmueller. In my hypothesis, Ernst Mesmueller, who graduated from Zurich University in 1930, heard about the volcano research and realized it was the ultimate weapon of mass destruction. He probably told Himmler about its potential value as an unstoppable weapon. It was easy to determine he was a student in one of Professor Snell's Geology classes in 1929. A list of students in 1929 classes had been transferred from paper and stored in their database. Hitler chose Mesmueller to manage the facility. He might have remembered the study.

The scientist rushes on before anyone else can break in, "The Soviets said they discovered the facility in the twilight days of the War, removed everything, and filled in the tunnels. However, it appears the facility that worked on weapons of mass destruction is likely to have developed the Doomsday Weapon. Thus, it had to have been moved since the Soviets did not find the Machine. Mesmueller protected the Doomsday Machine and had two possible locations to hide it should the allies discover it. The Machine was Hitler's ultimate weapon, so armed sentries painstakingly protected it from discovery or attack. It is not an enormous machine and could have easily been removed at the war's end and moved to Riese at Owl Mountain. It is only 531 km or 330 miles from one to the other. I theorize that approaching Red troops made the transfer necessary."

The Genius slowed down a little. "Now, let's revisit my discovery in the research study; I know the weak spot in the earth's crust that Professor Snell said would cause a massive explosion of earthquakes and volcanos if targeted by a powerful force. He said the energy would have to be far mightier than any force that existed in 1901. Professor Snell mentioned superflares from the sun and discounted them as the power needed. He said the power of the sun's superflares could release a giant burst of plasma equivalent to the energy released by 100 million one-megaton bombs. Power enough? Absolutely! Frequent enough or predictable enough? Absolutely not! We shall dismiss that theory for now."

Sir Winston jumped in again, "Albert, is all of this background necessary?" We know Dr. Einstein loves to talk about history and theories, and it is useless to nudge him toward another course no matter how much we need to move on.

Dr. E ignores Sir Winston and trudges on like a giant tank. "Then Professor Snell turned to new technology, electromagnetic manipulation! In fact, it existed only in theory in 1901. Yet, is that not where technology begins? It has been studied thoroughly yet secretly in the 21st Century. Electromagnetic manipulation uses a disrupter in the natural electromagnetic field. If the earth's electromagnetic field is sufficiently disrupted, it could trigger earthquakes and volcanos because the tectonic plates would be jarred with incredible force and vibration. The professor hypothesized this would be a likely and brilliant power source. This plan uses the earth's magnetic field to cause destruction. I read the following written by Aleksey Vsevolodovich Nikolayev from the Russian Academy of Sciences, 'A tectonic or seismic weapon would be the use of the accumulated tectonic energy of the Earth's deeper layers to induce a destructive earthquake.' The disrupter would use the tectonic energy available. Absolutely brilliant! The trigger must be precise and have enough power. That is all! According to Professor Snell, the process will feed on the earth's tectonic energy once the process begins. As the earthquakes start, they will trigger volcanoes one after the other. There are 1500 active volcanos and seven supervolcanos on earth. We have already talked about the devastation those massive powers could rain down on our planet. Possibly, even the end of the earth as we know it. Earth could become a dead planet similar to Mars. The Professor did not continue to the next step and suggest a possible triggering source."

Getting more excited as he nears the end, he exclaims, "I have read the study several times. According to the Professor, the weakest spots in the earth's crust are the asthenosphere, highly viscous, weak, and ductile regions of the upper mantle—located under the South American plate. The eastern edge of the plate is in the Atlantic Ocean. Professor Snell seemed to think anywhere along that edge beside the African Plate had a fatal weakness and could be activated. Since the area is so large, hitting it with whatever power the Doomsday Machine emanates will detonate it. This would not be challenging, theoretically. He theorized that the midpoint of the South American and African Plates boundary would be the optimal location. I have those coordinates. All of this is to say if we can change the coordinates, we prevent the epic devastation." Einstein stands and bows. He just solved our problem, well, in part. The genius has our full appreciation.

Then the dear man asks, "Do you have questions?" I run over to the genius and shake his hand. Bravo! Sir Winston salutes the Doc with his cigar.

Do we have questions? Does the sun rise in the east? David speaks up, "I need time to process this information, Professor before I can understand it well enough to ask intelligent questions. If everyone agrees, I suggest we share the information we have gathered on our separate tasks and then return to the Doomsday Machine target and process. I must say I am impressed with the work our Physicist has done, bravo! It may well be the answer we need. We will come back to it."

Visibly excited by the Professor's research, David moves on, "As you know, Angus and I have been studying the Machine diagram, which is relatively straightforward 1940s technology. I think we require some hands-on experience with the actual machine. There are several gauges and levers. A switch on the right side seems to activate it. Once we activate it, I assume we can read the coordinates. Since, thanks to Dr. Einstein, we have the coordinates suggested by Professor Snell, if we cannot disarm or destroy it, we can recalibrate it to a less destructive location as a last-ditch effort. Great work, Dr. Einstein! I assume the gauges tell us the count down until it is ready to engage and the power level. I have more bloody assumptions than solid facts." He looks at Angus for his input.

Angus looks as confused as the rest of us, "First, my sincere appreciation for Dr. Einstein's exceptional work! Getting back to David's statement, I agree until we see the physical machine, it is impossible to speculate with precision. The diagram does not label or explain the various gauges and levers. We know what it looks like in some detail. Indeed, I could draw it for you. I have spent so much time studying the beastly diagram I fear it is permanently imprinted on my brain. We could probably determine how it works if we had a few hours to study the machine itself. Regrettably, we will not have sufficient time to do that. I do not have bloody facts, either! However, I am excited to have a solid plan." Soph lifts her ears and nods in his direction. As long as Soph is onboard, we know we are traveling in the right direction.

Abigor jumps in with a look of terror, transforming his handsome face. "I pray I art wrong. A thought just occurred to me. I hast wondered why a demon wast involved in the project. Sadly, I know from experience demons hast tremendous power. Could black magic power the Machine?" We just fell down another rabbit hole.

Dr. Einstein calmly answers Abigor, "I have considered that possibility for a while. If we dismiss the monstrousness of your hypothesis, it is not impossible. We are best served by setting aside that discussion until we have more information. Our mission does not change whether the Machine operates using black magic or something more earthbound. We will do what we must when the time comes." At first, I am astounded by Dr. Einstein's calm. Yet, we have no time left for hysterics. We let out a collective sigh of resignation to fate.

Father Antonio crosses himself, reaches for his teacup, and Sir Winston sips his brandy.

David raises his hands in acceptance—it is what it is.

Then David loops us in on his trip to Innsbruck. "Angus and I were tasked with visiting the Innsbruck constables and reviewing their current file on Dr. Suggs. They have an encouraging lead that may pay off big. We decided to ask some questions as MI5 agents. The constable in charge thinks Suggs may have been taken to France. They are following leads from a private jet rental company, NetJets. An airline pilot said he saw a man who he thought at the time was inebriated helped into his plane by two men in black business suits. They said they were friends taking him home after a rowdy business trip. The private jet flew them to a small airport near Paris, Toussus-le-noble Airport. They stuck their faces in books as soon as they were airborne. The pilot said he could not describe either man. Generally, they were larger than average; one had dark hair, and the other was blonde. They reminded him of the movie *Men in Black*. I am optimistic, though, that this lead should have feet. When we are free to work on the case, Angus and I will track down the pilot and interview him and the staff at the airport, but we have one little rumble with demons before then." David winked at me as he said that and smiled. My hunk of a darling man is trying to calm my fears.

I shared intel on our visit to the Admiral and Thelma, "Thelma had a vision about our battle in the tunnel. Her vision was why the Admiral had previously said we would lose our *rumble*." I wink at David when I say that. He winks back. The wink tells him I am in the saddle, dying to tackle whatever pandemonium comes our way. "Thelma saw us lose and viciously crushed by our beastly, loathsome opponents. From what she said, it was not a pretty sight, something about bloodshed and scorching flames. Sir Winston and Abigor asked her to try to see the battle in the tunnel again. She agreed to attempt it for us but was not optimistic. She went into a trance, and this time the tide had turned. It was close, but we were not crushed again. We have a chance to win, that was exciting news! This vision favored our side slightly. I admit it was nerve-racking & spirit quelling waiting to hear what she would see." Father Antonio is grinning ear to ear as he hears the good news, well, better news. He whispers a prayer of gratitude.

I grin back at the dear Padre and continue, "If Thelma's vision is accurate, Aaii will not be alone. Luckily, he will not be surrounded by legions of demons. A few of his lieutenants will probably be there to support him. We pressed the Admiral for anything that might help us gain an edge over Aaii and his vile Tin Soldiers. Oh, Abigor told me they wear metal armor. They think they are Roman soldiers from the 2nd Century. Delusions seem to be trending in Hell." I asked Sir Winston if he wanted to relate this part since he had asked the Admiral for help. He agrees to tackle the Holy symbols.

Sir Winston stands and briskly paces the parlor, anxious to put our plan into motion. He comments, "Admiral Stallings had studied early religious symbology and drew a design first found in a manuscript discovered at a Catholic monastery. The manuscript was dated 1415. I assume fighting demons must have been quite fashionable then. Abigor has the drawing. The admiral said we should carry the design close to our hearts when entering the tunnel. He also agreed with the Holy Weapons David collected for us. And, of course, our spiritual super-weapon is Father Antonio." Sir Winston bowed toward Father Antonio with sincere appreciation for the spiritual weight he has added to our team. Sir Winston looks for his brandy. Soph anticipates his desire and pushes it toward him with her nose.

I am impressed by a 95-year-old man who leaves his home and joins us on a dangerous mission with no assurance he will ever return to his beloved cathedral. To my great sadness, I see a pink bike without its rider. A tear I quickly brush away runs down my cheek.

Sir Winston thanked David, Angus, and me for our reports and asked Dr. Einstein if he had anything further to add about the Doomsday Machine. The good doctor shook his head. Sir Winston says, "We must concentrate on preparations for our fierce battle."

At that moment, the door bursts open for the second time today, and Druid blasts into the room like a mighty tornado, all enormous and outraged. He took a few seconds to skewer each of us with his deadly stare. Astonished but also curious, we stared back expectantly. He boomed, "What are you doing? You now have two humans you are sacrificing to the gods of war? What did I tell you after you allowed the murder of innocents in your last mission? How many more will you sacrifice? If you battle with Aaii and his warriors, you will lose, and Bones and Father Antonio will surely die. I must fortify your righteous fighting spirit. I am taking over this mission and will meet you at the tunnel tomorrow. You also might be interested to know a team of ten Neo-Nazis are on their way to eliminate you. Two of whom you may recognize from the lab. Clearly, they do not understand who and what you are, but they can slaughter the humans. I suggest you prepare at once; they will be here in ten minutes. Do your worst! If anyone leaves this suite, I will deal with the bloody thug, and he will not enjoy it." A puff of smoke is the only lingering evidence of his final, fiery declaration. I think that is pure theater since he has never done that before.

David moves first. "Druid is dramatic, but he is never mistaken. Bones, please take Father Antonio to the study and protect him. You have your .38? Of course, you do! Since the Neo-Nazis are humans, we can neutralize them without breaking a sweat. Angus and I will wait on either side of the door. Sir Winston and Dr. Einstein, please stay seated on the sofa. We want them to see you when they enter. Abigor, stand by the door to the study out of sight. If anyone gets past us, they're yours." With a nod of assent, Abigor takes his place by the door to the study. As a guardian angel, Abigor is a master warrior of legendary strength. Sophie is sitting beside Sir Winston and is not impressed by the approaching minor confrontation. Soph is in her regal Zen mode. I bet she is yawning for effect.

I move quickly to the study with the Padre, checking my .38 as I walk. I love that little gun. It fits my hand nicely. Yep, loaded and ready to rock. I motion him to sit where they cannot see him from the door, in an armchair hidden by the massive oak bookcase. He calmly sits down and asks hopefully, "Do we have any tea and sandwiches left?" Dear God, this man is my kind of priest! I run over and quickly kiss him on the forehead before retaking my position.

As we wait inside the study, I am dying to know what is going on, and I desperately want to be part of the welcoming party. Yet, David gave me an assignment, and I am a good soldier. I will remain on my post until I am relieved or die, hopefully, the former. I don't have long to wait until all Hell breaks loose in the parlor. I hear the suite door slam against the wall with a loud bang! Then I hear the Nazis shouting orders to Sir Winston and Dr. Einstein. Soph is furiously growling and snapping to alert the thugs to extreme danger. Angus and David stoutly command Nazis to throw down their guns and lie flat on the floor with hands clasped behind their heads. David can make guns disintegrate in their hands when he has sufficient time to prepare. I assume he is doing that nifty trick right before their eyes. Drat, I hate not being able to see their faces. I hear more shouts, cursing, growls, and fists connecting, followed by screams of pain and shock. Our invaders have probably never seen guns disintegrate or guys with such extreme punch power. I snicker. We could even say otherworldly power.

The whole gun disintegrating thing got the Nazis' attention. It is getting quiet in there. A couple of them must have made a run for the door into the hall. I hear David yell, "The hall is dangerous, creeps! There be monsters out there!" Idiotic choice, guys! They are running into the arms of the highly enraged Druid. Hey, no sympathy. They attacked us first!

The door to the study opens slowly. I take my stance and point my .38 at the entrance. A big blonde guy in a black suit pokes his head in the door. Then I see a colossal fist punch him in the jaw and then the stomach. With a painful oof, he flies back about 20 feet. Bang! You go, Abigor! I peeked through the door. Yes, I know I am not supposed to look out. The blonde guy doesn't attempt to get up. His tires have been flattened, and his jaw is likely broken. I would feel sorry for him. Really, I would if I didn't know he would have shot my priest in cold blood without a second thought. That is an unnegotiable no, no!

The Padre and I dare peek into the parlor, where it appears quiet and controlled. Eight men in black suits, white shirts, black ties, and dress black oxfords are stretched out on the lovely wood floor in various states of agony. Personally, I think they are overdressed for this assignment, but who am I to judge since I wear red high heels and scuffed, faded jeans?

The debonair twits are grumbling, groaning, and/or cursing. To their credit, they are keeping the volume down to avoid further discomfort. Angus is not particularly sympathetic to their plight. He says to them in his best 21st Century vernacular, "As Buddha say, don't start none won't be none. So, here we are, guys. Stop moaning and complaining! Not a tough lot of bloody thugs, are you?" My guys are discussing what to do with our unwelcome and inconvenient guests. We are pressed for time and need to get rid of them. The two that flew into Druid's arms were unceremoniously hurled back into the suite and joined their fellows on the floor.

David, Angus, and Abigor have agreed to transport them to the prison cell in the sewers of London. The sewer is where we imprisoned Dr. Mengele and Franz during our first mission. Ironically, the Neo-Nazis on our floor may have helped the vile Doc to escape. That was naughty. We recognize two from the fight in the London lab on the night Mengele died and Franz shot Angus. One is the massively bulked, towering Captain Axel Fischer, the London Neo-Nazi group leader. David and Sir Winston interviewed that group while the Met Police held them for the lab fight indiscretion in London. They were into the strong silent type mode. In our last encounter, we learned Axel is called Bugsy behind his back. In my profession, we would say Axel has significant issues. Another familiar face belongs to Lieutenant Weber Weber, his second in command and who, by the way, is very sensitive about his name. With slicked-back blonde hair, dull hazel eyes, and a cleft chin, he would be Brad Pitt handsome if it were not for his reptilian glare. David looks into their cold, soulless eyes and says, "Well, gentlemen, I see we meet again. How lovely, you brought your playmates with you. You undoubtedly remember the cell in the London sewer from which you freed Mengele. That caused us a great many overtime hours. We are delighted to say you will have an opportunity to visit there again as our special guests. It will probably be a little crowded, but you can get to know each other better." I am ashamed to say I giggled, well, ok, maybe not entirely ashamed.

"More bad news, guys, in case you had forgotten, you rigged a bomb at the London sewer cell when you helped Mengele escape. The explosion killed and injured Met crime scene folks and the medical examiner. I will be cluing in the Met about your connection. When Franz was still lucid, he told us you planned everything. If you want to visit your old friend, he is now in an undisclosed nursing home abroad." Male bonding is a beautiful thing.

The bruised and battered hulks look at David with intense hatred. He smirks and walks away as Angus tries with little success not to laugh. Sophie is growling to show her utter contempt for the miscreants.

Sir Winston surveys the room and suggests, "David, Angus, and Abigor will have to pop over to the cell and transport our guests with them. We do not generally transport humans since it has occasionally been detrimental to them. Under these pressing circumstances, the world is crashing about our ears. It is the only satisfactory option. David, when you return, please call Spears Westbrook at the Met Police to see to our guests until we return from Poland. They will want their afternoon tea."

Sir Winston's eyes twinkle with mischievousness. "We must be cautious about the information we share with MI5 for the present. It pains me deeply to say or even suspect that we cannot trust someone at that honorable institution. The guys pop the Neo-Nazis over to the sewer cell. Yes, it is standing room only crowded. Spears will have to deal with that issue. If this influx of thugs continues, we will be forced to build another cell."

Dr. Einstein looks at the ceiling and says, “Reality is merely an illusion, albeit a very persistent one.” Please don’t ask me what he means. I am not a genius.

Chapter Twenty-One

The Plan

I am still furious with the Neo-Nazi blackguards, Sir Winston's term, who injudiciously attacked us, briefly interrupting our plans to rescue the planet from a fiery death. Happily, thoroughly trounced, they were rudely thrown into the London Sewer System to contemplate their errors in judgment. While we are again feverishly working on our plan to attack the vile tunnel creature and any loathsome lieutenants he may have recruited. That done, we shall grapple with the unpredictable beast machine.

Dr. Einstein suggests that each of us report on our part of the plan. David will begin with our transportation and supplies list. All of us will travel in the Rolls Royce to the airport to pick up the Netjet David reserved. He and Sir Winston have flown it before and feel comfortable handling the controls. I am not satisfied with one of the pilots—Sir Winston, whose flying experience was primarily crashing crude WW1 aircraft. After several near-fatal crashes, his wife, Clementine, warned Winston to choose between her and his crashing planes hobby. Thankfully, he chose Clemmie. Thus, when Fate smacked him on the shoulder in 1940, he was available to save the Western World.

Forehead furrowed in concentration, so darn cute, David reports on our supplies, "As I have said before, we are ready with protective gear for Bones and Father Antonio. We have the Holy relics blessed by Father Antonio. He will report on the items he brought. We have the Holy symbols Admiral Stallings drew, which according to the Monastic Holy men from 1415, have protective power against demons. We have not interviewed the Holy Men; hence we will take that on faith. Indeed, I hope they had their facts straight. I have the Met Police Department bomb kit, which is probably useless, but I do not want to overlook a potential tool. We are all armed with lethal weapons except Dr. Einstein, Abigor, and Father Antonio. Does anyone have questions?" We have been over this ground before, so we stand down.

Abigor has been speaking with Father Antonio, and he turns to us to report, "I do not have tools, weapons, or supplies to offer thee. We art well supplied and prepared for battle by David and Angus. I told you I would wait until the time came to discuss overcoming and controlling demons. I was one of them for thousands of years to mine eternal shame. We cannot kill or seriously injure them. We cannot, but one Holy warrior can mightily smite demons. He art not a member of our Team; thus, I shalt move past that for now. We shalt return to him later when the time is right." We all sit up as if we had been electrified. What!

After shocking us, Abigor goes on as if nothing of import was said, "The Ancients used words and names as weapons. Words have meaning and great power. I can conjure, Mashbia' ani 'Alekha, art the most widespread performative for conjuring and invoking demons. It is said that King Solomon could summon and control evil spirits. The words used were, ' "Come out demon, since I bind you with unbreakable adamantine fetters. And I deliver you to into the black chaos in perdition." ' The ancients wrote, draw a circle with four openings in front of the door to allow four spirits of the word to come in. Write a list of magic names inside a square. I shalt perform this ritual when we arrive at the tunnel, and the ritual shalt, I hope, weaken the lesser demons' powers. This shalt help protect Bones and enable the other team members to fight evil. I hast been talking with Father Antonio about the Holy protectors he has used. Father is ready. I shalt stay close to Bones." David discreetly growls. Sophie shakes her head at David and winks. We are all at a loss to understand our roles. What precisely, in laypeople's terms, do we do?

Sir Winston, who is cleaning his round black-framed glasses, needs details. "Are we supposed to fight them as we would fight mortal men? Naturally, we cannot harm them with bullet holes, and I desperately wish we could. It is a pity because I am a deadly shot, especially with my Prohibition Era Tommy gun." The Great Man sighs deeply as he says this. "It is splendid, and we are appreciative that you will have weakened them with the ritual. What does that mean to those of us fighting? I want more details, Abigor." We are all floundering in the dark.

David, listening to Abigor, grows more frustrated by the minute, "I agree with Sir Winston. I am thankful to learn that you have a comprehensive plan to help us, but what shall I do when we arrive in the tunnel chamber? When we rush in, what is our next move? I can fight with the best of them when my opponents are human. Believe it or not, I never fought demons when I was an MI5 agent, nor did Angus." Angus nods vigorously to support his former MI5 Deputy Director-General." David says with emotion, "I don't feel comfortable entering the arena blind and utterly unprepared for my role." Angus adds that he is just as confused about defeating the bloody hoodlums. They want details, and I agree. I am floundering without direction, also. Dr. Einstein listens to everyone. He does not usually participate in the slugging or shooting part. He plays a more subtle role.

Abigor nods and responds, "Thou shalt attack them as thou would mortals. Hit, kick, knockdown, slam against rocks, throw them outside. All these things shalt work in their weakened state. My ancient ritual will not weaken Aaii. He is why we asked the spiritually crushing Father Antonio to perform an exorcism. We cannot control Aaii in any other way. The good Padre does not know this, but he has grown mightier in spirit with each exorcism he performed. He art a mighty powerhouse of righteousness. As a demon, Aaii is a Behemoth. His foolish mistake is believing he is invincible. Aaii has met his match in Father Antonio. We know that, and mercifully for us, Aaii does not know." Whew, that is encouraging. Note to self, pack an extra pair of red high heels. Sophie snarls, showing her savage teeth. She is a stunningly unstoppable warrior.

Abigor returns to his discussion on all things demonic, "To answer your question, gentlemen, do precisely what thou would do in any other fight. Bones, we shalt use my code words and your compass to reach the Dark World if need be. We have not been given details. Red said thee must be there and bring the compass." He throws his hands up in confusion. I am proud that Abigor is improving his grasp of 21st Century English.

Abigor finishes by saying, "We shalt hope for words of clarity from Red and Druid. That is thine role, Bones." I am confused. I don't know what that means.

Sir Winston, who has resorted to chomping on his cigar while sipping, questions, "Is there anything else we need to know, Abigor? David? Albert, what do you wish to tell us? You have the map of the tunnel to the Demon's chamber and the diagram of the damn wretched machine. Then we will hear from Father Antonio."

Dr. Einstein looks solemn as he says, "Our time is vanishing. We have done everything possible to prepare ourselves for a successful Holy mission. Thank you, Abigor, for your plans to help us overcome the evil menace in the tunnel. David, you have done an excellent job planning travel arrangements and equipment. We are grateful. I will not attempt to explain Druid or the Admiral's messages. I have no facts. I will fight along with David, Angus, Abigor, and Winston. That is not my area of expertise, but I shall not falter in thrashing our grievous enemies to protect mankind. Bones, Father Antonio, and Abigor have specific duties to perform. Blessings on them. Father Antonio, would you honor us with your thoughts." Dr. E points his pipe toward the priest.

Father Antonio puts down his teacup and cake. He looks at us with obvious pity. "My dear friends, you have become precious to me in a brief time. Fighting evil together binds us in purpose and Holy duty. I have fought evil numerous times and was always alone except for the Master in my battles. Now, I have a team of friends who will go with me into the devil's den and fight fiercely. You have no idea how dear that is to this battered old warrior. I value Abigor's words, and I believe I can, with the power of God's Holy Spirit, banish Aaii to Hell. Do not worry about me. I am at peace." He made the sign of the cross and said, "My blessings on each of you as we enter the pit, walking with profound faith and devotion. I have given you blessed Holy water in tiny vials and relics. I blessed your sterling silver crosses. My bag of tools is with me and gives me hope and courage." He looks each of us in the eyes before he continues. "I love all of you." Tears well up in my eyes, then slide down my cheeks. I feel my throat closing. Dear God, the Padre is saying goodbye. I hear it in his voice. My heart is breaking. The others are not mortal, and they do not feel my deep despair and loss. David holds me close and dries my tears with his handkerchief.

When I look up through blurry eyes, I see a fireplug redhead with one eye patch. We all whip around to see him. We are amazed that he is standing here with us. Red, of course, knows Sir Winston and Angus. Sir Winston is the first to react. He jumps up, slaps Red on the back, and exclaims, "Dear boy, how splendid you look! It has been how many years since we worked together to save the world from a deadly dictator? Let me think. Yes, it must be at least eighty years. Now, many years later, our mission has not changed. It is splendid to see you again.

You, lad, have been at the center of our discussions about Owl Mountain, and now you are here in person. I believe you already know our team member, Angus. Didn't you work together at MI5?" Red shakes Angus' hand with enthusiasm. "You have had lunch with our dear Bones too." I reach out to hug him as I welcome him to our group.

Angus is the next to slap Red on the back and welcome him, "I cannot believe my eyes and not a day older than last I saw you. I am so pleased to welcome you, mate! I never thought I would see you again when you died so many decades ago. Yet, we have strange happenings on my Team. Let me introduce you to David Smythe, formerly Deputy Director-General of MI5. He left the Agency in 1965 when a bloody Nazi shot him in the head. You may know our Padre, Father Antonio, who traveled in intelligence circles during the War. And this gentleman is the renowned scientist Dr. Albert Einstein. Over here, next to Bones and in black and white weighing in at a vicious 120 pounds, is our immortal entity, Sophie." Everyone shook hands and marveled at our new visitor. Sophie nudged his hand, and he patted her back.

Red is beaming with delight. He says, "It is my immense pleasure to meet my new teammates and to see my old friends again. Angus was a first-rate MI5 agent. I always knew he had my back, no matter the danger. Who has not heard of the genius Dr. Einstein? Sir Winston, it is a great honor to see you again. Good to meet you, Padre, and big Sophie. I told the lovely Bones I would not be able to help your team in the coming dust-up. Despite that, I have been assisting President Kennedy's team, and I guess I earned enough merit points." He laughs heartily. Red has a wonderfully contagious laugh. We all have to join him. He continues, "I told the Beyond Powers I must be here to help you finish this mission. I love a good free-for-all, and you could use another experienced Tommy. Our friend Druid will meet us in the tunnel. I do not want to spoil his surprise, but I think you will be amazed."

I wonder what he means. When we talked, Red asked me if I knew who Druid was. An odd question. Druid is a force of nature, a giant in an 1890s suit and bowler hat with a fiery temper.

Angus questions him, "We have been trying to find your personnel file at MI5 to learn what happened to you, mate. Did you have cardiac arrest, as MI5 officials said when you suddenly died, or was something more sinister afoot? I never believed their neat little story, and your personnel file is lost. Odd that." We are accustomed to evil creeps murdering MI5 agents. We trust no one.

Red looked puzzled. "I do not know what happened. I suspect I was getting too close to the Owl Mountain secret, and perhaps someone stopped me with a bit of CIA heart attack drug. I noticed a tail on me. I planned to mention it to you, Angus, and never got the chance. The blokes were good, but not that good. Rumors were circulating about rogue agents who worked for the dark side. I don't know who they were or who they are now, for that matter. Certainly, we must be careful when sharing information with them. It makes me angry to have to say that about my old agency. I was listening when all of you were discussing the battle plan. I did not want to interrupt you. So, I know what you expect of me. I plan to narrow the odds." We would have a fighting chance if we had a few hundred more Rambos, just like Red.

Still excited to see Red, David informs him, "We will leave for Poland at 2:00 in the morning. Bones, you, and the Padre may want to catch a few winks while we put everything together. It may be a while before you get another chance to sleep."

Father Antonio is feeling the adrenaline rush before a battle. "I need truly little sleep, David. Thank you for thinking about me. Bones, you should sleep to be rested for the exhausting and dangerous day ahead of us." I told them I had slept well the night before and could not sleep now. My adrenaline is flowing, too; I am pumped for action. I will pack my hefty .40 caliber, though I don't know what I can shoot, and some snacks for the Padre and me. Sophie has been noticeably subdued as we have been making plans. She stays close to me and puts her massive head in my lap.

My phone rings, and it is Spears at the Met Police for David. I hand David the phone. "Hello, Spears. What is going on?" Spears says, "We had ears listening to our Neo-Nazi guests in the sewer cell, the bunch of wimpish grumblers. My guy overhead one of them say their group will be involved in a rumble tomorrow in Poland. The grousing creeps mentioned a tunnel and your name, David. Do you have any idea what they are talking about?" David looked at us and nodded. This is not good, guys. He answered, "No, Spears, I have no idea why they would mention my name. Thank you for giving me a heads up."

Spears replies," I told my guys these blokes are just bonkers. I will let you know if anything else comes up. Thanks to your lead, we are collecting evidence to confirm their involvement in the tunnel bomb massacre. I hope bleeding heart courts don't let them out on bail. We are moving them to jail for now. The softies think the sewer cell is too punitive.

"As you know, this case is very personal. Our team members and friends were the poor people killed and injured. Without your information, we wouldn't have our suspects in custody. We won't forget that, David." Well, I guess we know why we are bringing our weapons now. We might have something we can shoot.

This news pleased Sir Winston greatly.

Chapter Twenty-Two

The Journey

Although the luxurious old Rolls Royce is quite roomy, we cannot pack in all nine of us and our demon-fighting supplies. Abigor and Angus will pop ahead to wait for us at the tunnel near Ksiaz Castle in Poland. They will scout the area to stave off any nasty surprises. We were caught unaware by the planned Neo-Nazi welcoming committee. There is no logical reason for them to be a part of the war games. I would be willing to bet this is not Aaii's idea. He would loathe recruiting such paltry beings to bolster his legions. Recruiting the Neo-Nazi squad sounds more like the NGA crazies. They sorely overestimate their relevance and competency.

We cram ourselves into the Rolls to drive to the airport. Traffic is light at 2:00 am, so we don't have the usual nightmare fighting crazy London traffic. Father Antonio and Sir Winston have a rousing chat about WWII Generals. Gort and Auchlinleck were not Churchill's favorites. Sir Winston raises his volume and waves his cigar around to punctuate his points. The Padre is a fan of Field Marshal Montgomery. Lost in my own thoughts, I take this time to love London as we leave the city. I am awed and grateful to be part of London, however briefly, even with my, uh, scary "toil and trouble" life. I cherish the ancient cobblestone streets, dark alleys, musty structures, and the historically ingrained mettle that hangs triumphantly in the air. Sir Winston and the Padre continue their critique of long-dead military officers in the background.

Upon arriving at the airport, we walked to the NetJet counter to acquire our shiny Bombardier Challenger 300. Sir Winston passionately demanded a 1942 Boeing B29 bomber but darned the luck; they did not have a single B29 in their fleet. David had taken care of the paperwork days ago. He provided his usual false credentials to pilot an airplane of this type, and we are finally ready to take possession. I am uneasy with the name Challenger, but David assures me the plane is safe. Right.

David looks the plane over, follows his checklist, and gives it a passing grade. He reacquaints himself with the instruments and is soon ready to take off. He is also trying to prevent Sir Winston from totaling our rental, or as the NetJet literature says, our fractional-owned jet. The Great Man has more experience in crashing than flying. Sophie sticks close to me in her attack Dane from Hell (or whatever) mode. Father Antonio, Dr. Einstein, Red, and I are praying and putting on the armor of God as Abigor taught us. Red was not with us for the lesson, so I shared my notes with him.

As the only humans, the Padre and I are less armored than the immortals. Let's be honest. The Padre is a quantum leap ahead of me in Holy. Spiritually, I am the weak link. David and Sir Winston meditated before we left. I am concentrating on putting on all the armor, but I have no visible internal light—so far. Darn, I am not doing it right, and I keep reviewing my notes for clues I must be missing. I look around at Sophie, Father Antonio, Red, and Dr. Einstein, and I think I see a glow emanating from Father Antonio. Sophie always glows with righteousness; she is a given. Well, at least I am not the only non-glower.

Finally, all the effort to glow makes me hungry. I unpack hefty snacks for Father Antonio and me. Before leaving the Savoy, I asked room service to bring sandwiches and fruit for our flight. The dear priest looks around, signaling that he is ready to eat. I, of course, have hot Earl Gray tea for him with lemon and sugar. Breaking bread is a good time for me; I can relax and enjoy eating with the Padre. I share with him that I am concerned I am missing something vital in the whole armor thing. I inquire about his food choices, "Father, here is your tea and tuna salad sandwich with sharp New York cheddar cheese, or you can have a chicken salad sandwich. Is there anything else I can get for you?" He shrugs and reaches for his tuna salad sandwich.

"Father, I am stymied in my 'armoring up.' I studied my notes several times; I followed Abigor's words carefully. I can't seem to get it right. Could you help me?" Floundering is very frustrating for me. I strive to win.

He puts his hand on mine. "Bones, putting on the Armor of God is not an intellectual exercise you can force to happen; it is spiritual, an opening of the heart and soul to God's Word. You are trying too hard. Please sit back, relax, and let it come to you. It is not something you grab off a shelf in the store. If you are open and invite God in, He will find you." I wish I could say his thoughtful advice helped me. Maybe if I take a little nap, that will open my heart and soul.

We eat our food in silence. I tried to do what Father Antonio suggested to me. *I fall into a deep sleep and dream of a dark, frightening place. I cannot see anything. I raise my hand to my face, and I cannot see the large garnet ring on my right hand. The dark is deadly quiet. I think I am standing. Is this stimulus deprivation? I am getting frightened. I want to leave this terrible place.* When I awake, I am shaking. The Padre notices and puts his arm affectionately around me. "Dear Bones, are you alright? You were trembling."

I don't know what to say. I try, "I don't understand, Padre. I think I was dreaming, but it was very vivid, as if I had been in this dark, frightening place in the past. I could feel the terror rising in me." Sophie comes over and cocks her head as she looks at me. Even in Hell mode, Big Soph is loving and comforting.

Father Antonio pats my hand. "Do not be afraid of the dark, Bones. You are not alone, and it cannot harm you." Someone else told me that. Who said that?

Red is sitting on the other side of me. He says, "Bones, don't you remember? I sent a message to you telling you not to fear the darkness." I am bewildered now; why are they both saying the same thing at two different times? How did Red know I would have a dream about darkness? Just now, how did Red know what I was thinking? I'll ask him.

Red smiles at me and replies, "What do you mean? You just asked us who had warned you about the darkness." No, I did not. I let it go for now. I have other things to think about, like my survival. Father Antonio is meditating again. I remain silent and drink my coffee. Dr. Einstein is studying the diagram of the machine and the map of the tunnel. Sophie appears more terrifying by the minute, with dog black gums and sharp ripping teeth. I am eternally grateful she is on my side.

What the Hell is that? The jet begins to shudder and rock violently. Suddenly, I am thrown roughly out of my seat into the aisle. My right arm is twisted under me at an odd angle and hurts. I sit up, rub my elbow and try to move. The plane makes a horrible loud shrieking noise, and when I look out of my window, I notice we are flying low. What is happening to the plane? I hear an explosion, the plane jolts, and I smell smoke. We are losing altitude. Scraping, wrenching noises tell me the jet is tearing itself asunder. I look for Father Antonio. He is in the aisle a few feet from me.

I try to stand and fall several times. Finally, I just crawl toward him. I am afraid he is injured. He is still—too still. When I get to the Padre, I check for blood and don't see any. That is a great relief. The shuddering jet is still tossing me around as I try to hold onto the seat next to the fallen Priest. I check his eyes, and he is unconscious. I am a psychotherapist, not a physician. I don't know if he has a concussion or not.

Dr. Einstein walks over to help me. David runs down the aisle from the cockpit. Why can they stand up without flopping about like me? David yells to Red and Dr. Einstein. "Grab the equipment and be ready to pop to the Poznan Airport." Sir Winston is right behind him. David yells to him, "Transport with the Priest to the airport where our car is waiting. I have Bones!" Transport?

Sir Winston yells back, "We cannot do that! We might kill them, David! What are you thinking? You know how dangerous it is to transport!" I am seriously alarmed when I hear Sir Winston's fear and doubt. What will happen to our Priest? Can he survive such a dreadful shock? The dear man is 95 years old!

David screams back, "Of course, it is dangerous, but we have no choice. They would be killed when the plane crashed. We don't have time for parachutes, and I don't trust them. Let's move! Now!" Everyone is in a near state of panic, at least as panicked as immortals get. I want you to know I am damned panicked! They move quickly to carry out David's orders. He has no orders for Soph because she doesn't take orders. She throws a glowing yellow light around Father Antonio and me. Red and Dr. Einstein carry equipment and bags. I see them disappear. David picks me up. I feel sick, my stomach is lurching, and I am dizzy. The last thing I noticed was the plane splitting and leather seats flying out into the cloudless blue sky.

Then I am at the airport in Poznan, Poland. I am weaving back and forth like a drunk who staggered in from Czupito's Pub." David and I arrive first. The others are not far behind us. Fortunately, no random tourist is close enough to notice six people, and a red-eyed, enormous dog suddenly appear as if by magic. That would have been difficult to explain. Still, I am sure Sir Winston would have given it a go.

I feel fine after a few minutes, and the yellow light is gone, another manifestation not easily explained. I suddenly remember Father

Antonio and rush over to him. Sir Winston sat him down in a chair when they, uh, landed. Dr. Einstein is already checking him for injuries. The Genius says Padre is coming around now. He hit his head on a metal seat leg when he was thrown from his seat into the aisle. We are all gathered around, concerned about the beloved priest. Dr. Einstein pats me on my shoulder and reassures me, "Don't worry, Bones; Father Antonio is well. He has just a little bump on his head. His eyes look fine, no apparent concussion." Though the good doctor is not a physician either, he has picked up medical knowledge in his 142 years of, well, life.

Understandably, Padre looks confused as he peers at the unexpected airport. He stares at Sir Winston and asks, "Where are we, Sir Winston? The last thing I remember is sitting in my seat on the plane, eating my tuna sandwich on rye. Bones and I were enjoying lunch. Now, I am here, wherever here might be." He continues to look around, perplexed and lost.

Sir Winston leans close to him and reassures Father Antonio, "We are at the airport in Poznan, where our car is waiting. We will load up the rental car and drive toward the tunnel as soon as you have had time to recover. Bones was thrown into a dreadful state too. We have some matters to discuss. Then we shall carry on to meet Angus and Abigor." The Padre nods politely, still uncertain and muddled.

Red slaps him on the back and says, "We got this, Padre. No worries!" The Priest bounces forward. I must talk to Red about his well-intentioned but overly enthusiastic smacks.

All of us, except the Padre, huddle in a corner to discuss what happened to our perfectly operational jet. David tries to reason it out for himself and us, "I did the usual before we left London: ensured the aircraft had been released, completed visual inspections, tested emergency and safety systems, configured the GPS and instruments, checked the weather, routing, and weight and balance. I ensured I had everything, and all systems were a go. I suspect someone may have sabotaged the aircraft, undoubtedly one of our many freaky enemies. The list of freaky enemies seems to grow longer each day. Whoever rigged the plane was unaware that most of us could not be killed or injured. They slowed us down a little but not that much. I want to thank Sophie for cloaking the Padre and Bones with a protective light. Without that, it would have been more dangerous to transport them. Yet, we did the same with the Neo-Nazis and Franz, and they survived, more or less. Any guesses about who tried to kill us?"

Sir Winston jumps in to hazard a theory, "Evidently, the Neo-Nazis knew we were traveling to Poland. Spears told us about their conversation. They do not know about our, shall we say, advantages over the average human. I do not think they would have gone to that trouble just to kill Bones and Father Antonio. Spears also told us they would be waiting for us at the tunnel. If they believe we are dead, there will no longer be a reason for them to be at Owl Mountain. Also, they are supposed to be locked up in Spears' jail though I suppose they could communicate with comrades on the outside. Perhaps, we can cross one challenge off our list, or perhaps not. And, as we have said before, all of our enemies appear to be connected." Yes, the NGA goons, the Neo-Nazis ruffians, the demons, the MI5 traitor, and the Wagner scientists seem to be intertwined in a bizarre master plan. Then, we, weighing in at 7 to 8 warriors, are lined up on the other side. We are plus or minus Druid. Sigh.

David shakes his head. "To be certain, we can try to contact Angus and Abigor and find out if we have company. Our guys are there now. Usually, if I close my eyes and see Angus, he knows to contact me. We have worked together enough to have a routine." David closed his sensual blue eyes and concentrated on Angus. My phone rang. I hand it to

David. "Hello, Angus. We have had a slight problem and will arrive a little later than planned. How does it look there?" He put the phone on speaker. "David, I am sorry to hear that. It is quiet here in Poland, and we see no signs of the Neo-Nazi rubbish. Abigor and I checked out the location for miles and found nothing. It looks as if they have decided to skip the dance. Maybe they had another date."

David chuckled and responded, "Excellent news, Angus. We will be driving your way in about an hour. It is only a two-and-a-half-hour drive. If anything changes, let me know. We will arrive at about 6:30 am. I will catch you up on our adventure then. Remain watchful until we arrive; they are a sneaky bunch. Wait. Call Spears and ask if the Nazis are still safely tucked away in his jail. Thank you, Angus." Soon the Padre will be ready to travel, and we can go to find our rental. Hopefully, we will return the rental in better condition than the decimated jet. I pray we have insurance.

We have a short drive ahead of us to the Castle area. My anxiety will shift into high gear as we near ground zero. I want it over so we can tackle the NGA garbage. I feel better when I think ahead, past the tunnel skirmish to the more ordinary, ruthless psychopaths. They are undoubtedly disgusting, but they have no special powers, such as popping in and out of rooms or turning me into a frog or a tiki torch. I have never had a demon threatening to turn me into a frog, but I read enough Grimm Brothers as a child to know it is likely. I am at an advantage when fighting ordinary humans. I am fearless. I have fought much worse and so far survived.

We wait until Father Antonio downs a couple of cups of his favorite tea and begins to feel his usual robust self. He is remarkably spry and resilient, considering his advanced years. David, Red, and Dr. Einstein pack up the mammoth rental Hummer. According to their propaganda, our new Hummer will—test our limits. No harm intended, Hummer, but that vessel left the harbor long ago. Sir Winston and Sophie stayed close to the priest and me. They weren't taking any chances on another unexpected catastrophe. Soon we are loaded in the Hummer and driving merrily, well, not precisely merrily, toward Owl Mountain and the evil Demon's dungeon.

Red asks Sir Winston and David, "What exactly caused the jet to malfunction and crash? That is not a common occurrence with new jets. What happened?" With that question, we return to the stimulating conversation about our jet's untimely and almost fatal crash.

David thought for a moment and answered, "I wish I knew, Red. It started shuddering as if we were going through turbulent air or, perhaps, the rudder or ailerons were damaged. The air was not turbulent. It was tearing itself apart. It only stayed afloat a few seconds after we bailed out. It could be mechanical, but that would be unusual unless it had previous damage. The jet could have been sabotaged, which is the most likely scenario. Modern planes are relatively safe with multiple safety features. If the Neo-Nazis knew we were traveling to Poland, they could easily find the rental jet information. I assume they have the same talented hackers as everyone else. However, I don't use my real name to rent airplanes or cars. How many small rental jets were going to the same area of Poland early this morning? My guess is not many at all. We have been careless, and it almost cost Bones and Father Antonio their lives. That will not happen again." Sophie groans solemnly.

Sir Winston is hot! He shouts, "Are we agreed then, one of the bloody Nazi cretins or some other miscreant tried to kill our dear Bones and the good Padre? They rigged our jet? Such barbaric behavior is entirely unacceptable; we must find the vicious thugs and exact our revenge. I am furious! What a spineless thing to do! Were they too cowardly to face us man to man? Certainly, it could have been the Neo-Nazis. We know they had inside information about our travel. Another possibility is NGA and the buggers compromised at MI5. They are undoubtedly capable of tracking down our jet and the toothpaste brand I used in 1939." I consider everything David and Sir Winston have said. Suspecting that someone intentionally tried to kill us makes the plane crash more personal. Well, Bones, it is not as if people attempting to murder you are rare. Suck it up, girl, and move on. You have a demon and his buds to fight. There was something about a Dark World, too, ugh.

Thoroughly indignant, Red returns to the conversation, "We know an MI5 agent, at least two probably, have gone to the Dark Side. That makes them extremely dangerous to the ultimate success of our mission. They will be identified and destroyed, and I shall see to that! I have made it my business to watch the executive suite at MI5. Miles seems solid, but I am not as comfortable with Deputy Director-General Emory Tayor. Something about him sets off my bad-bloke alarm. I have been looking into his past, but I haven't found anything substantial yet. He is relatively new in this position. I am intrigued that the former Deputy Director-General, Staggs, just up and died suddenly, like me. David held Staggs' position, too. Not a prudent job choice, mates. We don't know what happened to Staggs, but I intend to uncover the truth. His sudden demise is just too convenient to satisfy me. I am also puzzled that Miles accepts his death with an 'oh, well, this is a stressful job' attitude. I wish I could say that bad lots at MI5 were not involved in our crash. I cannot."

Dr. Einstein throws in his genius opinion, "We have no facts confirming the plane was sabotaged. Were it sabotage, we have no evidence to identify the perpetrators. Because intentional incapacitation is possible, we must be more cautious in the future. We cannot dismiss NGA, a couple of MI5 traitors, or Neo-Nazis. Thus, we will monitor those individuals and groups. Logically, since they are all connected, when one is involved, they are all involved. We must destroy the entire organization and all of its tentacles. That shall be our focus after we deal with demons." I am grateful we have this time to discuss recent disasters and how those disasters screwed up our goals. That assumes we, Father Antonio and me, survive the tunnel encounter. Philosophically speaking, we have had the water pumps and the skilled crew to douse fires, but there were too many.

My hunky David has been unusually quiet. Finally, he says, "We must delve into all of these things when the time comes. I want to go over our plan for neutralizing the tunnel denizens and the creepy rust bucket. First, we will make certain no ragtag Neo-Nazis are in the area. Abigor will draw his anti-demon design at the entrance. We will carry our protective spiritual tools. Bones and the Padre will put on their bulletproof and injury-resistant gear. "The Padre interrupts to say, "I have protection, David. I will not be wearing bulletproof gear. I do not fear man." David sighs respectfully and continues, "I don't think bullets will be in play, but the Neo goons may be lurking about under rocks. Perhaps, they don't have complete faith in the jet crash. Red, Abigor, Angus, Sophie, and I will go in first. We are the fiercest warriors." Sir Winston puffs up to his vest buttons popping size in the back seat. He gasps, "David, my boy, I am afraid you left me off the list of warriors. That is where I belong!" I knew David's list would set off an indignant response by our former Prime Minister.

David apologizes profusely, "My mistake, Sir Winston. Of course, you will enter with the first group of warriors. After we clear the way, Bones, Father Antonio, and Dr. Einstein will enter. Abigor's entrance conjuring design may have weakened the lesser demons by this time. At least, we hope it will have done that. We will signal Bones, Father Antonio, and Dr. Einstein to enter with great caution when it is safe. Father Antonio will be free to begin the exorcism to banish Aaii. Abigor and Bones will attempt to enter the Dark World if necessary and find the device that may, according to Admiral Stallings, neutralize the Doomsday Machine. Abigor said he knew where to find the entrance to the Dark World. We will play the Dark World strategy by ear to determine whether it is necessary or viable. Angus, Red, and I will search for the confounded Machine to destroy, recalibrate, or "disconnect" it. Dr. Einstein, please give the diagram to Angus. Operational plan, for now, both groups will work to find the Machine since we cannot depend on the Dark World scheme. Bluntly, we have no guarantees it exists. Angus and Dr. Einstein will protect Father Antonio while he is performing the exorcism. Sophie will do whatever she deems best." Sophie stood ready. She is still morphing into her vicious, toothy look—all sharp, ripping canine teeth and wild beast.

Father Antonio responded from the back seat, "I have been in prayer, and I am ready to begin the exorcism. It will take about 20 to 90 minutes to complete if I am not interrupted. I feel the Holy Spirit working in me, and I have no doubt I can send Aaii back to the bowels of Hell where he belongs. God has strengthened this old priest for His Holy mission. God will not abandon me. He tells me, 'In this world, you will have troubles. But take heart! I have overcome the world.' I request that Angus and Dr. Einstein repeat the exorcism prayers as I say the words. Their righteous souls will empower my words. I have my vestments, Bible, and Holy Cross in my bag. God's Will be done."

Dr. Einstein agreed he would be honored to participate in the ancient ceremony.

We are a few miles away from our journey's end to meet with a fickle fate. A thoughtful, resigned, quiet settles over us like a familiar warm feather comforter. The skirmish with Aaii and the lads is not the first time we have been tested. We have said everything that must be said for now. We know where to begin. From there, we will be guided by intuition, courage, experience, God's Word, and circumstances.

Chapter Twenty-Three

The Last Crusade

As we approach the area, we can still see the ugly remnants of war after all these years. The gigantic Hummer gives us a bumpy ride on the uneven road near project Riese. There are seven underground structures in Lower Silesia, Poland. During the War, this area belonged to Germany. Ksiaz Castle is said to be one of the largest castles in Europe and the third largest in Poland. It tops the underground labyrinth. The Castle is known locally as the "Pearl of Silesia." Mary Theresa Olivia Cornwallis-West was unfortunate to be the owner of Castle Ksiaz when the Nazis arrived. They unceremoniously evicted her and took her magnificent home for their headquarters.

When she died in 1943, her loyal servants repeatedly moved her body to protect her burial location from plunder by Russian soldiers. We don't know where Daisy rests today. Rumors surround the Castle and the tunnels below; many locals hint at hidden treasure and ghosts. I ask you, what is a castle without at least one spirit? When she moved to the Castle, Princess Daisy shocked everyone by insisting a short humpbacked man haunted her chamber. Many years later, confirming Daisy's titillating tale, a humpbacked skeleton was discovered under the floor in her suite. Later, the Castle faced and survived monsters much worse than mere specters.

After the Nazis subjugated the Castle, in the latter part of the War, increased air firepower from the Allies forced the Nazis to go underground with factories and munitions. Building under a mountain was highly labor-intensive, but Germans had no shortage of captive workers, having used Gross Rosen concentration camp prisoners and Allied POWs for labor. These unfortunate prisoners were weakened by poor nutrition, disease, and overwork. The Red Army liberated the wretched humans who survived in May of 1945.

The Nazi tunnels were silent witnesses to unbelievable horrors. Weeping stone walls grieve for the humans who had bravely endured unimaginable cruelty. Sadness and grief poison the air. Echoes of cries and moans permeate every crevice of the cold stone walls.

Many reminders of that earlier time remain: hardened bags of cement, the foundation of guards barracks, a reservoir for water, a concrete monolith with pipes, drains, and culverts, old machinery, rusted mine cars, and numerous unfinished and ruined buildings scar the splendor of the majestic Polish mountains. To this day, rooms built by the Nazis in the castle's basement have never been opened. We can only imagine what horrors remain sealed inside. The Castle and tunnels have become the perfect tainted environment for the soulless Demon to make his home.

We arrived at the contaminated Castle area early in the morning. With David following the map, we find the general site quite easily. He pulled the Hummer to the mouth of the tunnel. An enchanting woodland of rustling leaves stirred by a mild breeze greets us at the entrance to our hell, where we will likely face the Demon and monsters. They are our prey now, and we intend to thrash them and send them back into the eternal weeping, wailing, gnashing of teeth, darkness, flames, and torments of Hell. We will show no mercy. We are aware they would destroy us or worse with unbridled glee. Father Antonio will humiliate and defeat Aaii and send him back to the pit, never to return to his earthly home, sanctify the area, and remove the stench of evil. The land will be as spiritually unblemished and fresh as before war criminals, and the Demon corrupted it.

We shifted into warriors as we drew closer. Sophie is in full Hell mode with red eyes and a hostile attitude. She is much larger than when we left London. Naturally, I have seen this impressive morph happen in the past, yet it is still scary stuff. David and Red are beasts, gladiators obsessed with their prey. Sir Winston has the heart of a lion. The old warhorse has fought many battles and is a fearless foe. Dr. Einstein is not a combatant but will not neglect his honorable duty, and I shall fight fiercely with everything I have, including killer red high heels. If I die, it will not be because I was an easy kill. I promise this; someone will be wearing nasty heel scars. The Padre is a Holy Crusader, and nothing on this planet has the power to stop him. Aaii, the poor monster, has no idea what awaits him.

Angus and Abigor are at the entrance. Abigor is an angel, a righteous titan. Recently dead Angus is unstoppable. After all, they cannot kill him twice. Our team is ready.

Abigor has already drawn the Holy conjuring design at the mouth of the tunnel. When they see us, they rush over to help us descend from the beast Hummer. Abigor helps Father Antonio with his bag. Angus tells David he spoke with Spears, and the Neo-Nazis were bailed out. He fought to prevent their release but could do nothing against the influential organization that paid the creep's bail. Angus and Abigor have not seen any indication of the Neo-Nazis here. They have checked every inch of ground within miles.

The Padre changes into traditional priestly exorcism vestments, an embroidered white tunic, and a purple stole. He hangs his huge silver cross around his neck and holds the Bible before him as a formidable shield against evil. The sun is just breaking the new day. Sunlight glints and glitters on the silver cross as if it were on fire. I have to look away as the light is blinding. I interpret the rising sun and the glowing cross as Divine signs of hope and protection for our Holy Crusaders.

Father Antonio, Dr. Einstein, and I will wait for David to call us after our warriors have dispatched the lesser demons back to their vile command center. Before the guys walk away, I hug David tightly to me. We both know it may be the last time we can hold each other. I don't want to let him go; the pain of this separation is sharp and unbearable. David turns from me, looks back, winks, and walks away with Sir Winston, Angus, Red, Sophie, and Abigor. They have their flashlights, weapons, and Holy relics. They put on the armor of God to protect themselves from the evil waiting for them at the end of their journey. We have the Admiral's ancient symbol close to our hearts, a talisman to draw upon for courage and protection. I drew mine on my chest with a Sharpie; I am not taking a chance on losing it.

The Padre, Dr. Einstein, and I dolefully watch them march into the forbidding dark hole. Father Antonio makes the sign of the cross five times. One cross for each warrior. For some reason, I think of the poem *The Charge of the Light Brigade*. "They that had fought so well, Came through the jaws of Death, Back from the mouth of Hell." Then it hits me. I know why I think about it—the words 'mouth of Hell' resonate with me." Tennyson described the carved-out passage perfectly. I know our guys cannot be killed or injured, but the fighting will be fierce even with the weakened lesser demons. The toll on their spiritual being will be tremendous. Though none have fought supernatural demons with incredible powers, the guys have all fought. Father Antonio has repeatedly wrestled in these battles, but he is with me. His role is to send Aaii back to his buddy Satan. My role is to help him wait and pray. Dr. Einstein will protect the Padre until he is needed. Now, the scientist is patrolling the area looking for threats.

Led by the savage Sophie and David, the men walk boldly but with due caution. Who knows what could be waiting for them behind the next curve in the tunnel? The walls weep water, the smell is foul and noxious, and the ground is rough and jagged. The frigid air greets them, though none are affected by the cold. They are silent as they march forward. Each warrior is a rock, confident in their ability and firm in their convictions. Sophie is the most dangerous entity there—she has no reason to fear demons. She is eternal and has known monsters for eons and defeated them. The demons have no idea what she brings to the table. If they knew, they would be terrified. She is also humble. She will do her part and then stand back while the others fight.

In the meantime, the priest and I work on my process of attaining God's armor. Finally, we see a very dim glow. I am thrilled and relieved.

I see a dark figure rushing toward us from the corner of my eye. The massive hulk grabs me and throws me against a wall of rock, and I tumble to the ground. Father Antonio runs toward him and grabs one arm. Our attacker swings him around as if he were a weightless rag. The Padre drops off on the ground. I recognize the creep—Axel! I jump up, my back screaming in pain, and hobble toward Father Antonio to help him. I yell for Dr. Einstein. The Padre manages to rise from the ground. Axel reaches for him, and I jump on Axel. All three of us are grappling, twisting, furiously writhing like a pile of angry eels. My team of two is struggling for dominance, but we are no match for the bodybuilder. He is Herculean. He lands a solid jab to the Padre's jaw. I hear myself screaming at Axel to get away from the Padre. I jump on the Nazi's back, infuriated that I cannot shred him with my nails and teeth. He easily throws me off.

I channel the fury. I use my legs to sweep his legs, jump up and kick his right knee inward, putting all my weight behind the kick. I hope to shatter his kneecap into tiny fragments of excruciating pain. He stumbles backward, falls, and roars, curses at us and our mothers. I land another kick to his stomach. He quickly bounces back up. Damn him! I thrust a wicked elbow into his ribs. Nothing phases him. He gets behind me, and massive hands circle my throat before I can react. He squeezes, cutting off my air; the priest pulls at him with every ounce of strength in his frail body, groaning. While Axel is trying to push away the Padre, I throw my arms straight up and drop from his grip to the ground. Gravity does the heavy lifting. My move takes Axel by surprise, and he grabs empty air. I jump up and kick his knee again with my sharp, high heel. He bends over, screeching in pain. Before I can get out of his arm's reach, he pulls me back toward him and uses a headlock gripping my neck in his elbow and tightening it. I cannot move or breathe. He furiously tries to break my neck!

The exhausted priest falls, hitting the ground. I pray he is not hurt, but I know we will die right here.

Thank God! I look up and see David running toward me. David! He stops, takes the stance, pulls out his .40, aims, and blasts, hitting Axel in the forehead. The big man slams the ground with a thud and yanks me down too. Blood and gray matter are gushing from the gaping exit wound in the back of his head. Axel is still. Blood splatters all over me, and I scream in rage. I hate blood! David is beside me, pulling me to my feet, crushing me in a desperate hug, and kissing my hair. David gently takes my sticky hand and guides me to a nearby stream, where I wash the blood from my hands, hair, and face. My Adrenaline slowly dissipates, and I am calmer.

Above, the sun is dazzling yellow against the clearest of blue skies. A lightning bolt and clap of thunder pierce the deceptive quiet and calm. David hears and understands the message. He is resigned.

Dazed, I finally remember Father Antonio and Axel's nasty jab to the jaw. I awkwardly stumble back to check on the old priest with David in tow. Father Antonio is on his back, moaning. Dr. Einstein, who just returned, is anxiously bending over him, checking for signs of a severe injury. His vitals are acceptable for a nonagenarian. We gently help the priest stand up and dust off his purple stole. His jaw is swollen and turning a patchy red. Father Antonio is the star of our show, plus we love him and want him uninjured. Frightened, we pester him with the question, are you alright? Nodding, though we can see he is in pain, the good Padre lurches over to Axel, kneels next to him, and makes the sign of the cross. He whispers a few words in Latin. The Padre is a kind and forgiving man. Still furious: I want to kick Axel in the other knee! Well, there goes my Armor of God dim glow. It is not in me to forgive an enemy who just tried to kill our saintly priest. Fine, my halo is tarnished.

David has to go back inside to help the others. He tells me to keep my .40 in my hand until he calls me to come in. Dr. Einstein and I guide Father Antonio to the steel behemoth we rode in on to rest in comfort. I have a thermos of his Earl Gray tea ready to pour. I will stand guard. This debacle would not have happened if I had been more aware of my surroundings—a sneak attack won't happen again. It is a good thing I brought a spare pair of killer red high heels. The recently deceased Axel destroyed one of my heels with his kneecap.

While Dr. Einstein and I attend to the Padre's needs, David, Abigor, Red, Big Soph, and Sir Winston arrive in the spacious chamber with the dazzling antique chandeliers. Four chandeliers provide light in the monstrous carved-out chamber. In a futile effort, the 20 feet tall double doors have been shut and bolted against them. Well, that will slow them down for two minutes. The guys decide to blow the doors out and storm the inner chamber, perhaps surprising Aaii and his minions. David stands in front of the doors, puts one finger on each door, and pushes forward, and without apparent effort, the doors fall in with a loud thud, boom! The Team laughs heartily at the idea that massive doors could have stopped them. They spread out across the opening with Sir Winston in the middle.

Aaii sits on his pilfered throne, impressive in his jousting garb. Ten random demons in 12th Century pageantry gear stand around him. Angus is stunned by the overripe opulence of the enormous room, the amassment of stolen royal portraits, and glittering chandeliers. Aaii is quite the spectacle in his full set of jousting armor; he clinks and clanks as he walks majestically toward them, lance in hand. Sarcasm is dripping as the fake knight addresses Sir Winston. "What a pleasure to meet the great Winston Churchill. How thoughtful of you to visit me here in my humble chambers. What a treat. I see you brought friends. May I offer you something to drink? Your legendary enjoyment of spirits precedes you. Oh dear, where are my manners? These are my pages and squires. Please do introduce your friends." Psychopaths feel compelled to ooze charm from every pore, even when their charm is clearly insincere and mocking.

Sir Winston, with a look dripping contempt, ignores Aaii. He steadfastly refused to negotiate with Hitler. He'll be damned if Aaii won't get the same treatment. With Abigor and Angus on either side, David faces Aaii precisely as he had faced other criminals and traitors in his career. He gives an order, "Aaii, I am not here to participate in your drama. We are here to find the Doomsday Machine. We will play nice if you show us where we can find it and get out of our way. Otherwise, it will get messy—your choice." Sadly, for Aaii, he takes too long to answer.

Abigor is alert. He can read Aaii and knows he is playing with them like a nasty cat with defenseless mice. He observes the other demons closely and concludes they are unwell. The ancient Holy Symbols are working. The lesser monsters are wilting and sluggish; the ravenous animal look is gone from their eyes. Abigor signals David to proceed. Sophie, following his lead, leaps to the forefront and attacks without the slightest warning. She is poetry in purposeful motion as she goes for the closest demon, the one with a red feather on his helmet. He is shocked and has no idea that she is anything other than an enormous bad-tempered dog. Big Soph knocks him to the ground and goes for his throat tearing at it with vicious teeth. His weakened powers are useless. He is terrified. He disappears, leaving the foul smell of sulfur behind. Sophie briefly sports a self-satisfied grin at her triumph, then tries to rid her sensitive nose of that hideous stench. David turns his attention back to Aaii, "We can continue this game if you wish. There are still a few of your ruffians left. Shall we continue? Or do you choose to be reasonable? By the way, you look ridiculous in that outfit." Aaii is beginning to understand he is in quicksand and sinking fast. What is the power these beings bring to bear? Enraged and full-on pride cometh before a fall. He screeches and orders his costumed devils to attack. The game is afoot! Aaii runs to the protection of his throne to watch.

The remaining demons attack. Two are on Abigor, who immediately shoots them across the massive room. They land with a deafening bang, crash, thud! He chases after them as if they are the football, and he needs a touchdown to win one for the Gipper. Sir Winston is grinning ear to ear; it has been a long time since he had this much fun. A devil dressed in bright blue tights tackles Churchill. The Great Man gives him a smashing right to the nose and a deadly chop to the kneecap. Blue goes down with Sir Winston on top of him, knocking off his helmet and plummeting him about his ugly head. Churchill claims the win without dropping his cigar. Blue disappears in a puff of smoke, not knowing who savaged him. The winner stands tall and makes a triumphant victory sign.

David grabs two monsters who are reconsidering their options at this point in the furious knockdown, drag-out clash. David knocks their heads together with fury. He keeps banging their heads like demon cymbals until they disappear from the field of battle, more sulfur, more stench. Aaii looks on in horror. His squires and pages should be terrifying the disrespectful invaders. The remaining weakened demons suffer from painful bites and deep scratches, courtesy of Big Soph, while an enraged Red savages them with his stout fists. Because the Holy Symbols weakened their powers, they are suffering pain for the first time in their existence. Pain is a traumatic shock and a rude awakening for them and Aaii. War is a game if you don't feel pain or fear. Aaii's little dress-up game just got agonizingly real.

Aaii is a major player, high ranking demon, and he is not affected by the Holy symbols drawn in the dirt. Abigor knew this; that was why he recruited Father Antonio. Time for the magnificent second act! David pops outside to summon Dr. Einstein, Father Antonio, and me. Refreshed by his rest, the Padre is eager to do his part in our righteous war. We walk in silence into the tunnel and along the path to Aaii, and whatever destiny awaits us.

As soon as we enter the inner chamber, Father Antonio begins the exorcism ritual with Dr.Einstein and Angus repeating the ancient words after him. Aaii begins to feel the jolting spiritual surge throughout his depraved body. The Padre continues to ram forward without pause, "in the name of Jesus Christ, our God and Lord, strengthened by the intercession of the Immaculate Virgin Mary Mother of God, of Blessed Michael the Archangel, of the Bless Apostles Peter and Paul and all the Saints. As smoke is driven away, so are they driven; as wax melts before the fire, so the wicked perish at the presence of God." Father Antonio continues repeating these Holy words as he holds up his brilliant, sparkling silver cross. Aaii is crouching on the floor, screaming in agony. His screams are echoed by lightning bolts that shear through the chamber, crackling and sizzling. I duck down to escape Aaii's deadly electrical tantrum. Father Antonio is a pillar of strength, utterly oblivious to the spectacular fire show. I watch, fascinated by the two powerful combatants and the electricity that hisses ominously in the air around me. David puts his hand on my shoulder and gently leads me away. The lightning fades as the screams wane.

Still staggered by what I have witnessed, I stumble along behind David and Abigor toward a gorgeous heavy tapestry hanging on the far wall. Abigor points to the tapestry, "The door to the Dark World art behind yond tapestry. Bones thou hast the compass, and I know the magic words to open yond door. We may find the fantastic device that might defuse the Doomsday Machine if it be there." Before attempting to enter a world that terrifies me and hides an unpredictable fate, I turn to David to fiercely embrace him and absorb his courage to stay the course. What? He is no longer standing beside me. Terror rises in me as I spin around, searching the chamber for him. David is gone! Dear God, what the hell just happened? Will this horror never end?

Desperate for reassurance, I run to Sir Winston. "Where is David? I don't understand?" My eyes silently plead with Sophie and Sir Winston. Please help me. I see their tears—pity is written across those dear faces. I drop to my knees.

Thunder and lightning

The End

Until we meet again

Epilogue

After David disappears, my world is unendurable, unimaginable pain. Grappling with the loss himself, Sir Winston reminds me, "All the greatest things are simple, and many can be expressed in a single word: freedom; justice; honor; duty; mercy; hope, grief. Listen to me, dear brave Bones you must attend to what I tell you." He puts his hands on my shoulders and looks deep into my eyes, "We are honor-bound to do our duty here and now. We must do everything possible to safeguard humanity. Then we shall fight or mourn, whatever we must do for David." I wish I could ignore the Great Man's words and curl up in a ball for all eternity. I cannot. Oddly, I am no longer afraid of entering a dark alien dimension. I am a tool sent to do a job. I learn that hopelessness crushes fear.

I strengthen my spine before I move away. Pausing momentarily on my way to meet Abigor, I am awed watching our heroic Padre still struggling against evil. Father Antonio is chanting the Holy words of the mystical exorcism mass. He is not alone, as Dr. Einstein and Angus concentrate their powers on repeating the ritual prayers. The ancient ritual is exhausting Father Antonio. He hunches over, breathing erratically and sweating profusely. I remind myself that Padre has fought many grueling battles in the last 75 years. Still, I worry about his physical stamina. Sophie stands close to me, and her eyes, like mine, are locked on the old priest. She shares some of her tremendous strength with him.

Angus sees the anguish on my face, reaches out to hold my hand, and gives it a little squeeze. He doesn't know David is missing, but he senses something is wrong. He assures me he is "bloody sure" we will win over Aaii, "Don't worry, Bones. We will mail the -knight- back to

Hell with Return to Sender stamped on his pretentious drawers." Thank God for Angus and his can-do attitude. He always lifts my spirits. I wish I could smile for him.

Sir Winston motions for me to come over and join him and Red. He is scrambling to revise our plan. David filled a vital role in our strategy. Without him, we must fill a vast void and adapt. The three of us design a simple, concise plan to get beyond our current disaster. As soon as Father Antonio rids us of the maddening Aaii, the Team will focus on finding the machine. If we find it, Abigor, Dr. Einstein, and Red will help Angus neutralize the vexing steel contraption. For now, we have paused my trip with Abigor into the darkness. If we cannot locate or destroy the machine, our journey will be back on the table and perhaps our last hope for survival.

I am furious with the brutal fate that took David away from me. My anger reinforces my resolve and sustains me. I desperately need the energy rage releases. Emotionally, I tighten my belt and pull up my bootstraps. I will keep putting one foot before another until we destroy that damned machine. I WILL find David when this is over. I make a scared vow to myself. I will find David! God have mercy on anyone who tries to stop me.

Outside the double doors to the inner chamber, a peculiar sound comes through the massive doors—I hear the beating of wings against the door—enormous wings.

About the Author

Dorothy McCoy has authored several books, all of which have been published. She worked in law enforcement as a South Carolina State Constable, taught in the South Carolina Justice Academy, created their Master Instructor Program, and worked briefly in the Richland County Sheriff's Department's Cold Case Squad. McCoy is an expert in counseling and psychology, having been licensed for almost 20 years. She has spoken at numerous international conferences on psychopaths and narcissists, and written books related to counseling.

The material for, *The Mysterious Secret Guardians Mysteries,* were pulled from McCoy's wealth of knowledge and experience. She also is a proficient researcher, a skill she heavily relies on in crafting her books. The history is accurate. The locations and science described are accurate. Before embarking on this project, McCoy read every book she could find on Churchill, as well as many of the 72 books he wrote. She also has read hundreds of mysteries. She has it down pat!

Upcoming New Release!

FINAL CHAPTER OF THE MYSTERIOUS SECRET GUARDIANS

BOOK 3

BY

DOROTHY MCCOY

Final Chapter of the Mysteries Secret Guardians, Book Three, of *Mysterious Secret Guardians*: Rasping, shrieking winds engulf the crumbling structure. Lightning strikes the turret; wood splinters fly into the deafening din. In the Demon's chamber deep beneath Castle Ksiaz, Good and Evil battle for the fate of all humanity. If the Guardians fail, the earth will be reduced to uninhabitable smoldering rubble and poisonous gases.

As the battle rages, a pivotal member of Sir Winston's team, Flight Marshall David Smythe, abruptly and mysteriously disappears, and another valiant warrior is mortally wounded.

Can Father Antonio, a 96-year-old exorcist, and a 14th Century Holy Incantation, turn the tide for the besieged Guardians and rescue humanity?

Owl Mountain shudders in terror.

Now Available!

DOROTHY MCCOY'S
MYSTERIOUS SECRET GUARDIANS
BOOK 1

For more information
visit: www.SpeakingVolumes.us

Now Available!

MATTHEW J. FLYNN'S
BERNIE WEBER: MATH GENIUS SERIES
BOOKS 1 - 2

For more information
visit: www.SpeakingVolumes.us

Made in the USA
Columbia, SC
13 September 2023

22838907R00157